I0590717

# MAGIC RECLAIMED

# MAGIC RECLAIMED

## THE WITCHES OF PRESSLER STREET™ BOOK EIGHT

MARTHA CARR

MICHAEL ANDERLE

LMBPN Publishing
PMB 196, 2540 South Maryland Pkwy
Las Vegas, NV 89109

First US edition, June 2020
eBook ISBN: 978-1-64202-968-0
Print ISBN: 978-1-64202-969-7

THE MAGIC RECLAIMED TEAM

**Thanks to our JIT Readers**

Kerry Mortimer
Diane L. Smith
Dorothy Lloyd

**Editor**

SkyHunter Editing Team

Special shout out to Grace Snokes, Lynne Stiegler, Judah Raine, Kelly O'Donnell and Stephen Campbell for their general badassery behind the scenes to keep everything running so smoothly.

*From Martha*

To all those who love to read, and like a good puzzle inside
a good story
To Michael Anderle for his generosity
to all his fellow authors
To Louie and Jackie
And in memory of my big sister,
Dr. Diana Deane Carr
who first taught me about magic, Star Trek,
DC Comics and flaming cherries jubilee

*From Michael*

To Family, Friends and
Those Who Love
To Read.
May We All Enjoy Grace
To Live The Life We Are
Called.

## CHAPTER ONE

"More? You're telling us we have *more* running around Austin to do before we can fix magic and be done with this whole thing?" Laura Hadstrom stared at the newly awakened Peabrain standing in front of her with wide eyes.

John gave her a small, understanding smile. "Sorry, Laura. That's pretty much it. And there's no way around it."

The oldest Hadstrom sister ran a hand over the top of her head in exasperation and turned away from her sisters, Chuck, Nathan, and John on the pebbly beach at the Barton Creek Greenbelt. The berm that had once been a small island growing from the center of the creek towered above them in a huge mound, the chasm in the ground covered from view again by the willow tree's draping branches. *What a mess.*

"Okay." Nickie Hadstrom folded her arms and shared a knowing glance with her boyfriend Chuck. "Where do we start?"

"Well..." John nodded toward the huge hill in the center

of the creek that marked the Gorafrex's now-destroyed prison. His eyes shimmered with two consciousnesses now —his, and that of the Gorafrex who'd joined with him as its first willing host. "We should probably start with her."

The ethereal being's previous host still lay unconscious at the top of the hill, kept safe somehow through the path of destruction the magical storm had swept across the Greenbelt until five minutes ago. The woman's lower half protruded from beneath the draping curtain of willow branches.

"Oh, boy." Emily shook her head and slowly pulled away from John's embrace. "This is gonna be one hell of a first step."

"Well, it's the best place to start." Laura nodded at her sisters, and they trudged back across the cool water of the creek in the middle of Austin's sweltering summer heat.

John followed them, gazing around the Greenbelt as if he'd never seen it before. *In a way, everything's brand-new to me now, isn't it?*

The woman lying half beneath the willow branches groaned. Laura, Nickie, and Emily scrambled up the side of the slick hill toward her.

"How do we explain this one?" Nickie muttered.

"Like all the others," Laura replied. "But we can only tell her so much."

John stopped where the hill met the creek and watched them. "Her name's Melissa."

Emily stopped climbing to look down at him. "That thing knows their names?"

He shrugged. "The thing knows a lot of things, Em. I guess…so do I."

"Huh. Can it read minds?"

A small smile cracked John's otherwise unconcerned expression. "Only mine."

"Well yeah, okay. That's kind of a given."

The sisters reached the newly awakened Peabrain lying partially beneath the tree. Laura pulled aside the closest draping branches so Melissa could see all three of them. When the woman opened her eyes, complete terror quickly replaced her instant confusion. She tried to scramble backward toward the tree but kept slipping on the slick, wet grass and moss.

"Where is it? That *thing* that—Oh my god. What am I doing here? Who are you?"

"We're here to help." Nickie smiled and lowered slowly to her knees. "It's Melissa, right?"

"Yeah." Melissa quickly glanced from one sister to the next, blinking heavily as she realized the world around her didn't look quite the same anymore. "Somebody better tell me what's going on."

"You've had a once-in-a-lifetime wake-up call." Emily nodded and extended her hand to help the woman to her feet. "Something most people unfortunately don't get to experience."

"I…" Melissa reached for the youngest Hadstrom sister's hand, then her eyes widened. "You're glowing."

"Perfectly normal," Laura muttered.

"No, it's not."

"For some of us, it is." Nickie nodded, and Melissa finally took Emily's hand and accepted the extra support to her feet.

"I have a concussion, don't I? That's what all these

flashing lights are, and…" Melissa's gaze landed on John at the bottom of the hill, standing in the creek with his hands in his pockets. "Do I know you?"

"Nope. I'm John."

"Melissa." She glanced suspiciously around, did a double-take at the weirdly familiar man down below with the oddly shimmering eyes, and drew a deep breath. "I don't remember coming out here."

"That's also normal." Nickie climbed down the hill, followed by her sisters and a highly skeptical Melissa.

"My name's Emily, Laura and Nickie are my sisters, and you're gonna be okay."

When they helped Melissa down and her feet slid into the startlingly cool water of the creek, the woman gasped. "Did I…did I hurt someone?"

"What do you mean?" Laura exchanged a quick glance with Nickie. *The curse is broken, sure. But we still need to be careful.*

"There was an old man. And a… You know, *you* look really familiar, too. All of you."

Emily snorted and tried to brush it off with a shrug. "We get that a lot."

"I don't think so…"

"The only thing that matters now is that you're safe," Laura cut in before the woman could dart down that rabbit hole where the Hadstrom sisters couldn't follow. "Can we take you home? It's the least we can do after a… Well, I'm sure it's pretty confusing to wake up in the middle of the Greenbelt that looks like a hurricane moved through and with no idea how you got here."

Melissa frowned at her. "It's a little disconcerting, yeah."

"It's a short hike out to the parking lot." Nickie pointed up the wall of limestone boulders toward the footpath yards above the pebbly beach. "Then we'll give you a ride."

"I don't care about the ride." Melissa stopped before they reached the beach, standing rigid in the water with her fists clenched at her sides. "I wanna know what the hell happened. All of you are staring at me like I have three extra arms growing out of my head, and I'm not going anywhere until someone tells me why I—" A burst of tiny silver bubbles streamed from her mouth. Melissa's eyes widened again, and she swallowed. "Why I—" More bubbles emerged, flashing with multi-colored lights and echoing her voice back at her. "What the hell *is* this?"

The Hadstrom sisters watched Melissa's untamed Peabrain magic floating around them. The first round of bubbles popped with sharp snaps, sending blue lights darting in every direction.

"Ow!" Emily flinched away from the lights crackling against her arm and scowled. "Let's get away from these firecrackers first, huh?"

The tiny magical bubbles snapped again like a twisted piece of bubble wrap, showering the beach with electrical sparks.

"This is—ow!" Chuck ducked and smacked the back of his neck. "This isn't what I expected."

"Well, what did you *expect*?" Melissa shouted. The rest of her bubbles popped at the same time, lighting up in a halo around her disheveled hair.

Emily raised her hands. "You're totally confused and a little angry, Melissa—"

"Ya think?"

5

"We get it."

"Please let us take you home," Laura added while trying to give the woman a reassuring nod but unable to stop staring at Melissa's mouth. *Please don't start freaking out with any more messed-up magic.* "Or anywhere that feels safe and comfortable for you so you can calm down—"

"Calm down? You're talking about this like you see this kind of thing every day! I spewed bubbles out of my mouth that started spitting fireworks! And everything I can see right now is totally... Something's wrong. What did you do to me?"

"Woah. Hold on." Nickie spread her arms. "We didn't do anything."

Emily scrunched up her face and used every inch of willpower she had not to say a word. *Sure, we didn't do anything. Only locked her Gorafrex-possessed body up in the Clubhouse for a few days and brought her here as part of our last spell that didn't fix magic.*

"Then tell me what's going on!"

John stepped up behind her and gently set a hand on her shoulder.

Melissa froze under his touch and turned slowly to look at him. "What are you doing?"

"Offering support." He smiled. "Which we can all keep doing once we get back to the car. Unless you'd rather we leave you alone. It's completely up to you."

His words took the frightened fight right out of her. Melissa sighed and glanced from one Hadstrom witch to the next. "No, I... I'd like to go home. I have no idea how I'm supposed to explain any of this."

"You're not." John removed his hand and nodded. "The

best thing to do is to let it happen. These three are doing everything they can to make things right."

Emily grinned at him. "And it could be a lot worse right now."

"I seriously doubt that, but whatever." With a determined nod, Melissa finally walked out of the creek and headed toward the limestone boulders, water sloshing out of her shoes with every step. She paused to look Nathan and Chuck up and down. "Who are you?"

"Chuck."

"Nathan."

Melissa pointed at the professor. "Your eyes are purple."

Nathan pressed his lips together to bite back a laugh and nodded.

Melissa shook her head and moved toward the wall, then climbed to the footpath as the Hadstrom witches and John followed closely behind her.

Chuck looked up at Nathan and cocked his head. "Seriously? Purple eyes?"

"Just a little."

"And of course, the one *human* wrapped up in all this can't see it, huh? Great." Chuck tossed his hands in the air and dropped them against his thighs with a slap. "That's like a Viking going to war with one hand or half an axe."

"We're not going to war with anyone, babe," Nickie called over her shoulder as she finished the climb. "I wouldn't mind seeing you walk around with a battle axe, though."

He chuckled. "Okay, note to self. And we should talk more about that later."

Nathan shook his head and followed Chuck toward the

wall to make their climb. The Hadstrom sisters headed down the footpath with Melissa, doing the best they could to answer the woman's dozens of questions without breaking the rules.

*Stupid rules, too.* Emily slapped two mosquitos that landed on her arm. *One dark Hadstrom thousands of years ago is responsible for Melissa's peabrain waking up, and we can't tell her that much. But at least we can keep her from losing it before she gets home. Or at least try.*

When they reached the access lot outside the Barton Creek Greenbelt, Laura pulled her keys out of her back pocket and frowned. "It looks so empty without the Club-house coin."

Nickie patted her big sister's shoulder and headed for Laura's car. "One of the things we had to give up. Like our rings."

"Yeah, that part still sucks." Emily smoothed her hair away from her face and looked at Melissa. "I guess you have some options. You can ride with us or Chuck and Nathan. Or I guess in John's truck?"

Melissa glanced at the tensely smiling faces around her and pointed at Laura's car. "I'm not about to get into a car with two men I don't know."

Chuck spread his arms. "Hey, we're nice guys."

She ignored him and opened the back door before sliding in.

"I'll come with you," John said.

Emily looked at his white truck again. "What about your ride?"

He set his hand on the small of her back and leaned in to

mutter, "We're gonna be driving around together for a while, Em. You can bring me back to get my truck when we've fixed everything that needs to be fixed." With a quick wink, John slid into the back seat beside Melissa. The woman widened her eyes when he smiled at her and had to look away.

"Okay. Carpool." Emily clapped her hands and jogged around the back of the car as Nickie got in the front passenger seat. "Move over, Peabrain. We need space for one more in there."

"Peabrain?"

Emily shut the door and blinked. "Oh."

In the passenger seat, Nickie sighed.

"It's like a term of endearment," John explained. "Applies to me too, actually."

"You?" Melissa stared at him. "Do my eyes do that weird flashy thing too?"

"No. That's only me."

Laura opened the driver-side door and turned toward Chuck and Nathan. "You guys wanna meet us at the house? This shouldn't take too long."

"It's not like we have a choice, right?" Chuck laughed and got into the car.

Nathan grinned at the oldest Hadstrom sister and nodded. "We'll be there waiting for you."

"Thanks. See you soon." Laura got behind the wheel and started the engine while watching the guys drive out of the parking lot in her rearview mirror. *Almost there. Then I won't have to keep telling him to wait for me all the time. Nathan's more patient than anyone I know, but everyone has their limits.*

"All right, Melissa." Nickie turned around in the passenger seat. "Where's home?"

"Crestview."

"Crestview it is." Emily smacked the back of Laura's seat and thrust a finger toward the ceiling. "Onward."

Laura shook her head as she turned the car around in the parking lot to head toward Melissa's house. "You're in a surprisingly good mood, Em."

"I'm making the best of a seriously weird situation." Emily shot Melissa a tight smile, then glanced at John. *There's a former witch-killer living forever inside my boyfriend. What else is new?*

## CHAPTER TWO

Melissa's questions didn't stop in the car. If anything, they only grew more frequent and more ridiculous. "If this is magic, and I'm not saying it is, but if it is, why is it bubbles? Do I need a wand? Oh my God, is this like *Harry Potter* in real life? Do I have to go back to school for this stuff? I graduated five years ago. I can't go back to school. Why did you call me Peabrain? That's a pretty insulting name for anyone you're *not* trying to insult. Is it because of the bubbles? 'Cause they were so tiny?"

Emily shot a quick look at the rearview mirror and met Laura's gaze in the reflection. *I don't know which one is worse. Dave's crazy magic in our house or trying to follow Melissa's train of thought.*

"Melissa, we can't—"

"Holy crap! Look at that guy!" Melissa practically smashed Emily back against the seat as she leaned over the witch's lap to get a better view out her window. "That guy has *wings*."

"That would be a fairy," Emily replied blandly.

"I saw someone with wings, didn't I?" Melissa shoved herself back in the seat between Emily and John and blinked. "That old guy."

"Oh, yep." Nickie nodded. "Leonidas is a fairy, too."

"A *fairy*? Jesus. Where do I know him from?"

"Um…"

Laura scrunched up her nose. "You may have—"

"Seen a lot of things that probably don't make sense right now," John cut in, turning slowly away from his window to meet Melissa's wide-eyed gaze. "The pieces will come back to you bit by bit, and they might seem pretty unbelievable. But when they do, you'll be ready for them. I promise."

"You guys still won't tell me what happened, huh?" Melissa swallowed, and the novelty of seeing the world through her newly awakened Peabrain eyes dimmed considerably. "Did I…did I hurt anybody?"

"No!" Emily startled herself with that shouted reply, which made Melissa jump in her seat, too. Then she cleared her throat. "No. *You* didn't hurt anyone. And you're not hurt, either, which is also super important."

"Remember that you're still you." Laura nodded and turned onto Melissa's street. "The same person with the same life, only a little extra."

"Extra." The woman closed her eyes. "The last thing I needed right now is *extra*."

"*Or*," Emily added, "it's exactly what you needed."

"Yeah, right."

"This has always been a part of who you are." John ran a hand through his hair and leaned his head back against the seat. "Like a skill you didn't know you had until you sat down and tried."

Melissa shot him a disbelieving look. "Bubble skills?"

Emily bit down on her lip before a laugh escaped her. "I like you, Melissa."

John shrugged. "You'll figure it out. That's what we do. Honestly, that's what *I'm* still doing, too. And it's not nearly as hard as it seems. Give it a few days, huh? Things will start making a lot more sense in a few days."

"Right. When we—" Emily stopped herself from saying anything else and looked up in the rearview mirror to see Laura's warning gaze. *Can't tell the baby Peabrain we broke magic and have to fix it, either. I seriously can't wait for this to be over.*

Laura pulled over in front of a small beige house and parked the car. "Is this you?"

Melissa sighed heavily. "Yeah. All me. My house isn't gonna start talking to me or anything, right?"

"Only if you want it to." Emily snorted at the woman's terrified expression and shook her head. "I'm kidding. Totally kidding. You'd have to call in a professional for something like that."

John opened his door and got out to let Melissa onto the sidewalk. She stood there rigidly, staring at her house, and swallowed. "Do you guys, uh...wanna come in with me? I still have more questions."

"I bet you do." Nickie chuckled.

"We have a bunch of stuff to work on today," Laura added.

"What, like you guys go around Austin pulling people

out of the creek to tell them absolutely nothing about new magic they suddenly have?"

Emily wrinkled her nose. "Something like that."

"Shit, I'm talking about this like it's *real*."

"It's definitely real." John gestured toward her house. "I can walk you to the door if you want."

"If that's all I'm gonna get, sure." Melissa turned back to the Hadstrom sisters in the car and looked like she had no idea why she'd done it. "Thanks, I think. I'm not sure what for other than the fact that none of you freaked out at my bubble vomit."

"Trust me, we've seen *way* worse." Emily shot her a thumbs-up. "You're good to go."

"Okay…"

"You got this, Melissa." Laura nodded. "And John's right. In a few days, everything's gonna be a lot easier for a lot of people. Including you."

"But you can't tell me why or how or who, blah, blah, blah. I get it." With a disbelieving laugh, Melissa turned and headed slowly toward her front door.

"Be right back." John shut the back door and caught up to the Peabrain who, until an hour ago, had been the host for the creature now sharing his body.

Nickie ran a hand through her long dark hair and sighed. "He looks like he's doing okay with that new setup."

"Who, John?" Emily laughed shrilly, then forced it back down. "Apparently, they're a good match."

Both of her sisters turned around in their seats to look at her directly.

"The Gorafrex. John and the Gorafrex, you guys. Not Melissa. Come on. I mean, we don't even know the lady."

Laura raised an eyebrow. "How are *you* doing?"

Emily patted the seat on either side of her. "I'm good. Enjoying the AC in this car. Way to keep *that* running smoothly."

Neither of her sisters found her deflection amusing. Nickie grabbed the back of her seat to twist farther around. "She means how are you doing after everything that happened."

"I know what she meant, Nickie."

"That was some serious stuff."

"Oh, you mean John being speared by a flying tree branch and almost bleeding out all over the beach?" Emily nodded and puffed out her lower lip. "Yeah, I'd say that was pretty serious. Traumatic, even. Maybe. But he's not dead. He's Gorafrex-flavored John. Still the same guy. With another guy in there somewhere." She leaned toward the opposite window and squinted at John and Melissa finishing up their conversation by her front door. "Or girl. Or whatever. It's hard to tell."

Nickie turned in her seat and muttered, "She's not gonna let us in right now with this one."

"Yeah, I'm getting that vibe, too." Laura watched their youngest sister peering out the window. "You know, Em, it's okay if everything's not okay. I mean, things worked out in a weirdly convenient way, but that doesn't mean you have to suddenly be happy about everything."

"Yeah, I know."

"If you need to vent or get something out of your system—"

"Ha!" Emily sat back in her seat and stared at her sisters

with a skeptically raised eyebrow. "You guys don't want me to *get it out of my system*. Not until magic's fixed."

"So you're not actually okay?"

"I'm *fine*. Maybe a little extra ecstatic that he's not dead and that I don't have to worry about keeping these secrets from him anymore. Or avoiding him." Another bitter laugh escaped her. "It's all out there on the table now, isn't it?"

"Like I said, Em. It's totally okay if you're not okay."

Emily looked at her oldest sister and nodded. "Thanks."

"For what it's worth," Nickie pointed at Melissa's front door as the woman finally stepped back into her house, "I think John has a much better way of handling new Peabrains than we do."

"Well, we're witches. We can only guess what it's like for them." Laura shrugged. "He knows."

"Yep." Emily watched him head back toward the car. "Anyone else weirded out by how calm he is?"

"He has an ancient ethereal being that's probably the most powerful thing on this ship cohabitating in his body, Em. If the Gorafrex is really in there to help them both, I don't think it's too much of a stretch to assume it's explaining things to John as they go."

"I hope you're right."

# CHAPTER THREE

When the Hadstrom sisters pulled back up to the witches' Victorian-style house on Pressler Street, John seemed on the verge of asking his own nonstop questions. Emily leaned toward him. "You okay?"

"What? Oh, yeah. Just taking it all in."

"Things really look that different, huh?"

He smiled. "Different and then exactly the same. You haven't changed, though."

"Well, that's encouraging."

They got out of the car and headed up the cement steps to the walkway on the hill toward the house.

"So, John." Laura turned around to give him a hopeful smile. "You think you'll be able to remember all the things we need to fix?"

"I think so, yeah."

"Might help to make a list."

"Seriously?" Emily frowned at her oldest sister. "You want him to sit the Gorafrex down and write out all its crimes in front of everyone?"

"That's not how I'd put it, Em. But at least if we have a list, we'll all be able to look at it and see what's coming up next. Plus, it helps us figure out if we're missing anything. Yeah, we broke the Hadstrom-Gorafrex curse, but magic obviously isn't coming back until we fix everything else first. We can't wing it."

"I don't mind," John said. "Really. It'll be good for me, too. And the Gorafrex wants to help clean up its mess as much as you do."

"You sound really sure about that."

He laughed. "I *am* sure, Em. It told me."

"Let's hope a Gorafrex freed from our family curse isn't capable of lying to us *or* John." Nickie turned around and nodded at her little sister. "Okay? We're gonna have to trust that thing if we want to finish this."

Emily squinted at her. "I know that."

"Do you trust *me*, Em?" John held his hand out to her.

*Crap. I can't say no to that smile.* She grabbed his hand and laced her fingers through his. "Yeah, I trust you. But I wouldn't be surprised or even offended, honestly, if you—"

A flutter of black feathers and shiny beaks burst around the hedges in the side yard and swarmed toward the witches. The grackles hopped and flapped at surprising speed, their beaks open soundlessly as they blocked the Hadstrom sisters off from the front porch.

"Woah." Nickie raised her arms and watched the huge black grackles stampeding around them. "Birds are freaking out again."

"Well, they were the first ones to warn us that things were heading downhill. Maybe they know what happened."

Emily stared at the birds rushing toward her and John.

"Or they're in attack mode. They've never acted like this before."

"They're birds who can't fly, Em." Nickie folded her arms. "How much attacking can they do?"

"Woah." John tried to step back and discovered his feet surrounded by grackles. The closest ones leapt onto his shoes and flapped against his legs. "Um... I'm pretty sure they—ah!"

He stepped back again, hastily picked up his foot when a grackle flapped furiously and gave his calf a sharp nip with its beak, then fell backward into the grass.

"Hey, cut it out!" Emily swatted at the birds, who hopped and skittered out of her way before redoubling their efforts to get to John. "We didn't order attack birds, and I didn't watch him almost die and get healed by a Gorafrex so you lot could try to peck him apart—*hey*!"

The grackles swarmed up onto John's lap, then hopped on his chest until he fell back in the grass, unmoving.

"Get off him!" Emily tried to shoo the birds away again and stopped when a low chuckle from John grew into full-throated laughter. "What?"

"Look at that." He picked his head up off the ground to watch the black birds hopping around on his chest as dozens more tried to climb their way up John Mountain. Another surprised laugh escaped him, and he extended his hand toward Emily. "We're good."

"No, that looks like they're trying to... Well, I *was* gonna say eat you, but now I have absolutely no idea what this is."

"This is a greeting." John pushed himself up onto his elbows, paused, then slowly straightened the rest of the way, giving the grackles plenty of time to hop off him and each other. "If they had their voices back right now, I bet you they'd be telling me welcome home."

"You don't live here."

"Em, I think he's talking about the Peabrain part." Laura carefully stepped through the excited grackles covering the front lawn, then offered John one hand while Emily helped him up with the other. "I've heard a few people say waking up feels like home."

"Oh, yeah? Who said that?'

Laura rolled her eyes. "Okay, I read about it."

"She's not wrong." John brushed dirt and stray blades of grass off his clothes. "Hell of a greeting, though."

"So you're not covered in beak-sized holes? Okay." Emily froze and narrowed her eyes. "Wait, how did you know they lost their voices?"

John spread his arms.

"Right. The Gorafrex that tells you everything. Your fast track through Magic 101, isn't it?" She puffed out a sigh. "That's gonna take some getting used to."

John laughed as he stepped around the fluttering, hopping birds and took her hand again, giving it a little squeeze. "You're pretty adaptable. It won't take as long as you think."

"Uh-huh. We'll see." The youngest Hadstrom sister gave the excited birds another dubious glance. "You guys really can't find another fun place to hang out until we get your wings flapping in the air again?"

"Think about it, Em." Nickie headed toward the front door. "If we were anyone else, and we knew that three witches were at the center of everything crazy that's happened in Austin over the last few weeks, where would *you* wanna hang out?"

"If you're trying to convince me of how cool we are, Nickie, I already know that. Honestly, I'd want to stay as far away from those three witches as I could get."

"Nah." John tugged playfully on her arm. "They know you three are the only ones who could put things back together again. They're not only birds."

She laughed. "Okay, just because the Gorafrex tells you things doesn't mean I don't already know."

He smirked. "Did you know these birds came straight from Arenya V?"

A sputtering choke burst from Emily's mouth, and she stared at her sisters. "He knows about the home planet, too."

"And the ship."

The older Hadstrom witches nodded, and Nickie tapped her temple. "Gorafrex, Em."

"Yeah, I *know*. It's so weird to hear you talking about this stuff like you know it as well as we do."

"Well I do, I guess." John shrugged as they stepped up onto the front stoop. "Only from a different perspective."

"Mm-hmm." Emily tried to hide a smile as they followed her sisters into the house, then leaned toward him. "And no. I didn't know our flightless feathery friends were direct descendants from this ship's homeworld."

"No, not descendants. Literally the same ones."

She jerked her hand out of his and playfully shoved him away. "Get outta here with that. I'm the one who's supposed to know stuff."

John chuckled, and a momentary frown flickered across his eyebrows. "Does it bother you that much?"

"That you know more things about magic and the world and this ship and freakin' immortal birds than I do? No, not really. I was kinda looking forward to getting to explain things to you, though. You know, like Nickie got to do with Chuck."

His eyes widened. "Did she explain everything?"

"Oh, yeah. His magic didn't wake up, but he sure got the full dose of reality in one fell swoop. You can ask your Gorafrex co-host about that one."

"Hmm." John frowned into the living room, where Chuck and Nathan watched him and the Hadstrom sisters walking back into the house. Then his eyes widened. "Oh."

"Yeah. Another minor casualty of your bodiless new friend's magical rampage."

John laughed. "He's handling that really well for not having his magic yet."

"Yeah, he is, isn't he?"

Chuck finished a long pull on his beer and watched them enter the foyer, his eyes wide. "Wow. That was literally the fastest you guys have returned from anything."

Nathan snorted.

John gave Emily a slow smile. "Does it usually take you guys a lot longer to drive someone home?"

"It's not the simple tasks that hold us up, usually. It's everything else."

"And this time, we didn't get sidetracked by the Gorafrex blowing something up or trying to kill us." Nickie turned toward John and shrugged. "No offense."

"None taken. By either of us."

Nickie slumped on the couch next to Chuck, who offered her his beer before he stood. "You guys want drinks? We picked up, like, a whole case on the way back. Figured we might as well, you know?"

"Definitely." Emily headed for the armchair next to Nathan.

Laura sat on the armrest of Nathan's chair, and he put a hand on her thigh. "Count me in too, Chuck. Thanks."

"Yep." Chuck disappeared into the kitchen, followed by the whump of the fridge and the clinking of glass bottles against each other.

The dog door popped open in the mudroom, then Speed scrambled into the living room from the back door, his claws clacking against the hardwood. When he saw John, he stopped, let out a low growl, then barreled toward him.

"Woah, Speed!" Emily tried to intercept him, but their usually lethargic immortal bulldog darted around her swiping hands and leapt up onto John's leg. "All the animals have lost it!"

Speed whined, his tongue lolling from his mouth, and pawed at John's leg while hopping back and forth. John laughed as he reached down to scratch behind the dog's ears, and his hand got a dog-tongue bath instead. "Hey, buddy."

Laura leaned forward on the armrest of Nathan's chair, ready to leap up and intervene if she had to. "I've only seen him move that fast one other time. And that was... Well, I guess *one* of you were here for that, huh?"

"You mean the night we—" John shook his head. "*It* kidnapped you?"

"Yeah, that night." Laura folded her arms and glanced at Nathan.

John finally got a good scratch in behind Speed's ears, and the dog settled almost instantly. "It's a funny thing about animals, you know? Birds. Dogs. They can always tell when something's off, but when whatever it is gets put right again, they're the fastest to forgive and forget."

Emily stuck her hands on her hips. "Yeah, like forgetting the fact that he knows he's not supposed to jump."

Nickie laughed. "That dog's been around literally forever, Em. Or as far back as forever goes on this ship. I don't think we can take credit for training him."

"And how do you train a dog who turns into a seven-foot fighting machine, anyway?" Laura frowned at their dog. "You really think he knows the Gorafrex is in there with you, John?"

"Yeah, he knows." John squatted and Speed immediately rolled over on his back with an urgent grunt. "Probably helps that he already knows me. Although I did *not* know that he could do all that."

"What, the whole were-bulldog thing? Neither did we."

"Well, no. I didn't know that either, but that's not what I'm talking about."

The Hadstrom sisters stared at their multi-generational family pet. Nickie tilted her head. "What else can he do?"

John stood while shaking his head and laughing silently. Then Chuck came back from the kitchen with their beers in a bucket of ice, a bag of tortilla chips, and a large tub of salsa. "Oh, hey, Speed. Finally decided to join the party, huh? Great, now we can—oh, *jeeze!*"

Chuck scowled, diverted his path toward the dog and

went all the way around the couch before setting everything down on the coffee table. "Immortal or not, that dog's rear end has some serious issues."

"Whew!" Emily fanned her hand in front of her face and went back to the empty armchair. "Please tell me that's not what you were talking about."

John chuckled and grinned down at Speed. "Should I tell 'em?"

The bulldog grunted and wiggled on the floor, begging for more belly rubs.

"No." Laura pointed at Speed and shook her head. "If you're about to tell us that dog rips magical farts, you can stop right there. It's already been a long day."

"It's, like, two o'clock." Chuck grabbed a beer, popped off the lid, and sat next to Nickie to throw his arm around her on the couch.

"I know." Laura grabbed a beer too and lifted it toward him in a toast. "And so much has happened, I don't even care that I don't drink this early."

Nathan laughed when she sat directly in his lap and took a long swig. "Now's a good time to start."

She wiped her mouth with the back of a hand and surprised everyone with a loud burp. "My thoughts exactly. Unleash a Gorafrex the day your baby sister graduates college—wrongly imprisoned, I might add—then spend two weeks trying to smash up ancient technology so it can't escape and blow a hole right through this ship. Toss in magic going completely bonkers with two—*two*—energy cores powered up, get kidnapped, rescue a few other kidnapped magicals, and try not to let Austin blow itself up. All that, only to realize that your family legacy isn't actually a legacy but a curse everyone forgot about. So you dig up your dead family members and cast the only spell that works right now to break a curse that also keeps a pretty decent guy from dying by teaming up with a witch-killer that is actually this benevolent being who now only wants to help. You guys, we never officially kicked off summer, and if now seems like the right time to do it by drinking a beer at two o'clock in the afternoon in the middle of the week, screw it. It's summer!"

Laura toasted to herself and took another huge gulp of beer.

Emily and Nickie exchanged a glance over the coffee table. "And she asked me if *I'm* okay."

"Yeah, that sounded a lot like one of *your* monologues, Em."

Nathan burst out laughing and clinked his beer against Laura's. "It's five o'clock somewhere, right?"

Laura grinned. "See? You get it." They both drank.

Chuck popped open another beer before leaning across the couch to offer it to John. "Welcome to the weird side of the Hadstrom house."

"I kinda like it."

## CHAPTER FOUR

With half the tortilla chips and salsa eaten and the bucket of beer freshly restocked on the coffee table, Laura stood and nodded resolutely. "I think it's time for that list now, right?"

John looked up at her from where he and Emily had moved to the floor to be closer to the snacks. "Sure."

"Half an hour?" Emily asked as Laura headed up the staircase in the foyer. "That's all we get before we're back to business as usual?"

"Magic's been broken for way too long already, Em. Besides, we still have to wait for Team John to make the list. It's not like we're going back out right this second." Laura's bedroom door opened and closed again behind her.

Emily raised an eyebrow at Nickie. "Well, one of *us* is driving this time."

"Wanna flip a coin?"

"Or whatever."

Nathan watched the top of the staircase. "She's only had two beers."

"That's one and a half beers over the Laura Hadstrom legal limit." Emily snorted and reached for the chips again. "You should see her drink margaritas."

"Oy." Chuck laughed and rolled his eyes.

John's face lit up. "Now *that* was a fun night."

"Yeah, before all the fun got sucked right out of everything we were doing. Just like the magic." The chip crunched loudly in Emily's mouth, then Laura bounded back down the stairs while steadying herself on the railing.

"Okay. I brought you a whole notebook, 'cause I don't want to assume anything about how much you'll end up putting on this list." Laura slapped the notebook down onto the coffee table, followed by a pen, and gave John a lopsided smile. "I hope it's not a long one."

"We'll have to see, right?" He slid the pen and paper toward him and opened to the first blank page. The pen hovered over the first line. Then he looked up at the five other people watching him intently. "Don't feel like you have to wait around for me or anything, if you have other stuff to do."

"Not really." Nickie slung her arm over the couch's armrest, her fresh beer dangling from her hand.

"Yeah, our schedules pretty much cleared themselves so we could get this done. Perfect timing, really." Emily stuck her elbows on the coffee table and looked up at John with an eager smile. "I mean, unless you don't want us around while you write everything out."

"I don't mind." When he blinked, a thin silver light

flashed behind his eyes. "You guys are gonna see it all put down here, anyway."

"Go for it, man." Chuck nodded and sipped his beer. "Nobody's here to judge."

Nickie turned to look at him with a smirk. "Listen to you."

"Hey, I like John. And I like not being 'the new guy' anymore."

"Babe." She scooted closer to him on the couch and snuggled in while patting his chest. "You were never the new guy."

"Well, except for the part where we've been together for four years and I only recently found out that you and your family are witches and magic is a thing."

"Fair enough."

"Plus, he's taking it a lot better than I did. Like, a lot."

John smiled down at the notebook. "I have a little help."

The second that pen touched down to paper, he didn't stop writing, engrossed in the information the Gorafrex fed him to funnel right out into a list. Emily watched him write for the first three minutes, then focused on going through more chips and salsa.

When the fifteen-minute mark passed in silence, Laura stood and almost fell back into Nathan's lap. "I'm going to the bathroom."

The sound of John turning one page after another filled the living room. Nickie got up and brought her acoustic guitar back to the couch with her. She draped her legs over Chuck's lap, winked, then started strumming the new tune she'd been working on.

"What's that?" John was still writing.

She stopped. "Something new." *I didn't think of that. My music and the Gorafrex now.* "Is it bothering either of you?"

"No, it helps. Keep going."

"Huh." She and Chuck shared a surprised glance, and she started playing again.

"Still working on finding you a new Strat, by the way." Chuck patted her legs. "Obviously, we've been a little busy."

"Don't worry about it. I'm not playing anything, anyway. Not until we get magic back on track."

"What happened to the other one?" John blinked, and the pen scratched faster against the notebook.

"I smashed it," Emily muttered. "It was a life-or-death situation, pretty much."

"Hmm."

"And then I lit a really nice guitar donated by another excellent musician on fire at the Mean-Eyed Cat," Nickie added. "That pretty much hit the pause button on public venues."

Emily pointed at her. "But it got us some Huldu friends."

"I've always liked your music, Nickie." John stared at the notebook with wide eyes, his hand moving furiously now in a way that could only have drawn scribbles but somehow wrote out legible words. He flipped the notebook over. "And I think the… I think we're both… fans."

Emily raised her eyebrows when John filled the last full page with the rest of the Gorafrex's list in five seconds flat. Then the pen dropped from his fingers, and he blinked rapidly while sitting back on his heels. "Woah."

Nickie stopped playing.

"Yeah?" John looked up at her. "It's only a few pages."

"A few?" She grabbed the notebook and turned back to the first page while counting. "Six pages filled with tiny writing. There's no way we can get through all of this in a few days. A few *weeks*, maybe."

"Let me see." John scanned the notebook again and frowned. "I... That's weird."

"What? Do you not remember writing all this down?"

"I remember. Mostly." He chuckled. "I think my passenger took a little backseat test drive."

Emily closed her eyes. "That's not reassuring at all."

"Em?"

"Yeah."

"I agreed to it, okay? Hey, look at me."

The youngest Hadstrom sister opened her eyes and focused on John's easygoing smile.

"See? Still me. I'm here. The Gorafrex isn't gonna pop out and take over at any second, okay?"

She drew a deep breath. "This is really weird."

"I know."

"Can I look at that?" Nickie asked. John handed over the notebook, and she flipped through the pages. "Em, it's not really as much as it looks like. I mean, yeah, there are a lot of items on this list. A lot of—jeeze, how did that thing do so much damage in so little time?"

John shrugged. "It was on a mission, I guess."

"Yeah, no kidding. And it laid out an explanation for what it did and why and how to fix it. For each thing on here."

"Which is a different stop for us now too, huh?" Emily blew the stray hair out of her face and drummed her fingers on the coffee table. "Well, I guess we better get crackin' then, right?"

"Not without Laura." Nickie glanced into the foyer as her big sister walked back into the living room, looking flushed but a lot steadier on her feet.

"Not without me, what?"

"John finished his list." Emily pointed at the notebook.

"Excellent." Laura took the list from Nickie and scanned the cramped writing, flipping quickly through the pages. "John."

"Yeah?"

"Is this everything?"

"Uh… I'm pretty sure, yeah. I mean, I'm working with what I'm being told, here."

"Okay." Laura flicked the notebook and nodded. "This is a big list. I wanna make sure we don't get to end of it only to open a whole new door into *one more thing* before this is over. Like we did with breaking the curse."

John scratched his head and nodded. "Yeah. The Gorafrex didn't hold anything back so what you see is at least everything it can remember. Wish I could be more certain about it."

"Okay." Laura flipped through the pages again. "Where do we start? We have all these past Peabrain hosts. Marlin, Jessica, Annie, Dave. I guess we already covered Melissa, right?"

"Right."

"Wait, *Dave?*" Chuck sat up straight on the couch. "You're gonna go pay Dave a visit with that thing inside John?"

"That's part of the deal, man." John spread his arms.

"Gotta hit everything on the list. Most of it is repairing some physical damage. And the rest is the Gorafrex making an offering, I think."

Chuck swallowed. "Dude, I told these guys no sacrifices, and I gotta put the same guidelines out there on this one, too."

"Nope. No sacrifices. Only making amends. This thing doesn't like what it's done, and it has to tie up loose ends. In a good way."

"And that's exactly how we're gonna get magic back." Nickie swung her legs off Chuck's lap, sat up, and threw her arms around him. "Then we'll all have a lot less to worry about. Things'll go right back to feeling normal. Mostly."

"I don't know." Chuck huffed out a laugh and pulled her closer. "This feels a lot like the new normal."

"Chuck, please don't jinx it," Laura muttered.

"Hey, I'm ready for a change too. And so we're clear, when you guys go talk to Dave for whatever *cleanup* you're gonna do with him, I wanna be there."

"Deal." Emily wrinkled her nose and looked at John. "Unless that's somehow against the rules of how this works. We learned that the hard way a few times."

"Nope. Chuck, you can come if you want. It might help, since Dave's the only one of this thing's former hosts who knows what's happening." John shrugged. "Or at least, he knew more about what happened to *him*."

"The perks of knowing the Hadstrom sisters." Chuck raised his beer high. "Am I right?"

Nathan snorted. "I'll drink to that."

They toasted each other from across the room. Laura

eyed them both, barely containing a tiny smile, and went back to scouring through the Gorafrex's list. "So after the hosts, we have the… Hmm. The witches that helped power the energy cores."

Nickie grimaced. "They didn't make it."

"That'll have to be more of a vigil-type thing." John frowned while trying to put the Gorafrex's thoughts into words. "I guess those witches didn't have any other family around, which is why it chose them. I think. So… You know what? I'll have a better explanation for how to handle that part once we get there."

"That works." Laura ran her finger down the list. "Then there are the kidnapped magicals. The first wizard named Mitchell."

"The one who tried to stab Dave." Emily nodded.

Chuck drank more beer and stared at the coffee table.

"Vanessa, who was swiped right out of her back yard at Nathan's party. And Leonidas. For kidnapping him *and* destroying his apothecary. Double whammy."

John burst out laughing, and everyone turned to look at him in confusion. Emily leaned forward, trying to catch his gaze. *Please don't let him go insane after all this.*

"Okay, spill it." Nathan shifted his weight in the armchair while smirking. "That thing made a joke inside your head, didn't it?"

Tilting his head from side to side, John calmed his surprising laughter and sighed. "Something like that. Leonidas the fairy. He has a lotta good stuff in that shop of his."

"Not anymore. The place torn was apart."

John looked up at Laura with an apologetic smile. "We

didn't—*the Gorafrex* didn't destroy everything. Or use it all."

"Oh, yeah? Did it take an inventory of the inventory, too?" Chuck snorted.

"Not exactly. It was working with a specific list."

"For the Tenebantur potion." Laura nodded. "We know. So after Leonidas, next is…aw, really?"

"Come on, Laura." Nickie waved for her sister to continue. "You're the only one holding that list."

"Astro."

"Ew." Emily wrinkled her nose and shoved her hand into the chip bag for another crunchy snack. "I thought we were done with that crotchety weirdo."

"Apparently not. Because…" Laura frowned at the written explanation and turned the page. "The Gorafrex stole the soothsayer's memories? He said it was more like fishing for information in a bunch of ethereal soup."

"There are different layers." John rubbed his chin. "Everybody has their take on it."

Laura's eyes flickered toward him briefly. "Okay… Wow, you really went all the way back to the beginning. We have the wizards who crashed their cars that night Nickie played at the laundromat."

"The night I almost played myself into a coma. Right. Good times."

Chuck slipped his arm over her shoulders again and pulled her closer.

"And the Peabrain boy who blew up his back yard downtown."

Emily grimaced. "The day the mess became public."

"Then we get to…what? Escort John and company to a

bunch of Huldus who want nothing to do with us." Laura turned the page again and tapped her fingers against her lips. "And Rutilda, for using her Velikan engineering against all of Austin."

"Rutilda's not around anymore, either," Nickie added.

John joined Emily in another round of chips and salsa. "We'll put her in with the witches who didn't make it. I think she'd appreciate the sentiment."

Emily's eyes widened. "You were passed out when I talked to her."

"I saw enough. And the Gorafrex knows way more about her than I think the giant Engineer realized. The Velikan are pretty sentimental, actually."

"Uh…" Nickie squinted at him. "If by sentimental you mean never throwing anything away and living literally on top of all her stuff, then yeah, maybe I'd agree."

"I mean with other magicals. She was losing her mind, but she really liked you guys. Especially you, Em."

Emily snorted and bumped her shoulder against John's. "I knew it. I liked her, too."

## CHAPTER FIVE

"Okay, hold on." Laura dropped the notebook by her side. "How do you know this stuff?"

John laughed. "Do I need to hang a sign around my neck that says, 'The Gorafrex told me'?"

"The Gorafrex was in that prison almost the entire time this ship's been floating around off course in an unplanned orbit. They weren't friends."

"No, but..." John blinked quickly. "I guess it's pulling this stuff out of that ethereal soup. Maybe?"

"It can access dead people's thoughts too, huh?" Chuck ran a hand through his hair and leaned all the way back against the couch. "That's a little creepy."

"It's more like accessing all the energy still floating around. I don't know how much of it still extends from back before we were all on this ship, but the ship does a great job of containing all its memories, anyway. And sustaining itself when everything's running the way it's supposed to."

Nickie pulled her legs up onto the couch and crossed

them beneath her. "Okay, John's sudden knowledge about all this stuff is starting to weird me out a little, too."

"Sorry."

"Dude, don't apologize for that," Chuck said. "I'd take instant knowledge over thinking I was losing my mind any day."

John shot him a crooked smile. "It's kinda weird that I don't think this is weird, isn't it?"

"A little." Nathan crossed one long leg over the other and shrugged. "But we're gonna have to deal. That's not really anything new, is it?" He nodded at Laura. "So, after this Astro guy is…"

"The Tree Folk. That makes sense."

"You're gonna have to give them something super important to the Gorafrex," Emily added. "That's how the Tree Folk do their thing."

John nodded. "We'll figure that one out as we go along."

"Looks like we have to revisit a bunch of those energy cores. Fix the damage done by the ones where we fought the Gorafrex and then… We seriously have to turn off the ones it activated?"

"Part of the package," John muttered. "The ship's mended a lot of the physical damage already, especially around the energy cores. But turning those two off is essential to bringing magic back. And the rest of this process is more about cleaning up the emotional and mental damage, I guess."

"Mental." Chuck lifted his beer to his lips and muttered, "You can say that again."

Laura frowned at the notebook. "The last two things don't have an explanation. Why the main library?"

"Oh." John scratched his head. "Because of what's in that secret room. All the Library at Alexandria books?"

Emily grimaced. "Yeah, but the Gorafrex didn't touch those. I'm the one who stole a restricted magical book and got away with it."

He laughed. "Way to go. The Gorafrex breaking magic is the only reason you didn't get your brain cells fried by those wards. I guess fixing things with the library is a way to pay everyone back for taking away all the resources in there?" With a snort, he shook his head. "Some of the stuff coming out of my mouth doesn't even sound like me anymore."

"There we go." Emily patted his back and grinned. "Now the weirdness is sinking in."

"It's a mixed bag, isn't it?"

"Welcome to our world, John."

"Okay, then this says Hadstroms." Laura pointed at the last item on the list. "Is that the three of us or literally everyone?"

"Oh, no." Nickie's shoulders sagged. "Grave robbing is only fun the first time."

Emily barked out a laugh and clapped her hands over her mouth.

"That's kind of a two-parter." John smiled sheepishly. "Saving the best for last, I guess."

"That's very thoughtful of you." Laura cocked her head. "Or I guess, thoughtful of the Gorafrex. This is weird. Are you two one person now, or two different brains in there, or what?"

He shook his head. "I honestly can't tell the difference between it and Peabrain magic, so…no clue."

"Right." With wide eyes, Laura turned back to the notebook and ripped out the pages. *It's impossible to get a straight answer these days. What happened to facts and the clear-cut process?* She tossed the notebook onto the table with a thud and waved the list by her head. "We better get goin' then, right? The sooner we clean up all the extra mess, the sooner magic can go back to doing exactly what it's supposed to do."

"You mean work at all?" Emily's mouth popped open in a goofy, expectant smile. When no one responded with anything more than a blank stare, she sighed. "Okay. Too soon. That's fine."

Nickie leaned forward and set her empty beer bottle in the bucket of ice. "John, are you sure we won't be getting in your way if we're tagging along all over Austin with you? Again."

"Actually, we need you guys."

Laura smirked. "Yeah, we've heard that one before."

"No, I mean most of this stuff won't work unless you're part of it."

"Because that dark-wizard ancestor of ours was part of the curse?" Nickie asked.

"Kinda. Mostly because you three are still the only ones who can use anything resembling working magic right now. You know, together."

"Hadstrom jumper cables for the win!" Emily pushed herself to her feet and offered John a hand up. "So you and Mr. G need a power boost to get the job done. Makes perfect sense."

Nathan cocked his head and blinked at Emily, trying not to burst out laughing. "Mr. G?"

"Oh, come on. I don't wanna have to say 'John and the Gorafrex' every single time. There's gotta be something better. And I mean, that thing's basically part of the team now, right?"

Chuck stroked his chin. "Does it *have* a name?"

"Uh…not one that I'm even gonna try to pronounce." John shoved his hands into his pockets. "The closest thing I can think of is the sound a giraffe makes."

Nickie laughed. "What sound does a giraffe make?"

"Exactly."

"Okay. I'm officially bringing *this* conversation to a close." Laura shook her head in disbelief as she folded up the list and stuffed it into her pocket. "Let's get to work."

Nickie turned to Chuck and ran her hand along his jaw. "You gonna be okay not coming along on all these extra missions with us?"

"Uh, yeah. I think I'll be fine. I have…" He eyed the half-full bucket of beer. "Three more beers to keep me company. And Nathan's cool, too."

"Yeah, thanks, man."

Chuck nodded at the professor, then kissed Nickie's temple. "I'm totally cool to let you guys finish all this up on your own. I mean, unless you guys need your magicless potions apprentice to whip up something—"

"*You're* making potions?" John asked.

"Well, I mean, I do what Emily tells me to do." Chuck shrugged. "Kinda the only thing I can do around here to help."

John's laughter filled the living room again, and he turned toward Emily. "But *you're* the one who started the whole potions thing, right?"

She grinned. "It's pretty much like cooking."

"Yeah, cooking seriously powerful alchemy magic." John wrinkled his nose. "I don't know why I think this is funny. But the Gorafrex was seriously impressed by what you managed to do with those potions, Em. That's how it got the idea for the Tenebantur. I mean, although it was pissed at the time."

The youngest Hadstrom sister stuck her hands on her hips and lifted her chin in pride. "I'll take that as a compliment straight from the...well, your mouth, I guess. Since that thing doesn't have its own. Okay. Let's get moving."

Nathan stood and pulled Laura back toward him while wrapping his arms around her. "Call me if you need any help, okay?"

"I will. But I'm pretty sure we'll need a lot less help now that the bad guy came over to our side. No offense, John."

John headed with Emily into the foyer. "You guys can stop saying that."

"Be careful, okay?" Nathan added. "It's not exactly safe yet with magic still all twisted like it is. And you and I still have quite a bit of unfinished business."

Laura huffed out a laugh, acutely aware of how hot her face was suddenly. *Great. I get to be the blushing sister who helps save magic.* Despite that, she couldn't look away from Nathan's glowing purple eyes. She leaned toward him and patted his chest. "I always finish what I start. You don't have to worry about that."

"Woo." Nickie stood from the couch. "Laura's getting frisky."

"Shut up."

"It's weird," Emily called while snatching up the library

book from the dining room table before she opened the front door and stepped outside with John. "Don't stop!"

Chuck quickly pulled Nickie down into his lap for a goodbye kiss. She laughed, grabbed his beer for a quick drink, kissed him again, and leapt to her feet. "You know the drill, babe. Hang out here if you want. And if you're not here when we come back, I'll call you."

"Yep. Just another day, right?" Chuck laughed and propped one leg up on the couch.

Nickie nudged Laura's shoulder as she passed her sister and wiggled her eyebrows. "Take your time. But, you know, not too much time. We have a city to clean up." Laura rolled her eyes as Nickie shoved her feet into her sneakers and opened the door. "Same applies to you, Nathan. You and Chuck have pretty much the same privileges around here. Well, with a few minor differences, of course."

"*Nickie.*" Laura shot her sister a warning glare, and Nickie laughed, then raised her hands in surrender before she slipped out the door and closed it behind her.

"Privileges, huh?" Nathan grinned down at her.

"Beer, couch, and waiting around privileges." Chuck drained the last of his beer.

Laura tossed the loose hair out of her face and met the part-Kashgar's violet gaze again. "I don't know what she's talking about. But you better know by now you're welcome to stay here 'til we get back."

"Thank you very much, Dr. Hadstrom."

"Yeah, okay." She started to turn toward the door, but Nathan pulled her back and surprised her with a deep kiss she couldn't pull away from if she tried. She didn't try.

Chuck glanced away, laughing silently as he cracked open another beer. *It's about time she let herself loosen up a little. Good work, Kashgar.*

When Nathan pulled away from her, Laura blinked furiously and wagged her finger at him. "Unfinished business."

"Yep."

"Okay. I'll call you later."

He grinned and held onto her hand a little longer than he had to before she turned and slipped out the front door.

Laura drew a deep breath when she stepped outside and let it all out again at once. Then she headed briskly down the walkway toward the cement stairs as Nickie, Emily, and John got into Nickie's car. *This better not take any longer than a few days. Hopefully less.*

# CHAPTER SIX

"Okay, John." Nickie started her car while everyone else strapped themselves in. "Please tell us your new friend knows where we can find these other Peabrains."

"It knows." In the back seat, John wrinkled his nose. "I know more about the Gorafrex's other hosts than I want to, honestly."

"Like, weird stuff?" Emily shot him a sidelong glance.

"Everything's weird when the thing in your head used to be in someone else's head. It's all mixed up together."

"But you can at least tell us where to go, right?" Laura turned around in the passenger seat and raised her eyebrows.

"Yeah. The first guy. Marlin. He's in South Congress. And I can tell you where to go from there."

"Okay." Nickie shifted into drive and pulled away from the house on Pressler Street, headed toward West 6th. "Even with the list, this still feels like a 'let's see what happens' kinda deal."

"Well, let's see what happens." Laura drew a deep breath while scanning the end of the street and the surrounding houses as they drove. "I'm looking forward to crossing things off that list."

Emily laughed and thumped her head back against the seat. "That's what brings you the most satisfaction in all this, huh?"

"No. The most satisfaction is in bringing magic back and putting all of this behind us. Finally." Laura looked out her window and smirked. "But I really do like crossing things off on a list."

Her sisters laughed, and John shook his head. "I think I get it now."

"Get what?"

"All the stuff you guys had to go take care of. All the *Hadstrom sister* stuff. That was Gorafrex-related, wasn't it?"

The car fell silent. Then Nickie snorted. "I guess we're busted."

"It's been our code for anything magic-related since... Well, I guess since we were old enough to pick up our wands." Laura tossed her hair out of her eyes. "It's worked pretty well for us so far."

"Yeah, and it makes for a compelling mystery." John chuckled. "I used to think I had to get into some kinda secret club before anyone would let me in on what the three of you got up to all the time."

"Well, yeah. It's the magic club." Emily looked up in the rearview mirror and met Nickie's gaze, both of them trying to hold back more laughter.

"But even Chuck and Nathan said this was normal stuff for you guys. And they've been in on it for a while, right?"

"Not quite," Nickie said. "I mean, Chuck and I have been together for a while. But he only found out about magic slightly after Nathan showed up in Laura's office doorway. It's pretty new for everybody. Except for us, honestly."

"But there's no point in trying to hide from any of you anymore," Emily added. "I don't know how that ended up working so well for all of us."

John grabbed her hand and gave her a small, knowing smile. "Everything's connected, and it all plays out for a reason."

The Gorafrex's shimmering light flashed behind his eyes again. Emily squeezed his hand. *That sounds like it's coming from both of them.* "Well, whatever the reason is, I kinda like the way things are working out."

"Save that for after we fix magic, Em." Laura turned over her shoulder to look at her little sister. "We still have to make sure *that* works out, first."

"Hey, I'm enjoying the little things. That's how we keep going until it's done."


The street Marlin lived on in South Congress was quiet and fairly empty for the middle of the day on a Wednesday. John directed them to a small brown house that didn't look like much more than a shack with a yellow-green door. When Nickie pulled up to the curb and turned off her car, the Hadstrom sisters drew a collective breath and readied themselves.

"So, we've only seen this guy once," Nickie said.

"Twice." Laura held up two fingers. "Or, I guess I've

seen him twice. I watched the Gorafrex go into him the first time."

"And it didn't take long at all for the thing to slip right back out again, did it?" Emily opened her door. "Maybe he's forgotten all about us cornering him in the parking lot."

Laura turned to look at John. "What do you think?"

He shrugged and slowly shook his head. "It could go either way, honestly. Marlin was a host for such a short time compared to the others. And he had a lot more time to work with his Peabrain magic before everything started falling apart. I'm still figuring this out as I go along, too."

"Okay." Laura opened her door and nodded at the brown shack. "Let's go see what happens, then."

John and the Hadstrom witches got out of the car and headed toward the gate in the chain-link fence around Marlin's small, square plot of land. By the time they got halfway across the front yard, they saw the dark-green smoke slipping through the cracks around the yellow-green front door. It rose in wispy tendrils and dissipated quickly.

"That doesn't look good," Laura muttered.

"Not much different from Astro's house, really."

Emily shot Nickie a sidelong glance. "Yeah, if he'd put green food-coloring in his scrying pool."

John reached the front door first and stared at the green smoke wafting around the tips of his shoes before finally knocking.

"Damnit!" The man's shout made them all freeze, followed by the sound of something heavy sliding and thumping around inside. Then nothing.

"Try again," Emily prompted.

John gave the door another polite but firm knock.

"What happens if any of these people don't want to be, you know, apologized to?" Nickie asked.

He shrugged, still staring at the door. "That would make things a little harder, probably. There are still ways around it, but the fastest is to talk face-to-face if we can. And the Gorafrex has something like…like an offering for each of them."

Laura looked the Gorafrex-inhabited Peabrain up and down. "Were you supposed to bring that with you?"

"Not for this one."

Nickie stuck a hand on her hip and tilted her head. "If he even comes to the door."

John raised his hand for another knock, and the door swung open before his knuckles met the wood. A burst of air and the dark-green smoke puffed through the open door around John and the witches. Laura coughed and waved her hand in front of her face.

"Hey, man." The man on the other side of the door wore nothing but a pair of thin, faded sweatpants. His long brown hair was pulled back in a loose ponytail, and he was unusually sweaty. "What's the deal, banging on my door in the middle of the day?"

"Marlin?" John asked.

"Yeah. Who are you?"

"My name's John. Can we come inside to talk for a few minutes?"

Marlin blinked, noticed the green smoke seeping out of his house, and shook his head. "Uh…no. Sorry, guy. Whoever you are. I'm not up for doin' business today, so roll on to the next house." He retreated and hastily shut the door.

Nickie leaned away, her nostrils flaring at the sweet-sour stink of the next puff of green smoke filtering into their faces. "Smells like Marlin put some green dye in his bong water."

"That wouldn't turn it green. I think."

"It would if it's magical dye, Em."

Laura shook her head. "Looks like one of these cases where we have to go the more complicated route."

"Maybe not." John lifted his hand toward the door again. "If you had magic for a week, then found out it didn't work the way you wanted it to and you can't control what's happening in your house, you'd be reluctant to let in a bunch of strangers standing here like traveling salespeople, too."

"Fair point."

He turned around to quickly eye each of the Hadstrom sisters. "You guys mind turning on a little Hadstrom magic for this one?"

Laura's eyes widened. "Like what?"

"Literally anything, to show Marlin we know what's going on with him."

"Sure." Nickie held her hands out to both her sisters and shrugged. "It's not like it has to be anything super powerful. This guy doesn't know what *he's* capable of, yet."

Emily slapped her hand down into Nickie's. "So, what are we thinking here?"

"Probably a light show or something." Laura took Nickie's other hand. "A small one, Em."

"I can do small, no problem. Is this gonna work without our wands?"

Laura frowned. "I have no idea. Didn't think about that one..."

"Try it." John nodded and turned for another knock on the door.

"Oh my God, *what*?" Marlin shouted. Two seconds later, the door flew open again, and he stared with wide eyes at the strangers on his porch. "I told you, I'm not doing any—"

"Hear us out for a second, okay?"

The instant John started talking, Emily and Laura raised their free hands, and a faded white orb of light sputtered to life on each of their palms. Nickie peered around John's shoulder and grinned.

Marlin stared at one glowing ball of light, then the other. "Shit, I thought I was the only one."

"You're not." John spread his arms with a reassuring smile. "Only a few minutes of your time. Please?"

"Well, yeah. Don't stand there with that stuff out where everybody can see. Come on." Marlin waved them inside and stood clear of the doorway to let them enter as he peered anxiously up and down the street. "Hurry."

When everyone had squeezed together in the shack's tiny entryway, the man closed the door and leaned back against it with a sigh.

"Thanks, man." John glanced around. "Is there somewhere we can sit for a quick chat?"

"Quick, huh?" Marlin wiped the sweat from his forehead despite the obviously functioning air conditioning in his home. "I don't believe this. Yeah, right in there. It's a mess. I'm kinda trying to fix something I messed up, I think."

Emily snorted. "So are we."

"Okay…" Giving her a confused glance, the man brushed past them and waved them after him into what served as his living room.

# CHAPTER SEVEN

The room had a worn leather couch and a recliner with frayed fabric. Dirty dishes, empty soda cans, wrappers, and crumpled pieces of paper were scattered across almost every surface. A medium-sized aquarium rested on a low bookcase against the far wall. The lights, fans, and filtration system filled the room with a low hum and the burble of tiny bubble streams as five colorful fish swam happily back and forth through colored strands of artificial kelp.

Nickie pressed her lips together when she took a quick glance at the items on the thin plank of wood set across stacked plastic crates as a makeshift coffee table. *Yep. Not a bong, but I was right about the smell.*

"Just, uh, move whatever you need to out of the way and sit." Marlin slumped into the recliner and caught Nickie staring at his paraphernalia on the table. "You want some?"

Emily barked out a laugh and quickly stuffed it back down.

Nickie shook her head. "No, thanks."

John sat on the couch, joined by Emily and Laura as Nickie sat halfway on the armrest beside them.

"What's this all about, then?" Marlin's gaze passed back and forth over the strangers in his living room. "I broke some kinda rule, didn't I? Man, I have no idea what's going on. I'm tryin' to live my life, man. Which totally turned upside down when this *thing*—"

"It's okay." Laura lifted a hand to stop him. "You're not in trouble."

Nickie shifted on the armrest. "Yeah, we're pretty much the last people to go around telling anyone else what they messed up."

"Oh. So what's up, then?"

"Finish what you were saying," John prompted. "About the thing."

"Right. Dude, I thought I lost my mind. You'll probably think I'm crazy too, but I'm not kidding. This thing, man. I was walkin' down the street a couple weeks ago, minding my business like the next guy, then I was trapped, man. By something else using my body. And believe me when I say I've put enough weird stuff in my body to know when I'm trippin' balls. But this wasn't that. This was something totally different. Like, a whole other freakin' *person* inside me." Marlin sighed and slumped back in the recliner. "And then it left maybe, like, a day later. And I was back in my body, man. Only everything looked different, and I could do stuff."

"We know," John revealed.

"See, I knew you'd think I lost my mind—wait. You know?" He looked from John to each of the Hadstrom sisters in turn, and his eyes widened. "Woah. No way. I *knew* you guys looked familiar. You were there, too!"

Laura nodded slowly. "We were there."

"Surprise." Emily wiggled her hands.

"But we were there trying to help," Nickie added. "That thing you felt ended up doing the same thing to a few other people."

"For real?" Marlin instantly straightened in the chair. "Damn, are they okay?"

"They will be." John shot the sisters a sidelong glance and nodded. "But we came here to make sure you're okay."

"I mean, I'm dealing with it."

"And because the being that borrowed your body wants to apologize."

Marlin stared at John as new beads of sweat formed on his brow. "Man, you have no idea what that thing can do."

"I do know, actually." John laughed. "I bet you've done some pretty crazy stuff yourself, right? You know, when you party sometimes."

"You're tellin' me that thing took over my body 'cause it was trippin' balls and now it wants to tell me it's sorry?"

"If that makes it easier for you to understand, then yeah. It's kinda like that."

Marlin puffed out a sigh. "Man, I want this craziness to stop. Don't get me wrong. I'm way into all the new stuff I can do. But the cool stuff got really freakin' weird after about a week, and now I can't—"

The fish tank at the back of the room bubbled loudly, then the surface of the water belched out another thick cloud of dark-green smoke that quickly filled the living room.

"Aw, now, see?" Marlin lurched out of the recliner and raced toward the fish tank. "I don't know what happened, but I can't get this crazy crap to turn off." He fanned at the smoke coming from the fish tank—the fish still unaffected as they darted around in the clear water. Every time he swiped his hand, a few sprays of brighter-green bubbles burst from his fingertips and settled onto the water's surface, only adding to the smoke. "This is insane. I only hope it's not making my fish sick, man. They can't be—"

A bright light flashed from both Marlin's hands, and the billowing smoke whooshed away from the fish tank and carried the man halfway across the room before suspending him in midair above the makeshift coffee table.

"See what I mean?" he shouted as he scrambled to find purchase on anything but the cloud. "I figured out how to feed my fish with this... I dunno. Magic or whatever."

John stood and held out his hand. Marlin took it and let John slowly pull him down out of the green cloud.

"Now that smoke keeps exploding, and I don't know how to turn it off. I thought I'd done my fair share of hot-boxin', man, but this is on a whole new level." His feet touched the floor again, and he nodded at John. "Thanks, man."

"No problem." John rubbed the back of his neck. "Here's the thing. I have the same kinda magic you do. And yeah, it *is* magic. But it's broken. So none of this is your fault."

"Thank God." Marlin wiped more sweat from his forehead. "I mean, it sucks that it's not working, but I thought *I* was the one who screwed it up."

"Nope." John frowned, then turned toward the fish tank. When he approached it and touched a finger softly against the glass, the green smoke still billowing from the tank cut off instantly. The fish swam right up to his finger and stayed there.

*Oh, nice.* Nickie folded her arms. *First the grackles, then Speed, now the Gorafrex is a fish-whisperer.*

"You'll be okay, Marlin." John turned back around and smiled at the other awakened Peabrain, who was stunned into silence by the whole situation. "The Gorafrex—that's what that being is—wants to apologize." He took a sweeping glance of the man's dirty house. "Magic will be up and running again in a few days. We're cleaning up a few messes, too. With these witches' help, obviously."

"Witches?"

"Yep." Emily shot him two thumbs-up. "The whole cleaning crew."

Marlin scratched his head. "And I didn't think things could get any weirder."

"Well, they might," Laura said. "But you'll figure out how to work with the weirdness."

The man chuckled. "Hey, that's why I moved to this city in the first place."

"So until we *do* get everything back on track," John continued as he returned to the center of the living room and stopped beside the couch, "things might be a lot easier for you if you cleaned up a little in here."

"If I cleaned?"

"Hey, I'm not judging. Trust me, I don't pretend to be a neat freak or anything, either." John shrugged and gestured toward the rest of the room. "But magic is a lot easier to handle when you're not buried in your stuff, you know? I have a feeling that when you're done, everything's gonna start working out the way it was headed when you first realized what you can do now."

"The magic part." Marlin glanced nervously at the fish tank.

"Yeah. The magic part."

"Okay." The man looked over the strangers in his living room one more time and widened his eyes. "I mean, I can clean, sure. Is that…is that it?"

"Uh… Yeah." John nodded, and his frown of concentration melted away into a reassuring smile. "That's it. Thanks for letting us in to talk."

"No problem." Marlin's eyes narrowed. "I guess this is as nuts as everything else, but I can roll with it."

"That's the spirit." Emily pointed at him and stood. "Maybe keep feeding your fish the old-fashioned way, huh?"

He chuckled. "Well now, yeah."

"We can let ourselves out." John extended a hand, and when Marlin took it, he saw the glimmering flash of the Gorafrex's light behind John's eyes.

"Uh, yeah. Thanks for stopping by."

"You're not on your own in this, Marlin." Emily nodded at the confused new Peabrain. "There are lots of other magicals rolling around Austin. You'll find them."

"And if you don't, they'll sure find you." Nickie chuckled. "In a good way."

"There *is* one rule, though." Laura paused in front of Marlin as her sisters headed toward the front door. "Or the only one that matters, anyway. We don't talk about this stuff with regular people. That causes a lot more problems for everybody."

"No problem." Marlin sniffed and eyed John as he passed out of the living room. "I have a hard enough time talking about it to myself."

He stared at his front door until John stepped out last and closed it behind him. Then Marlin laughed in disbelief and slumped back down into the recliner while smacking a hand against his head. "Okay, I was wrong. Things can definitely get weirder."

Outside in his front yard, Laura waited for John to catch up to them and leaned toward him to ask, "That's it? We show up, give these people a muddled explanation and a piece of advice, and we're good to go?"

John shrugged. "That one was admittedly pretty easy. Maybe because Marlin had some time to process his new magic before it went haywire. Maybe he has an open mind about the whole thing."

"Yeah, *real* open." Emily snorted and held open the gate for the others to pass through. "Sounds like the guy's been *expanding his consciousness* for a long time."

"Well, whatever he did before doesn't really matter as much as it used to."

"So the Gorafrex only wants to go around handing out life hacks to its former hosts?" Nickie opened the driver-side door of her car and raised an eyebrow. "That feels too easy."

"They're not all going to be like Marlin." John wrinkled his nose. "I think we started with the easiest one."

"Great." Laura hopped into the passenger seat and closed the door. "No one ever said the Hadstrom sisters don't like a good challenge."

"Challenge accepted." Emily strapped herself in and

paused when she saw John's troubled look. "Hey, we can do this. If we freed the Gorafrex and our entire ancestral line from that curse, we can help hand out a few apologies, no problem."

John cocked his head. "I hope you're right. The Gorafrex *wanted* to get rid of the curse. I'm worried about the Peabrains who won't wanna hear anything we have to say."

Nickie shifted into drive and pulled away from the curb. "We'll cross that magical bridge when we get there."

## CHAPTER EIGHT

"Next on the list." Laura smoothed out the folded papers in her lap. "The new Peabrain Jessica."

John shook his head. "She's at work."

"And how do you know that?" Nickie eyed him in the rearview mirror as she slowed in front of a stop sign.

"The answer hasn't changed since the last time someone asked that question."

"Right. Gorafrex in your head used to be in her head." Nickie let out a deep sigh.

"Okay...so, next is Annie. Host number three."

"She's at work, too."

Emily tossed a hand toward the window in frustration. "Super great that these people can keep going to work, and the whole 'we have to fix magic' issue doesn't take precedence over that. Wait, but you know where they work too, don't you?"

John shook his head. "I'm not bringing this stuff into their businesses or offices, Em. They already have too much going on, and that adds a lot of extra pressure."

"So we're gonna push it back and do this around their schedules?"

"Em, we have plenty of other stops to make. We can switch a few things around on the list." Laura turned over her shoulder to look at John. "We don't have to do these in order, do we?"

"No, as long as they all get done."

Emily groaned and dropped her head back against the seat. "Must be nice to have the really important issues wait 'til you get home from another regular day on the job."

John leaned toward her. "You okay?"

"Mostly, yeah. But I'm pretty sure I lost my job at Meadowlark because I had to call in again. Breaking curses and fixing magic doesn't wait for *us*, apparently."

"Did you quit?"

"Of course, I didn't quit." Emily finally looked at him and couldn't help a frown of disappointment. "But there's no way Chef Ansler's gonna want me in his kitchen if he can't rely on me to show up for my shifts. I've seen him fire people for a lot less."

"Hmm. I wouldn't be too worried about it, Em."

"Oh, yeah? Did your Gorafrex friend look into the future and tell you everything's gonna work out exactly the way it was supposed to before we messed it all up?"

He reached for her hand again and gently squeezed it.

Emily drew a deep breath when the rush of warm, calming energy seeped from his fingers into hers. She looked down at their interlaced fingers and muttered, "Okay, I can't tell who that's coming from."

"That's me, Em. My magic, anyway."

She tried not to laugh. "I appreciate the effort, John.

Really. But until we run all these errands and put magic back together, sharing your energy with me is more likely to electrocute me than anything else."

The warmth faded from her fingers, but John didn't let go of her hand.

He smirked at her and raised an eyebrow. "You're probably right."

"We'll head downtown, then," Nickie decided. "We can stop by the library and Brightwing Emporium while we're waiting for all these other people to get home from work. And we have to pick Chuck up anyway before we talk to Dave. But at least these places are all relatively close together."

"Good idea. Saves a lot on gas."

Nickie shot Laura a quick glance. "That wasn't my top reason, but sure. Saving gas is always a nice bonus."

They pulled up in front of Austin's main library first. Emily hugged the hardback magical library book to her chest and cast wary glances up and down the street as she followed her sisters toward the front doors. "I seriously hope returning a book this fast cancels out having taken it in the first place."

"Honestly, Em, I don't think Isabelle's gonna care that much." Nickie held the door open for her sister, but John took it instead and waited for Emily and Laura to go ahead of him. "She knows you took it. No one's gonna get you in trouble."

"As long as nobody thinks I have some kinda hyped-up thief magic." The youngest Hadstrom sister took a deep breath when they stepped through the security system at the front of the library. *Security for regular humans. Magicals get exploding wards that make your skin buzz for hours.*

The group hurried through the library toward the back, where Isabelle sat at her desk across the narrow hallway from the restricted magical section. The fairy librarian looked up at them with a smile, but it quickly morphed into wide-eyed surprise when she recognized the Hadstrom sisters. "You're back."

"Of course, we're back." Emily held out the slightly stolen magical book and grinned. "I have a library book to return."

Isabelle quickly took it from her and hid the heavy hardcover under her desk while peering over the raised counter to make sure no one was watching. "Thanks for that. It's a good thing no one's been able to get into the restricted section since the last time you were here. I can't even take inventory, so... Well, no one's looking for missing library books right now, are they?"

"That's probably the least of anyone's concerns, yeah."

The librarian cautiously snuck a peek at the first few pages of the returned book and quickly glanced up at Emily. "The pages aren't blank anymore."

"I had a theory about how to get them back." Emily shrugged. "Don't ask me how I did it. Trust me, a librarian does *not* want to know how that happened."

"Then I won't ask." Isabelle patted the top of her head and looked hopefully up at the Hadstrom sisters. "I guess you didn't find what you were looking for in this book, anyway."

"No, we did." Nickie nodded as she kept a wary eye on

the library patrons browsing the other regular sections in the back.

"But I thought whatever you needed from this book was supposed to help you fix things, right?" Isabelle looked like she was on the verge of tears. "And I'm usually an optimist, but things are definitely not fixed."

"We know," Laura said. "We were right about the spell we needed from that book, and it worked, but we still have a few things left on the to-do list, as it were. Which is another reason we're here." She stepped aside and gestured at John.

The man stared at Isabelle, his mouth slightly open.

Emily nudged him with her elbow. "You okay?"

"What? Yeah. I'm getting a whole different perspective." He blinked rapidly at the librarian, shook his head, then stepped forward and extended his hand. "You're a fairy."

Isabelle chuckled and shook his hand. "And you're a Peabrain. Nice to meet you."

"John." He gave the librarian another once-over, then cleared his throat. "I'm helping them clear a few things up before things can go back to normal in this place."

"That's nice of you."

"Well, I'm more involved now than I expected to be. Um, how do you get into the restricted section?"

Isabelle nodded toward the wall behind him. "Usually that wall isn't only a wall."

"Right." John turned and studied the blank wall, which this time didn't have any posters of cats or anything else. "How did you guys get through?"

Emily shrugged. "Hadstrom jumper cables. It's not a

good idea to try that one again, though. We almost got stuck *inside* the wall last time."

He winced. "Ouch."

"Definitely."

"Isabelle, is that the only issue the library's been having in the last few weeks?"

The librarian's face contorted in a frown of discomfort. "It's the only magical section we have, if that's what you're asking. The wards stopped working, obviously, and the wall isn't cooperating anymore. But as one of the few libraries in the world with the kind of powerful books we keep in the restricted section, we've definitely taken a hit in the..." She bowed her head and leaned forward to whisper, "The magical community. Now no one can get in, and they're starting to look for the information they want in all the wrong places. Yesterday, I overheard an elf saying she was going to try improving the protection charms around her house with a *sacrificial ritual* some bozo recommended on the internet. I overhear a lot in this library, and most of it's none of my business, but I had to beg the woman not to use a Facebook group for magicals as a reliable resource for spellwork. Especially right now. I can't even work in my garden with a simple spell anymore. Destroyed my flowerbed."

"You know who people *should* use as a resource?" Emily pointed at Isabelle. "Librarians. And somehow, nobody ever thinks about that."

"Magicals are still panicking." Isabelle shrugged. "It's only been a few weeks, but it's getting worse."

"Yeah, we've seen the panic," Nickie said.

Laura nodded. "And the rush for potion supplies as a backup."

Emily scoffed. "Most magicals should stick to spells, anyway. It's way too easy to mess up potions."

"I couldn't agree more." The fairy woman nervously licked her lips and peered around the Hadstrom sisters to see John experimentally pressing his hand against the restricted section's restricted wall. "That's the part that doesn't work, John."

"Hmm? Oh. I know. I wanted to check it out."

Isabelle leaned forward. "Is your friend doing okay?"

Laura smiled. "Peabrain just woke up."

"Oh, I see. When did *that* happen?"

Emily glanced at the clock on the wall behind the woman's desk. "About five hours ago."

"Really?" Isabelle's eyes widened as she looked back at John. "He's handling that surprisingly well."

"So far, yeah. We were thinking the same thing."

"John?" Emily turned to look at him. "Was there anything else you wanted to cover while we're here?"

"Hmm?" He patted the wall again and looked at her. "No, not really."

She squinted at him. *The library's on the list. There's no way we came here only to say hi to a fairy.* "Okay…"

"So now you have that book back." Laura tapped her finger on the raised counter at the front of the desk. "Hang in there, Isabelle. We're really close to wrapping this whole nightmare up and burying it for good."

"I'll keep my fingers crossed for you." The Hadstrom sisters turned to head back toward the front, and the librarian leapt out of her seat. "Oh! While you're here, it's probably a good idea to tell you what happened."

"What happened?" Laura glanced at her sisters before approaching the desk again.

"Well, you remember what happened the last time you were here, right? With that little flying book fiasco."

"Uh-oh." Emily scratched the back of her head. "Are we in trouble for that one, too?"

"Not exactly…" Isabelle rifled through a stack of loose papers on the desk, then pulled out a thinner collection of them and handed the paper on top to Laura. "You guys were pretty convincing with your magic show coverup, apparently. I've had parents of young children calling in and messaging the library's Facebook page asking when this magic show was gonna happen. I have no idea why there's such a sudden interest right now, but I had no way to get hold of you and some of these parents… They can be intense. Then the director heard about it and I didn't have much of a choice after that. It was either blow your cover story and tell him about the restricted book you…*checked out*, or cave in and give all these parents what they wanted. So I scheduled the event."

Laura stared at the flier in the fairy's outstretched hand. "You scheduled it."

"Scheduled what?" Emily peered over her big sister's shoulder, and her jaw dropped. "A for-real magic show."

Nickie closed her eyes with a sigh and slowly shook her head. "No way."

"It's been announced and everything." Isabelle smiled sheepishly and hunched her shoulders. "I guess I was banking on the fact that you're witches of your word and would bring that book back so I could tell you."

Laura took the flier and swallowed. "So we have to be in here on Saturday morning."

"Yep. Get here whenever you like. There's a little window of time in there after the library opens to get set up, if you need to. Then do your thing, I guess."

Emily looked at Laura and puffed out a breath through loose lips. "Then we better fix magic before Saturday."

John looked up and saw the woman in her early thirties lurking by one of the library shelves closest to the back hallway. He blinked, and the Gorafrex flooded his mind with the information he needed. *That's Jessica.*

He glanced over his shoulder at the Hadstrom sisters and Isabelle hashing out the details of their impromptu magic show, which wasn't exactly kept at library-approved volumes. None of them noticed him walking six feet down the hallway to talk to the Gorafrex's second human host on this ship. "You hear what's going on over there?"

Jessica's eyes darted toward him, and she frowned. "Are they really talking about a magic show?"

"Couldn't be the worst thing right now, right? And they're not always only for kids, you know."

"Maybe." She eyed the Hadstrom sisters again. "They're witches, aren't they?"

"Good eye."

"Well, I've seen them before. They helped me sort some things out a couple of weeks ago, but I really don't know them that well." Jessica turned toward him and cocked her head. "You're...you're like me, aren't you?"

"A Peabrain?" He rubbed the back of his neck with a

secretive smile. "Yeah. We have a few things in common." *Like hosting this Gorafrex, and that's about where we draw the line. Not the right time to bring that up.* "You should check out the show, anyway. Sounds like Saturday's the day."

When she opened her mouth to reply, a pale blue light bloomed between her lips. Jessica clamped a hand over her mouth and swallowed before giving him an apologetic smile. "I have enough magic in my life right now."

"Yeah, me too. Still. Might be a good way to take your mind off things for a while. Or learn something new, right? You never know."

"I don't know." She frowned at the Hadstrom sisters again, lifted a finger, then changed her mind about what she was about to say and turned toward the front of the library. "I gotta go. Have a good one."

"You, too." John stuck his hands in his pockets and watched her leave. *That went well.*

He returned to the hallway and stopped beside the solid wall into the restricted section. The Hadstrom sisters kept talking, and he ran his hand along the wall, searching for what he wanted.

"Even if it's a flop," Isabelle continued, "I'd be forever grateful to you three if you showed up anyway and did this silly thing. I hope the parents will leave me alone after this. So I wouldn't mind at all if you ended up doing silly beginner tricks for forty-five minutes. You know, the fake kind."

"Okay, then." Laura handed the flier to Nickie and smiled at the librarian. "We got ourselves into this mess, didn't we? It's the least we can do to pay the library back.

And you, Isabelle. For keeping the whole thing between us."

"Oh, I did this more for myself, honestly." Isabelle chuckled nervously. "With the restricted section out of order, I'm more or less a useless appendage in this place. Putting on this show might be the only thing keeping me from losing my job."

"Then we will definitely be here on Saturday." Emily nodded. "Promise."

"Thank you."

Nickie folded the flier in half with a crooked smile. "Any other surprise obligations you wanna spring on us?"

"Nope. That's it. I mean, beyond whatever you ladies have to do to get that stupid wall to open again."

"We're on it. Thank, Isabelle." Laura waved her sisters to follow her toward the front of the library.

"Won't be too much longer," Emily told the fairy. "Then you won't be able to keep me out of the restricted section no matter what you do."

Isabelle chuckled nervously and waved at them. When she met John's gaze, she saw the shimmering light flash in his eyes, and her smile wavered. "Good luck with everything."

"You too, Isabelle. Thanks."

The librarian watched the Hadstrom sisters and John until they disappeared through the library's front doors. Then she scratched her head and slowly pulled the returned spellbook from the shelf under the desk. *There's something different about that Peabrain. I don't care what it is, as long as this place starts working again.*

# CHAPTER NINE

"I can't believe this." Nickie ran a hand through her hair and turned on the sidewalk to stare at Emily. "You seriously haven't learned by now that habitual lying doesn't solve any of our problems?"

Emily stopped and spread her arms. "Should I have told all those humans and their kids the truth instead? 'Hey, sorry, guys. We're witches who cast the wrong spell, hence all the flying books. But don't worry, we've almost broken the curse on the super powerful being who's been using people like you as human meat puppets. Then it'll really be free, and you won't have to worry about seeing anything like this again.' Does that seem like a safer route to go than lying about a *fake* magic show?"

Nickie shook her head as she opened the driver-side door of her car. "No. But I'm sure we could've come up with something better if you hadn't blurted out 'magic show' and gotten everyone so excited about it." She slid behind the wheel and practically slammed the door.

"Nice. I'm not gonna shout my reply at the car." Emily

dropped her arms against her sides and looked at Laura. "I was trying to cover our asses."

"I know, Em. Let me talk to her for a second. You both have valid points."

"*Thank* you." Emily folded her arms and waited for her sisters to hash it out in the car.

John stepped up beside her with his hands in his pockets. "Does she hate magic shows or something?"

"Not that I know of. I have no idea why she's so upset right now. But she'll get over it. We kinda have a lot more important things to focus on. Like your special list." She shot him a sidelong glance and raised an eyebrow. "Which, by the way, didn't fully capture exactly *how* we're supposed to fix things in all those places. You didn't do anything in the library."

"Not explicitly." John shrugged. "That's the part where you guys come in."

Realization dawned on the youngest Hadstrom sister, and her mouth fell open with a laugh of disbelief. "We had to go to the library to find out about this magic show? Is that what you're trying to tell me right now?"

"Part of cleaning up the mess. Isabelle is really good at what she does, Em. She doesn't deserve to lose her job over this."

"Our ridiculous impromptu performance on Saturday is gonna be the last thing that puts all the pieces back together, huh?" Emily snorted. "Unbelievable. We get to fix magic in Austin by playing with pretend magic in front of a bunch of kids."

"On a surface level, I guess that's fairly accurate." John laughed.

"I'm trying really hard not to hit you right now."

"You don't actually wanna hit me."

Emily found it impossible not to laugh with him. "No, I don't. Because you have your extra little brain turned on right now, and the heavy-duty magic you won't be able to control would probably blow my head off."

"I wouldn't let that happen."

"Yeah, tell that to the magicals who thought they could do a few simple spells in the last few weeks with no problem. Magicals who've been doing this their whole lives. Our dad basically detonated a paint bomb in his house with that kinda thinking." She playfully shoved his shoulder.

He laughed again as he staggered across the sidewalk. "Feel better now?"

"A little."

John grabbed her hand and pulled her toward him, then wrapped his arms around her waist. "I don't mind you shoving me around a little, Em. When this is all over, if you still wanna hit me, go for it."

She rolled her eyes. "That's not gonna happen. See? I've lost the urge already."

"Good." He searched her gaze, grinning. "So now we can—"

"Sorry to break this up." Laura leaned out of the passenger seat and waved them back to the car. "We got a lot more places to hit. Come on."

Emily stepped out of John's embrace and gave him another playful shove. "To be continued."

"Not the first time I've heard that."

"Yeah, I know. But it's the first time I've said it without

wondering how I'm supposed to lie to you about everything, too. Now it doesn't matter."

"No, it doesn't."

They got into the back seat and closed the doors. Nickie looked up in the rearview mirror and caught Emily's gaze. "Sorry I snapped, Em."

"It's okay." Emily shrugged. "I didn't know you had a magic show button to push. My bad."

"I don't have anything against magic shows. I'm…" Nickie grimaced. "I'm not all that excited about that being my next performance when all my other gigs are on hold, you know? Sure, musician and magician sound the same, but that's about where it ends."

Emily chuckled. "No one's asking you to *be* a magician, Nickie. Only to pretend to be one. And, hey. Every magic show needs a little background music, right? If that's all you wanna do, bring your guitar and play in the background."

"Yeah, right. I'll end up setting the entire library on fire."

Laura laughed sharply, then cleared her throat. "Maybe not if we don't have our legacy rings anymore."

"Maybe. Not sure I wanna risk it in front of a bunch of kids."

"You guys will figure it out." John buckled his seatbelt and nodded. "I'm kinda looking forward to the whole thing."

"John, I liked you better as a fan of my music." Nickie smirked at him. "But thanks."

"Sure."

"Okay, so Brightwing Emporium, then?" Laura asked.

"Assuming Leonidas is back at his shop." Emily wrinkled her nose. "He was pretty shaken up when we pulled him out of that chamber."

"He'll be there." John nodded. "That apothecary is all he has."

"And it was destroyed." Laura sighed. "We're gonna be cleaning up a literal mess with this one, aren't we?"

They didn't have to drive far to get to the Brightwing Emporium apothecary. The place looked like all the other nightclubs on the street, most of which hadn't opened for the night, and the sign on the door was practically invisible in the daylight.

"Hard to forget a place like this, even without a visible sign," Nickie muttered as she joined her sisters on the sidewalk.

"He's open during the day, right?"

Laura shrugged. "I mean, people need an apothecary at all hours. Honestly, it'd make more sense if he stayed open during the day and closed at night."

"Well yeah. Nighttime break-ins tend to have that effect." Nickie grabbed the door handle and pulled it open.

The hallway they walked through this time was fully lit. Without the darkness and the black lights illuminating Leonidas Brightwing's display of magical taxidermy creatures and eerily glowing artifacts, the long hall into the main shop looked bleak and empty.

"Like a raided museum," Emily muttered.

As they neared the door into the main shop at the end of the hall, the fairy's grunts of frustration and aggravated mumbling seeped toward them. Something large and heavy thumped against the door, followed by a roar of outrage before glass shattered and a spray of blue sludge hit the small window in the top of the door.

"Looks like the trouble factor bumped up a notch." Nickie jogged toward the door, her sisters close on her heels. John walked slowly, his hands in his pockets as he gazed around the hallway.

Laura nearly ran into her sister when Nickie stopped short. "You gonna open the door?"

"It's locked."

Emily leaned around her sisters to knock fervently on the heavy metal door. "Leonidas? Everything okay in there?"

"We're closed today," the fairy shouted. "Come back—*oof*! Stop it. Come back when the whole world's not falling apart!"

"Go ahead, Laura." Emily set her hands on each of her sisters' shoulders and nodded. "You're good at unlocking stuff."

"That's called breaking and entering, Em."

"He obviously needs help with something in there, and that's what we came here for in the first place."

More glass shattered in the main shop. Leonidas shrieked. "Gah! I didn't come back here to be tossed around like a sack of—"

Through the tiny window in the door, the Hadstrom sisters caught a fleeting glance of the fairy apothecary owner flying across the room, followed by a thump and more items toppling over and shattering.

"Good enough for me." Laura nodded and pointed at

the doorknob. A yellow light flashed from her finger and sputtered out before her intended spell reached its target. "Seriously?"

"There's no way we ran out of juice," Nickie muttered.

"Maybe we should've brought our wands." Emily tightened her grip on her sisters' shoulders. "Should we go back and—"

"*I'm* the one calling the shots in *this* shop," Leonidas bellowed. "And I demand a semblance of—woah!"

A heavy metal box zipped across the room in the opposite direction.

"We don't have time for that." Laura scowled at the doorknob and shook out her hand. "We don't have our wands or the legacy rings, so we'll go back to old-school spellcasting somewhere in between, I guess. *Recludo.*"

The yellow light sparked at her finger again. This time, it zipped toward the doorknob with a crack and blasted the thing right out of its setting. Emily and Nickie ducked away from the flying doorknob, which darted past John's head and made him laugh.

Laura gritted her teeth. "Not what I was going for, but fine."

"At least there's still some kinda power in the actual words of a spell, right?"

"Sure, Em. Still the kind we can't control." Laura shoved on the door, but it stuck against something heavy jammed up against the other side. "How hard does it have to be to *help* somebody?"

"Come on." Nickie pressed her weight against the door, and the sisters pushed together. With a grating squeal, the door finally opened enough for them to slip into the apothecary's main room.

A two-foot wooden figurine sailed straight toward them, its carved mouth opening and closing as it let out an echoing cackle. The witches ducked, and the figurine thumped against the shelves on the back wall before bouncing around on the floor. Its eerie laughter didn't stop.

"Great. Magical possession doesn't stop with the Gorafrex." Emily glared at the mad figurine bouncing along the ground like a wind-up toy. "Now it's a whole apothecary."

"Leonidas!" Laura waved to catch the old fairy's attention. "Looks like you need a little help—"

"Don't!" He reached toward her with wide eyes, but she'd already taken her next step into the shop.

The floor buckled beneath her and moved in a rolling wave, scattering the Hadstrom sisters like they were being shaken off a blanket. Nickie stumbled against the side of the counter in the back and caught herself before a drawer whipped out of its own accord for a surprise blow to her belly. She doubled over with a grunt as it knocked the wind right out of her, and staggered backward.

Emily slipped on the potion-slick floor and landed on her butt with a yelp. Two old books leapt from the shelves along the opposite wall, their covers flapping like birds as they swooped toward her and fluttered around her face. She tried to bat them away, then found a broken chair leg rolling across the floor in the chaos and snatched it up. The books zipped away from her and doubled back for another attack.

"I'm warning you…"

The flying books ignored her warning and swooped toward her again. Emily swung the chair leg and bashed the first book across the shop.

"Nice swing, Em!" At Laura's shout, the second book veered away from Emily's makeshift club and headed for the oldest Hadstrom sister instead. "Crap."

"Here." Emily tossed the chair leg.

Before Laura could catch it, a tangled heap of fallen rope uncoiled and lashed out like a striking snake. It batted the chair leg aside, reaching for Laura's outstretched hand until it wrapped around the attacking book instead. The book let out a dusty squeak, and the rope jerked its impossibly animated prey back into its heaped coils. The sound of ripping paper filled the room.

"You shouldn't be here," Leonidas shouted as he battled with an old-fashioned cash register, the drawer opening and shutting again like a distended, snapping mouth.

"But we are." Emily kicked a set of shiny nesting dolls hopping out of each other and attempting to climb her leg. "And you could use the help."

"Oh, you have loads of experience fighting an entire shop back into submission, do you?"

"Do *you*?" Laura leapt away from the shelf behind her when a dozen small glass vials wrapped in wire sprouted wiry legs and tried to hop onto her back. She brushed the scrambling things off and stepped back when they skittered toward her across the floor. "What happened in here?"

"Careful with those!" The fairy's eyes widened as he

pointed at the spider-vials. "Highly dangerous. Don't let them break."

"Whose side are you on?"

"This is my shop!"

"Wow." John peered around the partially opened door and gazed at the swarm of animated potions ingredients and magical paraphernalia. "Looks like somebody's a little jumpy."

"I'm not jumpy," Laura shouted.

At the same time, Leonidas snarled, "You'll be jumping too, soon enough."

The second John stepped fully into the apothecary's main shop, the chaos froze. Every inanimate object hurtling across the room stopped and hovered mid-air. The walking furniture hesitated. The clack and bang of opening and shutting lids and drawers and latches ceased. Then everything tumbled to the floor at once, and the apothecary fell perfectly silent.

"Hmm." Leonidas scowled at the mess in his shop. "That's more like it."

"What did you do?" Laura glanced behind her to make sure she didn't step on any of the highly dangerous potions vials, their wire legs now returned to their original wrappings around the glass.

John shrugged. "Brought a little calming presence into the room, I guess."

"Ha!" Nickie staggered backward against the shelves behind her and fell into an uproarious fit of laughter, still clutching her belly where the counter's drawer had struck her.

Emily broke into a crooked smile. "I don't get it."

"*Calming…*" Nickie barked out another laugh and shook her head. "That definitely isn't…it isn't any of *us*!"

"Hey, I'm perfectly calm." Laura smoothed down the front of her shirt, then flinched away from the end of a long, gnarled stick poking out of the shelf when it brushed against her shoulder.

"Or maybe one that doesn't respond to everything like it's emergency," John added.

"This *is* an emergency." Leonidas blinked rapidly, his blue translucent wings twitching against his back as he jerked down on the sleeves of his long-sleeved button-down. "Or at least it was. Until you stepped in here and—"

Despite John's easygoing smile, the apothecary owner gaped when he saw the Gorafrex's shimmering light flare for a second behind the Peabrain's eyes.

"Oh, no. No, no, no. *You* need to leave."

"It's okay," Emily said, gesturing toward John. "He's with us."

"The last time a Gorafrex-infested Peabrain stepped foot in my shop, he was *with* one of you, too." Leonidas pointed at Laura, his chest heaving as he fought to catch his breath. "Before that night, this apothecary was one of the few sane places left. *Potions*, not magic! I don't care which Peabrain that monster's taken over this time. I will *not* let that thing rifle through my supplies again. That's what started this whole mess in the first place."

"The broken magic is what started this mess." Laura brushed loose hair away from her face and carefully chose her steps as she crossed the littered floor toward the fairy. "That's why we're here."

"N-no. I…I can't be a part of that anymore." Leonidas

stumbled backward, tripped on a ball of green-tinted glass that lit up when he touched it, and fell back into an open trunk shoved out from its place against the wall. The lid closed on the fairy's back with a thump, and Leonidas groaned.

After exchanging a cautious look with her sisters, Laura approached the frazzled apothecary owner and extended her hand. "The Gorafrex situation has changed."

"I don't care."

"Okay. Will you at least let us help you clean the place up?"

Leonidas squinted up at her, then let out a massive sigh. "If you can promise not to break anything or try to steal my inventory."

"Come on, Leonidas." Emily grinned and spread her arms. "You know us."

"Yes, and I thought I knew my shop, too."

"That's a promise we can definitely make." Laura nodded and glanced at her hand.

With a heavy sigh, the fairy took her hand and grunted as she hauled him quickly out of the trunk. The lid thunked closed behind him.

"Wow, Laura." Emily chuckled. "When were you gonna tell us you suddenly developed super strength?"

The oldest Hadstrom sister watched Leonidas brush bits of plaster and sawdust off his shimmering dark-purple vest. "Fairies and hollow bones, right?"

Leonidas glared at her, then chuckled despite himself. "Good for dislocating joints, escaping from ropes around our wrists, *and* making young witches look remarkably strong."

John laughed softly and shook his head. "Fairies."

The apothecary owner whipped his head toward the newly awakened Peabrain and pointed a crooked finger at him. "You stay out of this."

"That would be a mistake." Nickie stepped toward John and gave him a quick reassuring pat on the shoulder. "Without John, your shop would still be trying to eat you, or whatever. And we'd have absolutely no chance of fixing magic."

Leonidas sputtered in disbelief and scratched at his bald head. "John."

"Yes?"

"Not that thieving, kidnapping creature?"

John spread his arms. "It's both of us, actually. But I'm running the show for the most part. I think." He took another sweeping glance around the shop with a slowly growing smile.

"I watched you three fight that thing in a different body." Leonidas' gaze shifted from one Hadstrom sister to the next. "What happened?"

"Kind of a long story." Laura glanced at her watch and shrugged. "And we have plenty of time."

"Yep." Emily bent to pick up the scattered parts of the nesting dolls. "Helping you out here will be a lot more productive than sitting through rush-hour traffic, anyway."

Leonidas laughed. "I still haven't figured out the way you qualify your priorities."

She grinned at him. "It's an ever-evolving process."

"All right. I assume you three can clean up and talk at the same time."

"That's how we do it." Nickie pushed the counter drawer back in with a satisfying slam and nodded.

Leonidas studied John again with narrowed eyes. "Any funny business from that one, and I'll handle this mess on my own."

John raised his hands in surrender with an understanding smile. "I get it."

"Good." The fairy rubbed his almost bald head, then turned and pushed the trunk back into place against the wall. "Start talking, ladies."

## CHAPTER TEN

"So that's why we're here." Emily stood on her tiptoes and grabbed the shelf with one hand while she slid a small, lidless wooden box of dry herbs back into place above her head. "Call it a mission of apologies."

"And amends," Laura added while setting the newly recoiled rope back on its hook on the side of another bookshelf. "From the Gorafrex and from the three of us too, in a lot of ways. Who knows? Maybe we're the figure-heads for the entire Hadstrom family line, and we're making up for centuries of misunderstanding."

"A curse." Leonidas huffed out a sigh and stuck his hands on his hips as he turned to survey the mostly cleaned-up shop. "I'd like to say you should have come to me if you needed help. But I'm not sure I would have had what you needed, anyway."

Nickie smirked. "Not unless you're keeping a bunch of Hadstrom bones in a huge jar somewhere."

Leonidas laughed. "Now why would I—oh. You're serious?"

"Had to dig 'em up and everything." Emily dusted off her hands and nodded at her big sister. "Dream come true for Laura."

"Almost. I mean, it was fun." Her sisters snickered. "But we're a long way from finally putting this whole thing to bed."

"Not too long, I hope." The fairy swallowed thickly. "I don't know how much more of this nonsense I can take."

"You're not the only one." Nickie ran a hand through her hair. "But we're a lot closer than we were the last time you saw us."

"And we know a *lot* more about the truth." Laura glanced at John and nodded. "And what it'll take from all of us to make it right."

"Well. I suppose I'll know the minute you do." Leonidas headed across the shop toward the counter in the back. "Thank you for your help. And the explanation. It wasn't necessary, but I always appreciate insider knowledge."

"It was necessary," John said.

The fairy blinked at him from behind the counter. "Is that so?"

John pursed his lips in thought and gazed around the apothecary. "The Gorafrex wants me to share a few things with you. Are you open to hearing them?"

"Well, that depends." The fairy shifted uncomfortably and swiped the scattered dust off the countertop, trying to be nonchalant about it. "That creature has already insulted me enough as it is."

"Not an insult. An apology."

"Eh?" Leonidas blinked quickly and cleared his throat. "Admittedly, young man, I'd say you have my attention."

"Thank you." Jon scanned the shelves beside him as he took a few slow steps toward the counter. Leonidas leaned away, watching the Peabrain with wary curiosity. "The apology comes first. For breaking into your shop and ransacking your supplies."

The fairy snorted. "That's a start."

"And then for tying you up and leaving you here to wait before the Gorafrex came back with Laura." John turned briefly toward the oldest Hadstrom sister with a knowing smile. "This doesn't count as *your* apology, by the way."

"I'm fine waiting for that one."

"And the last part is for stealing your working knowledge of the Tenebantur potion." John shrugged, his hands still in his pockets. "You had every single ingredient for that in your shop."

"Of course, I did. Those items are used for all manner of other potions and charms. It's the—"

"The way you put them all together for the Tenebantur. That's what makes it so dangerous. That, and how accessible it is to most magicals with any working knowledge of potions. I know."

Leonidas opened his mouth and drew a deep breath, then seemed to forget what he was about to say and asked instead, "How do you know all that?"

Emily laughed. "Maybe you do need a sign."

John pointed to his temple. "I have all the information the Gorafrex has. So far, it's been pretty helpful in filling in the blanks for me."

"I see. Does that creature have anything else to say to me?"

"Yeah." A wide grin spread across John's face. "It's pretty

impressed by the way you and Astro built that illegal potion. I'm, uh…" He wrinkled his nose and closed his eyes, listening to the other voice in his mind. "Well, now I know who to go to for potions. I mean, if Em's ever too busy."

Leonidas snorted. "What in the world would a Peabrain ever possibly need a potion for?"

"Just in case."

The fairy tried to hold his smile back, but his building laughter was too much. He slapped a hand down on the countertop while chuckling to himself and shaking his head. "I never thought I'd live to see the day. You look happy, young man. And if that's still the rose-colored glasses of your little peabrain waking up to this brand-new world with a better instruction manual than most of you ever see, that's all right. The happiness may fade, but I daresay you'll be pretty damn content with this new arrangement of yours."

"It's growing on me, yeah. I'm still alive, the Gorafrex gets to stay with someone not constantly trying to push it out, and we get to fix magic in Austin. Thanks for listening."

"Would that thing have made you tie me up again if I hadn't agreed?"

John laughed. "No. It would only make our job a lot harder than it has to be."

"Well, all right." Leonidas chuckled again and watched John studying another small case of potion vials on the bookshelf. "Any advice for how to keep my shop from trying to kill me again?"

John leaned toward the vials. "Try settling back into

your normal day, I guess. Once magic kicks back on, you'll already be prepared for it."

"Uh-huh."

John gently lifted a vial of glowing blue liquid from the case and turned toward Leonidas. "Is this for sale?"

"As much as I tried to pull it off in the front hallway, young man, this is in fact still an apothecary and not a museum." Leonidas smoothed his hands over the counter-top. "But that's a rather expensive item."

"Hmm." John turned the vial over and over in both hands. "Kind of out of a server's price range, huh?"

Emily forced back a laugh. *The only Peabrain on this ship with a Gorafrex as an added bonus, and he's still a server. As long as he hasn't lost his job by now, too.*

"What about a trade?"

Leonidas leaned forward. "A trade? I appreciate the offer, but I'm not sure you have anything that quite matches up to the value of that. Especially when you've only had your magic for half a day. You're holding a—"

"Eternal Heart. I know. You sell empty vials too, don't you?"

"Two twenty-five apiece." Leonidas shot Laura a skeptical glance. The witch shrugged.

"Okay." John pulled out his wallet and unraveled three one-dollar bills. "Then only an empty vial, please."

Without looking away from the Peabrain, Leonidas reached under the counter and pulled out a cardboard box filled with vials in different shapes and colors of glass. "Take your pick, son."

John pulled a vial from the box and set the bills on the

counter with the glowing blue Eternal Heart potion. "Thanks."

Leonidas pursed his lips and made change for the three dollars. "Why do I feel like this is some type of trick?"

"No trick." John chuckled. "I'm simply working with what I got."

Nickie stepped silently toward Emily and leaned toward her little sister. "Any idea what he's up to?"

"Nope. But it feels a lot like one of those Gorafrexy peace offerings he mentioned." Emily folded her arms. "Little weird that he thinks buying an empty vial will do that, but whatever."

John uncorked the empty vial and reached deep into one pocket to pull out what looked like absolutely nothing between his fingers. He sprinkled the nothing into the vial, brought the glass to his lips, and gently blew into the opening.

A pearly-white bubble floated between his lips and drifted slowly down to the bottom of the vial. Then the entire thing flashed with a bright-white light, and when John held the vial up toward the fairy again, a viscous substance not quite liquid and not quite gas filled the glass. It pulsed with bright-orange light.

*Looks like a heartbeat.* Emily squinted and headed toward the counter for a better look.

Leonidas' eyes widened as he stared at the orange-glowing vial. He clenched his eyes shut, opened them quickly, and his mouth dropped open. "Is that…"

"Yep."

"How in the world did you…" The fairy reached slowly toward the potion in John's hand, grinning. "Honestly, at this point, it doesn't matter. This is a once-in-a-lifetime sight. Yes, even once in a fairy's lifetime."

"Would you take this in trade for the Eternal Heart?"

Leonidas chuckled and rubbed his aged, hairless chin. "My boy, you could take half my wares for that item in your hand. Are you sure you don't want more?"

"I'm sure."

"Then you have yourself a deal, and I daresay I'm getting the better end of it." The fairy stuck out his hand. When John took it for a brief shake, the Gorafrex's light flashed again behind his eyes. Leonidas slowly lowered his open palm to take the orange potion and looked at John sidelong. "Why do I feel like your suddenly benevolent passenger is laughing at me?"

"It's glad it knew what you wanted."

"Is it?" When John set the vial in the fairy's hand, Leonidas cupped it in both palms and drew in an awed, shaky breath. "So am I, my boy. So am I."

"Pleasure doing business with you." John picked up the blue Eternal Heart vial, raised it toward the preoccupied apothecary owner with a nod, and slid it into his pocket.

"Yes, you... Feel free to come back any time." Leonidas licked his lips, his eyes reflecting the potion's bright-orange glow. "And good luck to all of you. You may be a few of who knows how many unsung heroes on this ship, but if you succeed in fixing this city's magic—"

"*When* we succeed." Emily pointed at the elderly fairy and raised an eyebrow. "You better believe it."

"I do now." Leonidas looked up at her with a breathless laugh. "Most people won't know what you've done. This is me thanking all of you in advance."

"You're welcome. In advance." Nickie followed John and her sisters toward the door into the hallway. "See you around."

"Mm-hmm."

"Oh, I'll definitely be back," Emily called, leaning backward into the shop. "You can count on it."

"I won't hold my breath, young lady, but you're welcome any time."

As the Hadstrom sisters let the door close behind them, Leonidas pulled a small black box from beneath the counter and slowly opened it. He nestled the orange potion into the padding and sighed. "In all my days… Ha. And from a brand-new Peabrain. Ha, ha."

## CHAPTER ELEVEN

"That was definitely weirder than visiting Marlin."
Nickie pushed open the front door of Brightwing
Emporium, and the balmy evening air washed over them
as they stepped out onto the sidewalk.

"And at least we didn't have to agree to another magic
show, am I right?" Emily's grin faded when Nickie shot her
a warning look. "Too soon? Okay. Fair enough."

"What was in that vial?" Laura asked as they all got into
Nickie's car.

John pulled the back door shut behind him and smiled.
"Magic older than that fairy, I guess."

Emily buckled her seatbelt and narrowed her eyes at
him. "Not *your* magic."

"Nope. I simply…" He chuckled. "Breathed a little life
into it."

"Into what?" Nickie started the car and glanced quickly
up at his reflection in the rearview mirror. "I saw you pull
absolutely nothing out of your pocket."

"A little dust from the library, actually."

Laura cocked her head. "Dust?"

"From the restricted section. The wall." John picked at his fingernails, then dusted off his hands. When he looked up and saw all three Hadstrom witches staring at him, he laughed. "That's not a real wall."

"Yeah, we know that."

"Those books weren't the only things saved from the Library at Alexandria when it burned down. Some of the magic used to build *that* library was used to make the restricted section of Austin's library, too. And probably the others around the world like it holding the rest of the rescued collection. You guys didn't know this?"

"Nope." Nickie let out an exaggerated laugh and pulled away from the curb to head down the street. "I don't think it occurred to any of us to scrape off a piece of a wall that doesn't normally exist as a wall."

"Well, that's where all the wards get their power."

Emily gaped at him. "You mean I stole a book through wards that used to run around the *Library at Alexandria*?"

"Yep."

She smacked her palm against her forehead and sat back in her seat. "Good thing magic broke before *that* happened."

"You wouldn't have done it if magic was working the right way, Em." Laura tapped a finger against her lips and watched the rest of downtown Austin blur past them in the early evening light. "We wouldn't have done a lot of things if magic was working."

"What about that Eternal Heart?" Nickie asked. "Em, do you know what that is?"

"Never heard of it."

John shot her a knowing smile, then slowly turned to look out his window. "It's something I thought might come in handy."

"You or the Gorafrex?"

He shrugged. "Not much of a difference at this point."

Emily blinked and turned toward her window to hide her troubled expression. *He's not only John anymore. And I'm... What? Dating the Gorafrex, too?*

"The museum's not too far away." Laura was oblivious to her sister's reaction. "Next stop?"

"I don't see why—woah." Emily pressed herself against her window while looking as far back as she could until the plume of flashing purple smoke and spraying bubbles disappeared behind the next building they passed. "Did you guys see that?"

"What?" Nickie glanced around the street.

"No, way out there. Nickie, turn around."

"What's going on, Em?"

"That Peabrain kid. The one who blew up his back yard. I think that should be our next stop."

Laura and Nickie shared a quick glance. "What happened?"

"Looked like another minor explosion." Emily leaned forward and gripped the back of Nickie's seat. "We can't put this one off. That kid's on the list too, right?"

"Yep."

"Next stop, then."

Nickie made a U-turn at the next light, then headed back toward Mueller. When they drove past the main library again, a plume of green bubbles spewed up into the air from the center of a neighborhood miles away.

"Yeah." Emily slumped back in her seat with wide eyes. "That's the same place I saw the explosion that day from the library window. It's gotta be the kid."

"Any thoughts, John?"

"Other than that I agree with you? No, not really."

They made it into the neighborhood in Mueller eight minutes later.

"Not here." John pointed straight ahead. "The next street over."

"Are you—You know what? I'm gonna stop asking." Nickie pulled away from the stop sign and took a right at the end of the next block. The neighborhood was mostly quiet, although there were plenty of people sitting out on their porches for a late dinner now that the temperature had cooled enough not to be scorching. One man waved to them from a lawn chair in his front yard, where he'd surrounded himself with multi-colored pinwheels stuck into the grass.

Laura gave him a hesitant wave as they drove slowly past. "Anyone know that guy?"

"Nope. Looks like he's the friendly neighborhood waver. Every neighborhood has one."

"Oh, yeah? Who's ours, Em?"

"Uh…" She laughed. "You know what? Maybe it's me."

"You don't sit out in the yard like that."

"Yeah, but I don't mind a quick hello every—oh! There. Right there. Yellow house on the right."

The nonstop plume of bubbles rose from the yellow house's thin chimney, surrounded now by a flock of barn swallows screeching and flapping around the now-yellow Peabrain magic.

"Yeah, somebody's bound to notice this sooner or later." Nickie pulled over on the other side of the driveway and parked. "At least nothing's exploding."

"Not yet. So we need to be fast. Poor kid. He's probably had enough attention from the last time."

The Hadstrom sisters got out of the car. John closed his door softly behind him and followed the witches down the driveway toward the yellow house's front door while craning his neck to look all the way up at the highest bubbles bursting within the flock of barn swallows.

When they reached the front doorstep, the shouting from inside the house made them pause.

"Anthony, *please!*"

"I don't know how!" The boy couldn't have been older than twelve. "Mom, do something."

"There's nothing *to* do. Anything I try right now is gonna make it worse."

"Do the vacuum thing."

"Honey, that's more likely to suck up either one of us than your magic. Just—"

"Make it stop!"

Laura cleared her throat and knocked as hard as she could on the door. The shouting stopped instantly, then a baby started crying.

"Oh, no. No, no, no. Get back here!"

"Mom, someone's at the door."

"Don't you dare."

The drapes covering the window beside the door peeled aside, and a young boy's wide brown eyes blinked at

MARTHA CARR & MICHAEL ANDERLE

the Hadstrom sisters and John. His dirty-blond hair stuck up on one side, and a flash of yellow light illuminated the rest of the room behind him. Emily smiled and gave him a friendly wave. The boy dropped the curtains back into place and disappeared.

"Guess there's a time and a place for waving." She dropped her hand against her thigh. "Try knocking again."

"They know we're here, Em."

"They're probably thinking we'll leave. Try again."

Laura turned to shoot her sister an exasperated glance, and Nickie stepped up to the door and knocked again instead.

"We're here to help," she called. "Please open up."

The baby's crying rose even louder, then three sets of locks turned in the front door before it finally opened. The woman standing on the other side had dark circles under her eyes, her hair scattered around her face as she bounced the screaming baby up and down in her arms. "Can I help you?"

"Mom, they're *witches*—"

"Anthony, go wait for me in the kitchen."

"But what about—"

The woman shot him a fierce look, and the boy darted across the entryway toward the other side of the house, his wide eyes taking in the strangers at the door before he disappeared.

"We're sorry to bother you," Laura said. "We couldn't help noticing—"

"That the boy who blew up the neighborhood lives here? Yeah. Magicals in this town really like to talk."

"Actually, there's a beacon shooting up out of your house." Emily pointed straight up into the air.

"What?" The woman blinked and glanced at the ceiling of the narrow awning over the front stoop. "You've gotta be kidding me."

"It's not nearly as bad as... Well, as last time." Nickie gave the woman a reassuring smile. "But it caught our attention. And we'd like to help. You know, to keep it from getting worse."

"Oh, sure." The woman rolled her eyes. "Everyone always assumes it *will* get worse. He's only a boy."

"We know." Laura tried not to stare at the still-screaming baby. "And he's not the only one having a hard time with their magic right now."

"Then I don't see how you could possibly help us." The woman gave each of the sisters a fleeting once-over. "Unless you're carrying around a cache of potions made specifically for a Peabrain going through a lot more than puberty right now."

Emily pursed her lips. *I gotta start keeping emergency potions all the time.*

"We've managed so far with a little magic," Laura said.

"Yeah, it works most of the time."

Nickie elbowed Emily and kept smiling at the woman.

"I don't know who you people are or why you think you can walk right up to my front door." The woman jerked her head away from her infant when the child let out a renewed scream. Then she sighed and closed her eyes. "But we can handle it. Like everyone else in this town is trying to handle this broken mess."

"He's feeding the birds with that." John still stood in the

MARTHA CARR & MICHAEL ANDERLE

driveway as he gazed up at the barn swallows circling around the bubbles spraying out of the narrow chimney.

The Hadstrom sisters turned on the porch to stare at him.

"That's what he does when he's scared, right? Your son?"

The woman's mouth popped open in an O of surprise.

"Because it reminds him of Michigan." John lowered his gaze and looked at the woman.

Nickie frowned and tucked her hair behind her ear. *He sounds like a crazy person.*

"I…" The woman in the doorway let out a heavy breath and resumed bouncing the baby up and down while absently patting her infant's back. "How do you know that?"

John shrugged. "I'm happy to sit down and tell you all about it. Can we come inside first?"

"Well…" The woman looked at the three witches at her doorstep, searching for an answer none of them had for her. "It's not really safe in here. Even for another Peabrain."

"We can help with that, too."

"I don't…" The woman turned over her shoulder to see her son peering around the corner from the kitchen. He disappeared when she caught him spying, and she let out an uncertain chuckle. "If you think you can do something about this, then come on in."

She stepped back to let the group of strangers into her home while cooing to her baby and shifting the child to her other arm, still bouncing up and down. Behind her in the living room, the walls crawled with swarms of different insects—ants, caterpillars, tiny flies, a handful of spiders, all of them wrapped in tiny glowing bubbles of magic. The bugs pulsed at random with yellow light, and some bubbles detached from the walls to float sporadically around the room.

John closed the front door when he stepped inside and calmly watched a thick trail of the bugs in glowing bubbles float across the ceiling toward the kitchen.

"Wow." Emily stared at the infested walls. "Your kid did all this?"

"His name's Anthony." The woman bit her lip. "Mine's Stephanie."

"How long has the room been like that?" John pointed behind him into the living room as he watched the trail of floating magical insects move across the entryway.

"Since this morning." Stephanie's eyes filled with tears. "They don't do anything but crawl around on the walls. And I can't do anything to make it stop. He was doing so well after the last incident, but he's going through such a rough—" The baby screamed in her ear again and made her flinch. "Sorry about this. We're all going through… Well." A few tears spilled from the corners of the woman's eyes.

"What's her name?" Nickie asked.

"This is Amanda." Stephanie smiled weakly. "She's picking up on all this chaos, and none of us have been getting any sleep."

"What about help?"

Stephanie swallowed thickly and kept bouncing the baby, unable to answer the question.

"I'm happy to hold her for a little if you want a break."

Emily frowned at her sister. "I didn't know you liked babies."

"When I get to hand them back later? Sure."

"Thank you." Sniffing, Stephanie handed her child to Nickie, and the baby kept crying in the same way, no matter who was holding her.

"Okay." Nickie patted the baby's back with wide eyes. "We'll be fine."

"I don't… I don't know why I handed you my kid. I have no idea who you are."

Emily shrugged. "We all need a little break sometimes. Oh, that's Nickie. Laura. I'm Emily. And this is… John?" She spun around, grimacing at the room of swarming bubble bugs before they found John heading slowly into the kitchen.

"Wait." Stephanie took off after him while wiping the tears from her cheeks. "Hold on. He's a little—"

"Mom?" Anthony's terrified voice rose from the kitchen. John paused in the doorway and turned to wait for Stephanie.

"You good over here?" Laura raised her voice so Nickie would hear her over the crying baby in her arms.

"Yeah." Nickie looked down at Amanda's red face and chuckled. "We'll stay right here."

"Okay." Laura and Emily headed toward the kitchen. "There's a lot more going on in here than broken magic."

Emily bit her lip. "Probably why that kid ended up blowing up his magic in the first place. I can relate."

"But we're not gonna be able to help with everything."

"A little goes a long way, right?"

# CHAPTER TWELVE

"Everything's okay, kiddo." Stephanie gestured for John to wait a moment, then stepped into the kitchen and bent over in front of her son with her hands on her thighs. "These people saw we were having a little trouble and wanted to see if they could help."

"Do you know them?"

"I do now, sure. This is John."

"Hey, bud." John raised a hand and smiled.

Anthony looked him up and down and frowned. "What's wrong with your eyes?"

John chuckled. "I'm kinda going through a few things myself. Wanna sit down and talk about it with me?"

"No. Mom, why'd you let them in our house? You said you wouldn't let anyone in the house after those pissed-off gnomes."

"Anthony, that was because of what happened in the—"

"Everything's about that!" The boy clenched his fists, his face reddening by the second. "And before that, it was all Amanda. Then before that it was *Dad*."

"Sweetheart, this isn't the right time."

"It's never the right time!" Anthony's eyes widened and shimmered with tears. "I messed up once. Just *once*. I'm not trying to do any of this."

"I know, kiddo. Try to—" Stephanie stepped back when another stream of translucent bubbles burst from her son's clenched fists. "Anthony. Take a breath, buddy."

"I *can't!*"

The bubbles burst on the floor and scattered scalding water wherever they landed. Steam rose from the puddles, and the boy leapt away when some of it splashed up against his bare calf.

"Mom."

"It's okay. We'll—ow." She stepped away from him and watched the steaming puddles grow across her kitchen. "We'll wait for it to settle down."

"Hey, what are you doing?" Anthony peered around his mom to watch John walk calmly across the kitchen toward the back door. "Mom, why's that guy walking through our house?"

"I don't… John?"

"I'm letting in a little fresh air." John opened the back door and drew a deep breath. "Hey, it's cooled off a lot." He stepped outside while leaving the door open, and walked across the grass of the back yard. "Wow. Now *this* is awesome."

Anthony splashed across the wet floor and hurried after the adult Peabrain. The bubbles had stopped streaming from his fists, but his body still trembled. "That's private."

"The whole back yard?" John looked at the kid with a crooked smile.

"Yeah, the whole back yard. Our entire house, too. You can't simply go wherever you want in other people's houses."

Stephanie sighed and lifted her bare foot out of the cooling puddle of water in front of her.

"Are you okay?" Laura asked from the doorway.

"Could've been worse." The woman huffed out a humorless laugh. "It *has* been."

"What's outside?"

Stephanie looked up at Emily with a pained frown. "His treehouse. Or what's left of it now, anyway. He built it with his dad."

"And his dad's not here anymore, is he?"

The woman's lips trembled, one eyelid fluttering as she tried to hold back more tears. "No. He's not. It's only been a few months, and we don't…we don't have a lot here. Kind of hard to meet people with a six-month-old and an eleven-year-old who's pissed off about being dragged across the country halfway through his second semester of sixth grade." Stephanie covered her mouth with a trembling hand and stared at the witches. "I'm sorry. You don't need to hear all that."

"Doesn't matter what we do or don't need. Sounds like you needed to say it," Laura soothed.

"So you guys don't know anyone around here?"

"Not really. Anthony hasn't made many friends. And I don't get out much."

Emily and Laura looked at each other, and the younger sister glanced up at the stream of floating insects in yellow bubbles now making their way through the open back door instead. "And he's handling it the best way he can."

"Which isn't very well." Stephanie swallowed a bitter laugh. "And when magic stopped doing what it's supposed to do…" A shout came from the back yard, and her eyes widened before she lunged for the door. "Anthony?"

The shout turned into a full-bellied laugh, and the woman braced herself against the doorframe. Her son jumped up and down while pointing at the birds now swooping down from above the house to snatch up the conveniently floating bugs from his uncontrolled Peabrain bubbles. John chuckled and raised his hand. "All good out here. So you like birds, huh?"

"Yeah." Anthony laughed again when a bubble popped and another barn swallow snatched up the caterpillar inside it. "My dad and I used to go watch them. When we lived in Michigan, at least. It's so much better there than stupid Texas."

John smirked. "Even the cold?"

"Especially the cold. That makes everything clean, you know?"

"I've never been."

"You should. It gets hot there too, but this town stinks. I mean, like, it smells."

"Huh."

Stephanie leaned her head against the doorframe and watched her son mill around the back yard as he talked to John.

"Everything okay?" Emily stepped carefully through the puddles of water in the kitchen.

"I think so." Stephanie turned around to look at the witches. "What's the deal with your friend out there?"

"With John?" Emily laughed. "Brand-new Peabrain. He woke up this morning."

"Wow. I would've thought he's one of us. You know, born with all magical eyes wide open."

"Yeah, he's handling it like a pro."

Stephanie frowned. "How did he know where we used to live?"

"What?"

"Michigan. He knew about Anthony feeding the birds and Michigan."

Laura shrugged. "It's one of his gifts." *If John's not gonna tell her about the Gorafrex, neither are we.*

"Well, whatever it is, I'm glad you all showed up. I haven't heard my kid laugh like that since we told him we were moving. And now I..." Stephanie's breath hitched in her throat, and she cocked her head. "Do you hear that?"

"Uh... Nope."

"Exactly." The woman nearly knocked Emily over when she darted back through the kitchen, water sloshing up beneath her bare feet. Laura moved out of the way just in time, and Stephanie skidded into the entryway before stumbling toward Nickie. "What's wrong?"

Nickie stopped humming and looked up at her. "What?"

"Why isn't she crying? What's happened?"

"Um... I think she fell asleep." The witch lowered the quiet, sleeping baby so her mother could see.

Stephanie's legs wobbled, and she clutched at the banister at the bottom of the staircase to steady herself. "She's sleeping."

"Yeah. I was humming a little. And I think she liked it."

"You're literally a miracle." The woman brushed her

disheveled hair out of her face and closed her eyes. "That kid hasn't taken a nap in weeks."

"Wow. That sounds exhausting."

"You have no idea."

"Nickie?"

"All good." Nickie nodded at Laura and gently readjusted the baby in her arms. "Somebody fell asleep."

Emily poked her head out of the kitchen and cocked her head. "Anyone ever tell you a baby looks good on you?"

"No, Em. And don't even think about telling Chuck."

The youngest Hadstrom sister laughed softly and raised both hands. "Just sayin'."

"Do you want her back?"

Stephanie shook her head with wide eyes. "Not even a little. If she fell asleep, I don't wanna change a single thing about how you got that to happen. So keep doing what you're doing. I mean, unless you have to go."

"Not really." Emily nodded toward the open back door. "I think John and Anthony are in the middle of a pretty intense conversation, so we'll wait 'til they're done, I guess."

"Intense conversation?" Stephanie took another relieved glance at her baby, then headed past the sisters one more time through the kitchen.

Emily scratched the back of her head and watched the woman peeking out into the back yard. *She's being pulled in a million different directions.*

"Oh…" Stephanie leaned against the doorframe again, oblivious to the much thicker column of bubbled insects floating over her head and into the air behind her house. John and Anthony sat cross-legged in the grass beside the pile of splintered wood the boy had blasted off the side of his tree house almost two weeks before. Anthony shrugged and tossed a chunk of wood across the yard, answering John's question with words his mother couldn't hear. The woman slipped back into the kitchen and closed her eyes.

"Where do you keep your towels?" Emily asked.

"What?"

"I'm gonna get this water out of here."

Stephanie blinked quickly and finally let the tears run down her cheeks as she stared at the ceiling. "He's finally talking. I don't know how or why, but you showing up here... It's exactly what we needed."

"Good." Emily smiled and waited for the answer to her question.

"This is... I'm just..." With a squeak of emotion, Stephanie grabbed Emily in a tight embrace and let out a small sob. "Thank you."

"You're welcome." Emily looked over her shoulder at Laura and gently patted the woman's back. "Happy to do it."

Stephanie released her equally quickly and wiped the tears off her cheeks. "I'm a mess. I can't remember the last time I took a shower. I'm gonna take a shower. Do you mind?"

"Not at all," Laura said.

"Okay. Bathroom upstairs if anything happens. If you need me. It's upstairs."

"We got it covered." Emily rubbed the woman's back and nodded toward the stairs. "Go ahead."

"Okay, I... Okay. Thank you. I'm a mess." The woman

laughed as she headed for the stairs. "You don't happen to make these kinds of visits on a regular basis, do you?"

Nickie grinned. "This is a first for us."

"Well, you should do it more. Whatever you brought with you when you stepped inside, it's… Keep doing it. Whatever it is. Oh, kitchen towels are in the closet under the stairs."

The sisters nodded silently, and Stephanie climbed the staircase, dragging herself up in exhaustion and chuckling to herself. The Hadstrom witches watched her until she disappeared into the bathroom and shut the door. Then Emily let out a small laugh of disbelief. "I don't think Austin could handle us doing this whole thing all over again."

"That's not what she meant." Laura walked toward Nickie and the sleeping baby.

"I know. But it's kinda funny to think about. Out of everything we've been doing to fix things, the most positive effect we've had on anyone else is by singing a baby to sleep and getting a kid to talk outside in the yard."

"And leave the door open for all the bugs." Laura smiled at the living room. "Only a few more stragglers waiting to be buoyed out to a swift end by bird-lunch."

Nickie looked down at the sleeping baby in her arms. "Is this really all we came here to do?"

"Hey, don't jinx it, huh?" Emily knocked softly against the staircase banister and approached her sisters to study the almost bug-free living room. "Whatever we came here to do, I'd say it's working so far."

"Looks like it. And John's sitting out there talking with Anthony?"

Emily folded her arms. "Yep. Last time I checked, that was it."

Laura tapped a finger against her lips. "Which is apparently what *he* came here to do. And now we wait, right?"

"Now we wait." Nickie swayed back and forth while humming softly again. She interrupted herself to add, "Tell me when all the bugs are outta there, okay? This little girl's tiny, but she already feels like forty pounds."

"That's where the mom strength comes from." Emily snorted. "Holding a baby all the time."

"And ours did it three times?" Laura rolled her eyes and couldn't help a small smile. "I don't know why."

Nickie shrugged. "I mean, there's something to be said about holding a sleeping baby."

"Yeah." Emily snickered as she headed for the towels in the closet. "'Cause you get to give that one back."

## CHAPTER THIRTEEN

When Stephanie came back downstairs after her shower looking like a completely different person, she found Nickie Hadstrom sitting on her couch with Amanda in her arms. "I'm so sorry that took so long. I lost track of time in the shower, and I—Oh my God, is she still sleeping?"

"Yep."

"Wow." The woman paused at the bottom of the stairs, one hand still wrapped around the banister. "She didn't wake up at all?"

"Nope."

"It's been almost an hour. How did you *do* that?"

"Trust me, if I had an answer for you, I'd share the secret in a heartbeat."

Stephanie's mouth popped open. "The living room."

"Oh. Yeah. That issue took care of itself, pretty much." Nickie tried not to laugh at the overwhelmed surprise on the woman's face. "Everyone else is in the kitchen."

"The kitchen." Stephanie hunched her shoulders and

raised her hands toward her daughter, but her loud exclamation didn't bother Amanda one bit. She lowered her voice anyway. "I'll be right back."

"No problem."

Stephanie quickly headed into the kitchen and froze in the doorway.

"Hey, Mom."

"Hey, kiddo." She settled her wide-eyed gaze on Laura as her mouth fell open again.

The oldest Hadstrom sister smiled. "He said he was hungry."

"And you made him dinner…"

"Lucky kid, right here. My sister's a chef at a five-star restaurant."

Emily wrinkled her nose. "I *was*. And I'll get back into it eventually. Gotta keep the skills as sharp as the knife, though, so I put something together really quick. I hope that's okay."

"You didn't have to do that." Stephanie approached the table and ran a hand over her son's disheveled hair. "How you doin', bud?"

"Fine." Anthony pointed at his plate with his fork. "This is really good, Mom. You should have some."

"No, that's okay. You're eating broccoli. Keep that up."

John folded his arms in his chair and chuckled. "It's gotta be good the way he's been puttin' it away like that."

"Don't get any ideas." Emily pointed at him. "I only made enough for Anthony and his mom. Stephanie, there's an extra plate with tinfoil in the fridge. Didn't know when you'd wanna eat, but it's in there."

The woman combed her fingers through her son's hair

again and glanced from John to Laura to Emily. "Thank you," she whispered.

John watched Anthony shovel more food into his mouth. "It's all good. We had an okay time, huh?"

"I guess." The boy shrugged and reached for his water glass. "Mom, you ever heard of a grackle?"

"Nope." She pressed her other hand to her mouth and closed her eyes.

"I guess there's only one kind back home, and they're not there very long in the spring. Probably why Dad and I never saw any, but John said to look out for 'em here. There's like some kinda huge flock of them that's supposed to show up around now. Can we go out to one of those rivers around here? I can bring my binoculars."

Stephanie sniffed and blinked back more tears. "Yeah, buddy. We can do that."

"Wait a few days." John stood from the table and winked at her. "Trust me, when they come through, you'll hear it."

The woman nodded vigorously as she watched him with wide, glistening eyes.

"Later, dude." John extended a fist toward Anthony, who bumped it with his before diving right back into his dinner.

Laura and Emily stood and followed John and Stephanie into the entryway. Nickie looked up at them from the couch. "Time to go?"

"I think so."

Standing slowly, Nickie joined them with the still-sleeping Amanda and gently returned the baby to her mother.

Stephanie hummed in appreciation and shook her head. "That was really, *really*… You didn't have to do all this."

"No, we didn't." John gently patted her shoulder. "But when magic breaks down in a whole city, we gotta look out for each other a little more than normal, right?"

She let out a breathless laugh. "Are you sure you just found your magic today?"

"Pretty sure." He grinned as the Gorafrex's light shimmered for a split second behind his eyes, and turned toward the door. "Feels like a lot longer, though."

"Okay, don't get too far ahead of yourself." Emily smirked and held the door open for her sisters as John stepped outside.

"I can't tell you how much this means to me. To all of us." Stephanie glanced at her baby. "Do you guys live close by?"

"On the other side of downtown." Emily grinned. "Look for the witches on Pressler Street. Big Victorian house. You can come by any time you want."

"Okay. Yeah, we might do that."

"Have a good night, Stephanie." Nickie slipped through the door.

"You too. Thank you."

"G'night." Emily pulled the door shut behind her and hurried down the driveway to catch up to the others. "That was it, huh?"

"Yep." John stopped and turned, spreading his arm to wrap it around her shoulders when she reached him. "That was part of the deal."

"And you've never seen that kid before?"

"Nope."

"What about the Gorafrex?"

"No, Em." He pulled her closer and chuckled. "It saw the explosion a few weeks ago. And that marked the beginning of things going nuts in the city, didn't it?"

"Well, yeah…"

They got back into the car, and Nickie started the engine. "That lady has a lot on her plate."

Laura closed her door and strapped herself in. "And we helped her clear it, I guess. So Emily could slap a gourmet meal down on it instead."

Emily laughed. "It wasn't *that* fancy."

"Probably been a while since anyone's cooked her a meal or held her baby or cleaned up a mess for her."

"Or talked to her kid like that, apparently." Nickie glanced at John in the rearview mirror as she pulled away from the curb. "What *did* you guys talk about?"

"I promised not to tell anyone."

"Well that settles it, then." Laura propped her elbow on the doorframe and scratched her cheek. "Can't break a promise to a twelve-year-old Peabrain who blew up half of downtown."

"He's eleven, actually."

Emily laughed. "You told a little boy about the whole Gorafrex thing and the curse and why magic's broken. And he knows we're taking care of everything to fix it again, right?"

John shot her a coy smile and dipped his head. "None of that ever came up."

"You're kidding."

He shook his head. "Not even once."

"Wait, but we're running around so the Gorafrex can

*make amends.*" Nickie turned out of the neighborhood and shot John a quick glance in the mirror. "How's that supposed to work if the people on our list don't know that's what we're trying to do? To put everything back together again?"

"And we didn't use any slightly less broken Hadstrom magic, either." Emily folded her arms and stared at John in the back seat beside her. "Why was this on the list?"

He drew a deep breath. "The kid's going through a lotta stuff right now. His dad died, his sister was born right before they moved. New school, new town, barely any time to make friends before a new school let out for the summer. And no one to talk to about it. Add on top of that the huge explosion he let off before everyone else knew this wasn't simply a magical hiccup but something seriously overturned in the whole balance of things…"

Laura puffed out a sigh. "Stephanie thought we were there to berate him about that some more. There must've been tons of magicals showing up to ask what the hell was going on."

"He mentioned the gnomes." Emily dragged a hand down her cheek and grimaced. "The Huldus have been cleaning up after the biggest messes since we stopped being able to contain them all. Somehow, I can't see them being overly understanding and polite when they had to chase down the source of that explosion afterward."

"And we thought *our* world was falling apart." The car rolled to a stop at the next red light, and Nickie tossed her hair out of her eyes. "Poor kid."

"So you literally talked to him about everything *but* magic?" Emily asked.

"Yeah. And it looked like everything else fell into place after that, didn't it?" John set the back of his hand on the seat between them while wiggling his fingers. "Sometimes, the most powerful magic doesn't need any spells at all."

Emily's mouth popped open in a wide smile, and she walked her fingers across the seat before slipping them between his. "You are full of surprises."

"I better be. What would that say about *us* if I can't pull out a few good lines even with a Gorafrex mixed up in my head?"

She snorted. "That wasn't only a line, John."

He held her gaze, a crooked smile blooming on his lips. "No. It wasn't."

Nickie looked at them in the mirror and chuckled. "Let's be clear about this, guys. I am *not* driving you around in a lovemobile right now. Whatever's going on back there, keep it PG, huh?"

"Oh, right. Coming from the least PG Hadstrom sister."

"What? I'm not that bad."

Laura snorted. "Nickie, I walked in on you and Chuck gettin' it on in the mudroom."

"That was weeks ago!"

"Please. That's only because we've had this whole Gorafrex-curse-broken-magic fiasco to deal with, and you know it."

"Yeah? Well, everyone heard you and Nathan up in your room the other day."

Laura straightened in the passenger seat, her cheeks reddening with an instant blush, and stared straight ahead.

Emily pressed her lips together so hard, they practically

disappeared as she turned slowly toward John with wide eyes.

"That's none of your business," Laura muttered. "And I actually closed a door."

Nickie laughed. "Okay, fair enough. Your room, your business."

"Damn straight it is."

The car fell silent. Emily slowly leaned forward. "Was it at least good?"

"I'm not talking to you about that!" Laura thumped her fist against the doorframe, and the sisters burst out laughing.

John looked from Emily to her sisters in the front and shook his head. "It's stuff like this that makes me glad I'm an only child."

"I wouldn't compare us to other people with siblings, though," Nickie said.

"We have our thing," Laura added. "Comes with being a Hadstrom, I guess."

"Oh, ew." Emily burst out laughing again. "I just pictured Dad having this conversation with Aunt Julie and Uncle Mark."

"Come on, Em…"

Nickie hissed out another laugh. "I did not need that bonus image in my head."

"Well, Dad's not keeping it PG either, is he?"

"Emily!"

The youngest Hadstrom sister slumped back against the seat and gave John's hand another squeeze. "You sure you still wanna be a part of this when all this magic-fixing business is over?"

"I honestly can't picture what it would be like without it, Em." He returned the squeeze. "I'm in."

"Okay. I'll remember you said that." *No way am I asking if the Gorafrex feels the same way. And I have to stop thinking about that.*

## CHAPTER FOURTEEN

"Anyone else we want to pay a little visit to tonight?" Nickie asked as they stopped at the next light.

"I don't know. John, do we have time to call it a night?" Laura turned in her seat. "Or do we have to keep hashing this out until we come up against a roadblock?"

He shrugged. "I mean, magic's still doing weird things either way. And we all need to sleep at some point. Yes, even me and even with the Gorafrex."

"Does that thing sleep?" Emily cast him a sidelong glance.

"How should I know? I haven't slept yet."

"You know what else we need?" Nickie pointed out Laura's window. "Food."

"Now that I can definitely get behind." Emily looked out the window. "We going with burgers or Tex-Mex?"

"Feels like a burger kinda night, Em." Laura nodded. "Let's do it."

Nickie pulled over behind the line of cars parked along the street and whipped her keys out of the ignition. "I don't care what Chuck says. Chips, salsa, and beer are not a real lunch."

"I thought it was perfect." Emily hopped out of the car and waited for John and her sisters on the sidewalk.

"Not what I expected the chef to say, but okay."

"Hey, just because I have an advanced appreciation for gourmet cuisine doesn't mean I turn my nose up at the simple stuff. I let Nathan make me eggs."

"Those were really good eggs."

Laura brushed past her sisters and headed for the front door of the newest mom-and-pop burger place. "Talking about food isn't gonna get us dinner."

"So very true."

The oldest Hadstrom sister held the door open for everyone else as they filed into the relatively busy restaurant. They stepped into the line stretching back from the order counter and scanned the menu. The other customers moved around them, the place filled with conversation and laughter and the sounds of the fast-paced kitchen cooking up quick meals in the back.

An abnormally thin elf with long black hair hanging down to his waist walked past the line with his order on a tray. He nodded at the Hadstrom sisters, and his eyes widened when he saw John.

John jerked his chin up at the elf and glanced briefly at the man's pointed ears poking above his dark hair. "Hey."

The elf opened his mouth to reply, then caught sight of the odd but short-lived flash of shimmering light in the Peabrain's eyes. He closed his mouth and leaned away while frowning before he took his tray with him to find an empty table.

John nodded toward after him. "I didn't think elves had a problem with Peabrains."

"They usually don't," Laura muttered. "But there aren't a lot of awakened Peabrains running around Austin."

Emily bumped her shoulder against his. "You think they can tell you're a little different?"

"Is it that obvious to complete strangers?"

"No clue. We're not complete strangers."

The line moved forward again. A dwarf and a wizard—his wand barely concealed in the messenger bag slung over his shoulder—laughed beside the drink cooler. The dwarf thumped his friend on the shoulder and nodded toward John and the Hadstrom sisters.

"We can't seriously be drawing that much attention right now." Emily linked her arm through John's and leaned toward him. "You're not doing any kind of covert *extra* magic, are you?"

"Not beyond walking around with two consciousness-es." He snorted and gave her a reassuring smile. "Whatever it is, it doesn't matter."

"It might if people think they have a reason to do something about it," Laura muttered through the side of her mouth. "I'm not sure I like the way they're looking at you."

John laughed. "I appreciate the chivalry, Laura. As crazy as it sounds, I'm not a damsel in distress needing a champion."

Emily snorted and playfully slapped his arm. "You sure?"

Laura folded her arms. "That's not what I meant."

"I know. I know." He laughed and wrapped his arm around Emily's shoulders. "I couldn't help it."

"Nobody's gonna start throwing around unpredictable magic right now." Nickie stepped up in the line again and pulled her big sister after her. "Especially not in a public place."

"When people get scared, though…"

"Look at this face, Laura." Emily raised her palm under John's chin, and he batted his eyelashes. "Who's gonna be scared of this face?"

"I don't think it's John's face making people nervous."

"Let's quit making ourselves nervous, okay? I don't think we have anything to worry about." Nickie stepped up again as second in line and had to spin Laura around to keep her sister from mean-mugging the handful of magicals casting them wary looks across the restaurant. "Will you cut it out? Maybe you're the one making everyone else nervous."

"I am not." Laura tossed her hair out of her eyes and looked up at the menu again. "What are you getting?"

They ordered their dinner and walked down beside the counter to wait for their order to be called out from the kitchen.

"You never know how hungry you really are until you're standing in the middle of a bunch of people stuffing their faces." Emily peered hungrily at a little girl's massive burger and raised her eyebrows. The little girl smashed the burger into her mouth while spilling sauce and loose pickles all over the wrapper, and stared right back at the youngest Hadstrom sister. Emily laughed and turned back toward the others. "Touché."

"Do you guys wanna find us a table?" Nickie asked. "The place is filling up pretty quickly."

"Yeah, Nickie and I can wait for the food." Laura nodded toward the other booths and tables behind them.

"Hey, look at that." Emily grabbed John's hand and gave him a goofy smile. "We're being *dismissed*."

John smirked. "Well, we *could* use some nice, quiet, intimate alone time."

Nickie rolled her eyes. "Go, already."

Emily laughed as she pulled John away from her sisters and hunted for an empty table. "So, between you and me," she muttered while scanning the restaurant. "Do you have any idea why people were staring at you?"

He shrugged. "I'm not doing any secret magic, Em. But we all recognize another magical when we see one, right?"

"Sure. Pretty easy to spot if you know what you're looking for. Unless someone puts up a serious illusion to hide it from everyone else."

"Right. So I don't know. Maybe all the other magicals in here are surprised to find a brand-new Peabrain walking around right now, especially with magic not doing what it's supposed to do." John rubbed the back of his neck and studied the floor as Emily pulled him along. "I mean, after hearing a little about what's been going on with Anthony and his mom, it wouldn't surprise me if magicals in Austin are a little scared of us right now."

"Of Peabrains?" She chuckled, then remembered how much destruction Anthony's accidental explosion had brought to the city two weeks before. "Peabrains generally don't instill fear into the hearts of other magicals, but I get your point. Oh, hey. Open booth right there. Plenty of room for four."

"Works for me."

They hurried toward the table, and Emily hastily swiped the last few crumbs off the tabletop before sliding into the booth. John sat across from her and folded his hands in his lap. They sat there for a moment in the busy background noise of the restaurant's customers and the kitchen whipping up fast meals. Emily drew a deep breath and leaned forward. "Obviously, now's not really the right time to go into it a whole lot. I mean, it's pretty much a given at this point that we'll be interrupted, anyway."

John chuckled and studied her wry smile. "Well, you can't stop there."

"I know. I just…" Emily pressed her hands against her thighs as her knee bounced up and down under the table. "When all this is over and we're not racing against the magical clock, you and I still need to sit down and talk about everything. You know, about what we're doing. How your extra passenger comes into play. Maybe lay down some ground rules."

John's gaze flickered away from her face for a quick glance at the woman sitting in the booth behind Emily. *Uh-oh.* His eyes widened. "Em, I think that's—"

"Hadstrom!" The shout came from the pickup counter at the same second that Annie—the Gorafrex's third host right before it found Dave—looked up and saw that pale, shimmering light flashing behind John's eyes.

"No!" Annie tossed her hand toward John, as if she meant to throw him against the wall beside the booth. Two huge bubbles of pink light burst from her fingertips as she scrambled to climb out of her seat.

The first bubble burst with a deafening crack beside Emily's ear. The Hadstrom witch jumped away and clapped a hand over her ear. The second bubble struck the booth cushion above John's shoulder with a whump and a harsh rip of fabric. Pink light sparked from inside the hole in the booth.

"It's okay. It's okay!" John raised both of his hands and slid out of his seat to stand.

The fact that he was talking to her surprised Annie so much that she froze, her chest heaving and her eyes wide. Emily whirled around in the booth to see one of the Gorafrex hosts on their list, and her mouth popped open. "Annie, right?"

"Get away from me. I'm not going through that again." Annie took a faltering step backward, shaking her head.

"It's safe, Annie." John slowly stood from the booth, his hands still raised. "If you let me explain, I can—"

Blue light flashed around the terrified Peabrain's hands, and a spray of dark blue bubbles blasted into the floor. They burst where they landed, and coated the floor in a slick layer of blue-tinged slime that looked oily beneath the bright restaurant lights.

Emily glanced at the bursting bubbles. *Is that dish soap?*

"Things have changed," John said calmly. "And we can talk about—"

"No!" Annie spun around and darted down the narrow aisle of booths, blue bubbles trailing behind her as she fled to the front door.

"Wait."

"John, watch out."

He stepped forward to go after his fellow Peabrain, and his sneakers slipped in the blue oily liquid on the floor. Both feet whisked out from under him, and he landed on his outstretched hands that couldn't get any traction in the slippery substance. John crashed down onto his elbow and his stomach, then flailed and slid around more when he tried to stand.

"Woah, woah. Hold on." Emily reached down and offered him both of her hands, but they couldn't get a good grip on each other because of Annie's unintended and slippery defense mechanism.

The last of the bubbles streaming behind the frightened Peabrain as she darted onto the sidewalk floated up to the ceiling. Half of them burst and dropped the same slimy soap onto the diners sitting below. Shouts of surprise, disgust, and outrage rose from the tables, and the diners tried to leap away from the mess splattering all over their food and onto the floor. Two of them almost fell like John, then the other bubbles burst with a crackling pop like more magical fireworks. Green sparks crackled across the restaurant ceiling, letting out bright yellow smoke. The electric buzz shorted out two of the overhead lights with a loud zap. Then the smoke detectors went off, followed immediately by the emergency sprinklers.

CHAPTER FIFTEEN

"Are you serious?"
    "Come *on...*"
"Damnit, I just sat down!"

The diners shouted and rose quickly, everyone filtering toward the door at once and squeezing past each other to get outside.

"What the hell's going on out here?" The manager came out from around the back and saw the last glimmer of the yellow smoke and the still-sparking green bursts along the ceiling. "That's not right..."

Emily stood and braced herself against the side of the booth to help John up off the floor. He finally grabbed hold of the booth Annie had been sitting in and pulled himself up, stepping carefully where it was now soaked beneath the sprinklers but not covered in slime. "You okay?"

"Yeah." John swiped at the blue goo all over his front and tentatively sniffed at his hand. "That's soap."

"That was my guess, too." She glanced at the floor behind him, where the spattering water from the sprinklers now made a thick layer of soapy suds slowly spreading across the floor. Then she looked up across the quickly emptying restaurant toward the order counter and saw both her sisters standing there, staring at her. They each held a tray, water pouring down their faces and soaking into their clothes. Laura scowled back at her little sister. Nickie laughed and tried to peer up at the ceiling before she set the tray of their sopping food down on the closest table.

"Y'all need to get out." The manager stormed toward the oldest witches while sputtering and swiping water out of his eyes. "Fire alarms went off."

"Yeah, we know." Nickie nodded at him. "Fire in the kitchen, maybe?"

"Nope. But that sure as hell doesn't look like something I wanna be around any longer than I have to." The man pointed up at the ceiling, where the crackling green sparks still traveled in zigzagging patterns across the ceiling. A light fixture burst and swung down over the center of the restaurant, and the yellow smoke grew thicker and descended.

"Oh." Nickie cocked her head. "Yeah, that looks like an issue."

"I'm in charge of this place right now. Fire department's on their way for whatever *that* is. And y'all need to clear outta here, or this place is gonna get ripped apart for going against emergency regulations. Go on."

Laura dropped her tray on a table with a wet smack and stormed across the restaurant toward the door. Nickie followed her, eyes wide when she met Emily's gaze.

"What happened?" Laura seethed. She snatched her

youngest sister's wrist and pulled her along toward the door.

"It wasn't us, Laura. Annie was in here."

Laura jerked open the front door and stormed outside into the warm evening. Nickie caught the door before it closed and held it open for John, who now had soap bubbles coating his shoulders and chest. All along the sidewalk, the soaked restaurant customers grumbled and tried to flick water off themselves, pulling out phones and wallets to check for damage.

"Annie, the Peabrain host on our list?" Laura stuck her hands on her hips and glanced between Emily and John.

"That one, yeah." John tried to swipe the bubbles off himself, only smeared them around more, and gave up. "She saw me, and I think she recognized the Gorafrex. Or something about it, at least. She freaked out."

"And then she tried to use her magic, right?" Nickie tossed her hair back with a spray of water.

"I don't think she tried," Emily said. "She was terrified."

"Great. It's gonna be even harder to find her now, isn't it?"

"Not if she goes home," John replied. "She might react the same way if she sees me or Emily again. I don't know."

Emily shrugged. "Or maybe she'll have some time to let what you said sink in. That things are different and you just wanna talk to—"

A brilliant burst of green light came from inside the restaurant, followed by a loud crack and a boom that shuddered the windows. The people on the sidewalk shouted and ducked away from the blast, quickly spreading up and down the street when the thick yellow smoke ballooned against the windows and seeped out under the door.

"One more mess for us to clean up." Laura rubbed her forehead while frowning. "This isn't helping."

"Well, we can't—"

"All right, everybody. Fire department's on their way. Anybody who's seen something crazy-weird this evening, all eyes on me!"

The Hadstrom sisters turned to see six Huldus walking down the street toward them. The one with the bright-orange beard in denim overalls waved his hands above his head.

"Is that Ronan?" Nickie asked.

"Have we met any other mechanics with orange beards?" Laura rolled her eyes. "We were supposed to get through this *without* making anything worse."

"It might not be worse, though." John raised his eyebrows when Laura frowned at him, then he gestured toward the Huldus gathering the disgruntled customers closer down the street. "We gotta make a stop with the mechanics eventually, anyway. If they're already here…"

"If they even want anything to do with us." Nickie wrinkled her nose. "Ronan wasn't all that happy about seeing us the last time. And we needed help from the trees to convince him to hand over a shiny gnome screw."

John scrunched up his face with a confused chuckle. "You had to do what, now?"

"Long story." Emily bumped her shoulder against his. "And we'll have time later to go over that piece of it. The Gorafrex was still in the Clubhouse at that point. And Melissa."

"So what about this?" Nickie pointed at the yellow smoke roiling inside the restaurant.

"I mean, we can try to clean it up." Laura sighed heavily. "Or maybe it'll clear out on its own?"

Another crack echoed inside the dining room, rattling the glass front door in its frame and sending a little shudder through the sidewalk as the yellow smoke burst with green sparks.

"I don't think that's gonna happen." Emily held her hands out toward her sisters. "Time to juice up."

"Here we go." Nickie grabbed her little sister's hand.

Pink light bloomed down the street as the Huldus stood together in a line, their legs spread and the outside of their boots touching their neighbors' boots as they conjured the pink bubbles that would wipe the clueless humans' memories of what they'd seen.

Emily scowled. "I hate that spell."

"Kinda necessary though, Em." Nickie squeezed her sister's hand. "With most people."

"Looks like they took a page out of our book, too." Laura slowly reached for Emily's other outstretched hand. "Linking up like that to power their magic right now."

"It worked when the museum was falling apart." Emily sighed. "Let's do this."

The Huldus' bright-pink spell flared in a brilliant light and disappeared.

"All right. Nothin' to see here, people," Ronan shouted, his orange beard fluttering as he waved away the memory-wiped onlookers. "Go on home and get yourselves dried off. Go on. Scram."

"That part's taken care of." Laura nodded toward the

restaurant as the firetruck sirens wailed and grew steadily closer and louder. "Let's do our part, too."

The Hadstrom sisters all turned to face the restaurant, holding hands. "Just a quick cleanup. We'll pull the smoke—"

"Oh, no. Uh-uh!" The harsh shout made them turn again. Tiberius marched toward them, waving a hand in front of him and shaking his head. "Don't even think about it."

"Hi, Tiberius." Nickie gave him a tight smile. Laura rolled her eyes.

"Everywhere I freakin' look, you three are starting even more crap around here. Hey, break it up." The black-haired gnome batted at Emily's hands until she finally let go of her sisters. "I don't know what you're trying to pull but you're going too far." He finally saw the yellow smoke inside the restaurant and leaned away with wide eyes. "I love this place. Great burgers. What did you *do?*"

"We didn't do anything." Emily folded her arms. "One of those new Peabrains we're trying to help had a minor freak-out."

"What? You're not supposed to help *any* Peabrains. That's how this works."

"Not explicitly," Laura said. "We know that, Tiberius. You don't have to keep shouting at us, either."

"I'm not shouting!" The gnome sucked in a deep breath and let it out in a growling sigh. His eyes narrowed when he saw John standing behind the sisters. "This Peabrain?"

"No." Emily stepped toward John and glared at the mechanic. "He's still off-limits."

"Off-limits? Girl, what in the world are you—" Tiberius

blinked quickly and pointed at John. "This is the guy? Your friend?"

"Oh, now you recognize him, huh?"

He rubbed his head and shrugged. "Well, now that you're standing right next to each other, yeah. That night's coming back to me pretty quickly. He wasn't a Peabrain then."

"You mean when you wiped his memory? No. He wasn't."

"I'm John."

Tiberius stared at John's outstretched hands and folded his arms. "Okay. Something funny's happening with your eyes, Peabrain. You might wanna get that checked. And we all need to quit dancing around the pink elephant on the sidewalk. You witches promised me you were gonna fix magic. That's why I gave you my screw, isn't it?"

"That was for our spell." Laura flicked droplets of water off her hands. "The one we thought would fix magic, yeah?"

"*What?* Are you telling me I gave you a family heirloom just so you could test drive a massive spell and screw it all up? I need coffee." Tiberius thumped his palm against his forehead. "And half a dozen donuts."

"No, the spell worked," Nickie added. "We have a few things to clean up and make right again before magic stops dishing out all the wrong surprises."

"Yeah, no kidding." Tiberius pointed at the yellow smoke. "You really suck at cleaning up, you know that?"

"Again, that was another Peabrain. Not us."

"Well, I don't care who it was. We need to make this go away before the fire department gets here and we have to wipe a bunch of firefighters this city might need for a *real* fire." The gnome stuck two fingers in his mouth and let out a piercing whistle.

The other mechanics hurried toward him from down the street. When Ronan saw the Hadstrom sisters, he rolled his eyes. "You three again? Come on."

Laura folded her arms. "Okay, I'm done trying to explain. We're not the problem, here."

"No, but you sure aren't helping, are ya? Come on, fellas. Line up and clean up. Let's go."

Emily reached for her sisters' hands again.

"Ah-ah-ah!" Tiberius jabbed a finger at her and raised an eyebrow. "Let us do our jobs, huh? You sit tight."

The mechanics lined up boot-to-boot and shot streams of milky-white bubbles through the restaurant's windows. The yellow smoke slowly dissipated, drawn into the white bubbles working like dozens of floating vacuums until the restaurant was clear again. The now-yellow bubbles swelled before blinking out of existence one by one. The sprinklers still rained down on the dining area, where several booths had been ripped from their bolts and scattered across more tables.

Tiberius sighed, peered at the ceiling, and sent a stream of clear bubbles toward the green sparks. When the bubbles burst, the sparks cut out. "There. That's—ow!" The gnome's finger sparked with green light next, and he shook it out before sticking it quickly in his mouth. Then he popped it out again and stared at it. "And stay down."

"You guys have been practicing with the Huldu supercharge, huh?" Nickie gestured toward the gnomes' boots linking them together to power their magic.

Tiberius stepped out of the line and brushed imaginary dust off his sleeve. "Yeah. I guess I can give you guys credit for that one. But it's still not anywhere near as good as the real shebang. Which you were supposed to have fixed by now!"

"We *know*." Laura spread her arms. "We're working on it, okay?"

"Well, work faster. How the hell did you not know that spell of yours wasn't the last piece of this screwed-up puzzle?"

"We were still missing one piece." Emily glanced at John. "Now we have it."

"The *Peabrain*? Look at him. He's brand-spanking new! He has nothing to do with that cockamamy story you told me about your family legacy and the Gorafrex and all this craziness with possessing sleeping Peabrains and—" Tiberius blinked at John. "Seriously, kid. Whatever's happening with your eyes, stop already. It's freaking me out."

John looked the mechanic up and down before giving him a slow, gentle smile. "Want any help with that control center for McKinney Falls?"

## CHAPTER SIXTEEN

"McKinney Falls?" The Huldu blinked rapidly and snorted. "McKinney Falls is none of your business, Peabrain. What makes you think we'd need any help with that?"

Ronan's eyes widened as he shifted his gaze from one Hadstrom sister to the next. "How does he know about that?"

"Well, maybe he didn't, and now you told him." Tiberius glared at his fellow mechanic. "Nice one."

"I can help." John's smile widened.

"I seriously doubt that. As far as magic is concerned, you're still a baby. Besides, anything you could do is out of order until that magic gets pieced back together by these witches." The gnome folded his arms. "We're all waiting for it."

"We're doing everything we can," Nickie said. "And it would help us if you let John help you with whatever this McKinney Falls problem is."

"I call bull, witch. You're not pullin' another one over on me. No way."

John cleared his throat. "You have a problem with the falls. Half the water falls up, and none of the mechanics can get the lever in the control room to move. Emergency magic generator, right?"

Tiberius and Ronan stared at him, both of their mouths falling open.

"I mean, not any magic *we* can use. But it's part of the ship's built-in system for at least keeping the natural balance. 'Cause the top of the falls are flooding, the bottom is running dry, and you guys can't figure out how to fix it because the control room isn't doing its job, and that's keeping you from doing yours."

"Who *is* this guy?"

"He already told you his name."

Tiberius snorted. "I mean, how does he know all this?"

The Gorafrex's light flashed in John's eyes again, and the mechanics leaned away from him.

"He's part of bringing magic back." Laura waited for that bit of information to sink in.

Ronan tugged on his orange beard. "No way."

"Yes, way." John shrugged. "I can fix the control room for you. Get rid of the issues you're having with McKinney Falls. And I'm more than happy to explain how all this is possible on the way."

"Yeah, right. You expect us to believe you know all about our jobs, but you don't know where you're going when you get down into our level?"

"Pretty much."

Tiberius narrowed his eyes and slowly turned away from John while waving the five other Huldus toward him for a quick huddle. The gnomes wrapped their arms around each other's shoulders and leaned their heads together for a lot of harsh whispering and muttered consulting.

Emily leaned toward John. "Is that really what you have to fix to cross the Huldus off the list?"

"Yep. I'm trying to seize the opportunity while they're standing right here in front of us demanding to know why magic isn't back yet." He smiled down at her and raised his eyebrows. "Maybe they'll settle down after this. Or at least let go of their grudge against you guys a little."

"That would be nice." Emily puffed out a sigh. "You know Tiberius is the one who wiped your memory and knocked you out that night, right?"

"Yeah, I know." John wrapped his arm around her shoulders and pulled her closer. "Can't blame the guy for doing his job."

"Oh, yes, I can."

"Come on, Em. We're all trying to fix our mistakes."

She snorted and leaned against him. "You haven't made any mistakes."

"Well, you know what I mean."

Laura glanced at her wristwatch while bouncing impatiently on her toes. "How long does it take to decide? It's a simple yes or no."

"If you were in their shoes, you'd take a lot longer than this to decide what to do," Nickie pointed out.

"But I'm not in their shoes. And *I* know that the only way to bring magic back is to get John down into whatever control room he needs to get into. How do these guys not see that?"

"Um…" Nickie frowned at her sister. "Because they're missing the giant piece of information about us breaking the curse and John harboring a Gorafrex who doesn't wanna blow up Austin anymore."

"Oh. We should tell them that."

"That's the plan," John agreed. "Whenever they decide they're ready to listen."

Emily looked up at him and studied his light eyes. *At least the Gorafrex isn't flashing around right now to say hello.* "How are you so calm about all this?"

"What do you mean?"

"You're patiently standing here waiting for these mechanics to talk themselves in or out of helping us. I would've been shouting it at them by now." Her eyes widened. "And I'm trying *really* hard not to."

"We're all in this together, Em. Whether they know it or not. Making things right with somebody doesn't work if they're not willing to accept the gesture. That was obvious with Annie."

"Right." She leaned her temple against his shoulder and wrapped her arm around his waist. A sharp laugh escaped her. "Is the Gorafrex some kinda Zen guru or something? 'Cause you've been spouting some seriously deep things that don't really sound like you."

"The Gorafrex is simply trying to help. Same as all of us." John chuckled. "It helps to have something else in my head constantly reminding me that things are all working out the way they're supposed to."

"And you listen to the voices in your head, huh?"

They both laughed. "This one, yeah. That's probably the only reason I'm not freaking out, too."

"It's a lot different than the first time things got weird at Meadowlark."

"Oh, yeah… That was right after we started hanging out, wasn't it?" John grinned. "You cooked an orgy into that soup."

"Ew. Don't say it like that."

"All right." Tiberius clapped his hands and spun around from the Huldu huddle to point at the Hadstrom sisters, sweeping his finger back and forth. "We'll take you and the grownup baby Peabrain to the control room. But I swear on my daddy's toolbelt that if there's any kinda funny business from any of you—and yeah, that includes you too, Creepy Eyes—the deal's off. And we won't be nearly as fun to hang out with the next time we run into you witches and a bunch of trouble in the same place."

"Deal." Laura nodded. "Can we get going now?"

"I wanna hear it from this one first." Tiberius swung his finger toward John. "No funny business."

"I don't know enough about what I'm doing with magic to even try." John spread his arms with a crooked smile. "Jokes aren't included in the funny business, right?"

Emily choked down a laugh and shook her head.

"Very funny, Peabrain. I'd laugh if my skin weren't crawling all over me when your eyes start flashing like that. What is that, anyway?"

"We can talk about that on the way too, if you want." John leaned toward the gnome and lowered his voice. "But we should probably get down to that control room as soon

147

as possible. You know, so things don't get too out of control."

Ronan elbowed Tiberius in the ribs. "He's right. We're not doing ourselves any favors by taking longer than we have to with this. Lots more work for us if—"

"I know what happens *if*, man." Tiberius shoved his fellow Huldu away and rolled his eyes. "Come on, then. Everybody fall in line and partner up with a gnome. And cross your fingers that we have enough juice to get you all down there without burying you alive."

"Oh, what a happy thought." Nickie shot him a tight smile and stepped toward Ronan. "So how do we…"

"I'm not holding your hand, witch. Grab my shoulder or something."

Laura stepped up beside the next gnome lining up after Ronan and put her hand on his shoulder. The Huldu frowned up at her and shook his head but didn't say anything.

Emily and John walked past them to partner up with other Huldus.

"Uh-uh." Tiberius snapped his fingers and pointed at John. "You're up here with me. I wanna keep an eye on you."

"Are you serious?" Emily leaned sideways and stared at the black-haired gnome. "After what you did to him?"

"Hey, he's obviously recovered." Tiberius gestured toward John. "Which isn't supposed to be possible, but whatever. The whole damn city's breaking the rules."

"It's all good, Em." John nodded at her and reached out to set his hand on Tiberius's head. "Don't worry about it."

"What…you…" Tiberius grunted and slapped John's

hand off his head. "Strike one on the funny business, Peabrain."

"No, it's not." John set his hand on the Huldu's shoulder instead and leaned toward the gnome while lowering his voice. "This would be a lot easier if you tried not to be so angry about everything."

"I don't care who you are or what you know, man. Not my job to make things easier for you."

John looked straight ahead and shrugged. "I meant easier for you."

"Hey, if I feel like grumbling, I'll freakin' grumble. Maybe that's what makes me happy. You ever think of that?"

"Just a thought."

Tiberius snorted and turned over his other shoulder. "You fellas ready?"

The other mechanics nodded and mumbled agreement, then they each reached out and touched the opposite shoulder of the gnome in front of them.

"Focus. On the count of three. One...two...three!"

The sidewalk trembled, and before the Hadstrom sisters knew what was happening, the entire party fell through the cement and the dirt beneath the street as if they were being dropped right out of the sky instead.

Emily gasped as her stomach flipped and immediately found herself with a mouthful of loose dirt. Then boots clomped down on metal, and the falling stopped. Emily's knees buckled when she hit the solid surface beneath them.

"Woah!" Laura stumbled away from the Huldu beside her while spinning her arms to keep her balance.

Nickie landed on the grate of a walkway beneath the

street and fell to her knees, bracing herself with both hands before she got a face full of metal.

Tiberius huffed and folded his arms. "None of you have taken a trip down like that before, have you?" He looked at John, who looked up at the densely packed dirt serving as the ceiling above them, and eyed him up and down. "Except for you, maybe."

"First time."

Emily spit the dirt out of her mouth and wiped her tongue. "No. We tend to go down manholes and unfolding staircases into the belly of the ship."

"Well, don't get used to it. Not like you have a choice, anyway. This is the first and last time you witches get to take the Huldu bus into *our* world. Come on." Tiberius waved the group forward as he tromped down the metal grate. "We have places to go, people. Or one, at least. That park isn't gonna unscrew itself."

The other mechanics chuckled as Emily rubbed dirt and thin broken roots from her dark hair, scattering it across the grated walkway. Then she looked down and saw the miles of open chasm beneath her with dozens of other walkways like this one. Two of them swung in different directions as a group of Huldus marched across toward their destination. *That's a long way down.*

"You okay?" Nickie gave her little sister a hand up and helped brush more dirt off Emily's back.

Emily spit out another glob of dirt and coughed. "I know we missed dinner, but I'm not nearly hungry enough to eat dirt."

"It's good for ya," one gnome called as he turned halfway around and thumped a fist against his chest. "All those extra minerals. How do you think I got *these* guns, huh?" He flexed his bicep, and his fellow mechanics burst into laughter.

Laura chuckled and turned to follow John and the Huldus. "Come on. I think it's a good sign if they're making jokes right now."

"I'm not eating dirt."

Nickie gave her little sister a quick pat on the back. "We know, Em. Don't worry. You'll come up with something witty, and then those gnomes will realize who they're messin' with."

Emily looked at her sister in surprise as they hurried across the walkway to catch up with their guides. "You know, that makes me feel better."

"As long as you time it right."

"But wait until John fixes their control room for them, huh?" Laura eyed the Huldus warily. "I wouldn't put it past Tiberius to change his mind about this little detour."

"No funny business. I know." Emily smirked. "I'll time it right."

# CHAPTER SEVENTEEN

Tiberius grunted when John finished telling them as much of the story as he thought was appropriate. "Come on, man. You honestly expect us to believe that you're walking around of your own free will with one of the most dangerous and destructive beings straight from the homeworld living inside you? And that you're *cool* with it? I've been around a long time, Peabrain, and that story's even more unbelievable than what your witch friends cooked up about letting that Gorafrex loose in the first place."

"It would definitely explain the eyes, though," Ronan muttered behind him.

"Are you trailing along behind me to contradict everything I say, Ronan?"

"No. But think about it—"

"I *am* thinking about it!" Tiberius pressed his hand against a huge black button on a panel in the underground wall, and a large metal door slid open with a rusty squeal. "That *would* explain the creepy eyes."

"I don't have any reason to lie to you." John stepped through the open doorway behind Tiberius.

"Neither do we," Laura added. "Trust me, we wanna put everything back together again as soon as possible."

"Yeah, I bet you do. Since you're the ones who screwed it up."

"And if they hadn't," John said calmly, "they wouldn't have broken the curse between the Gorafrex and their family line going back since before this ship was even drawn out in blueprints."

"Well, I don't know anything about that." Tiberius scratched his head. "Haven't been around *that* long. But if I were to believe this highly suspicious story, what's the Gorafrex telling you about this control room for McKinney Falls?"

"Pretty much exactly what I told you up on the street. What's happening with the falls and that you guys can't fix it from down here."

"Yeah, it's been a real pain in my ass for the last few weeks." The Huldu stopped at another door on the other side of the chamber, his hand poised over an identical black button on the wall. Then he turned around and narrowed his eyes at John. "What I don't get is why that thing is so damn interested in our work down here. And how your alleged ability to get this control room working again is even remotely tied to fixing magic. Which, lemme tell ya, is way more important in the long run than a little upward-falling water."

John spread his arms. "Call it making up for all the trouble."

"Uh-huh. And?"

"There's an energy core in the Velikan's escape pod about a mile outside the falls. The Gorafrex tried to activate it and caused some serious issues. The ship's pulled most of the pieces back together—"

"I know what the ship can do, Peabrain. We're the ones keeping it running. Tell me something I don't know."

"Okay." John stuck his hands in his pockets. "The magic released by the Gorafrex trying to power that energy core caused a few earthquakes. Small ones, but that's what jammed up your control room, and the leftover magic funneled right into the falls. Made the water act all weird, and the issues with that come directly down to what the Gorafrex did when it was...cursed and confused, right?"

Ronan chuckled but stopped abruptly when Tiberius shot him a warning glare. "What? That's a good one."

"So that thing's trying to say, 'Sorry, I messed up. I'm not evil anymore so let me help you do your job?' I'm not saying I believe this crap, but if it's true, is that what you're telling me?"

"You got it." John nodded at the door in front of them. "Is that the control room?"

"Maybe." Tiberius squinted even more at the new Peabrain, then turned his attention to the Hadstrom sisters. "Have you seen this guy succeed in making these so-called amends?"

Nickie nodded. "Yep."

"About..." Emily counted on her fingers. "Four times already today. That's a good track record, since John's magic woke up *this morning*."

"That fast, huh?" Tiberius snorted at John and punched

the black button on the panel. "Failed to tell me the time-line, Peabrain."

"It didn't feel like a particularly important detail."

"You know what? Why don't you let me be the judge of that, huh?"

Emily rolled her eyes. "Yeah, we all know how impeccable your judgement is."

Nickie nudged her little sister and shook her head.

The youngest Hadstrom witch gritted her teeth and forced herself not to say anything else. *If the mechanics can accept this peace offering, I need to forget about the memory wipe. Which isn't an issue anymore.*

The next metal door slid open into the wall and revealed another circular metal chamber with a few raised control panels blinking with blue and yellow lights. Two large iron wheels were attached to the far wall, and the Huldu sitting in the command chair bolted to the floor swiveled toward the open door and spread his arms. "Tiberius! You came to keep me company, huh?"

"Not really. Got a bunch of witches and a Peabrain saying they can help us out with your little lever problem."

"Mine?" The gnome hopped off the chair with a grunt and pulled down the front of his overly stretched sweater in stripes of neon-yellow and a puke-ish orange-green. "This is *our* problem, buddy. I'm not about to take the fall for every little thing that goes wrong on this ship." His words whistled through the gap between his front teeth. "One mistake. *One mistake*, and I'll never hear the end of it. Wait, did you say Peabrain?"

Tiberius stepped aside into the chamber and gestured toward John. "Yeah. A new one."

"A new…" The other Huldu clapped a hand to his head and stared. "Popping up outta the ground like daisies now, huh?"

"John." John walked across the chamber and extended his hand.

The gnome looked him up and down and turned his head away. "Uh-huh."

"This is Bernie." Tiberius stared at the Hadstrom sisters as they entered the chamber with the other Huldus behind them. "And Bernie, these are the witches I told you about."

"These?" Bernie squinted at the Hadstrom sisters. "Oh, you mean the ones breaking magic and running all over with a Kashgar friend, huh?" His eyes widened. "Tell me you didn't bring him with you. I'm not lettin' one of those tall bastards in here. Uh-uh. No way."

"Hey, none of this would've been possible without that tall bastard." Emily folded her arms. "You need to get over it."

Laura shot her a disapproving frown. "And he's only part Kashgar."

"Oh, only *part*, huh?" Bernie looked back and forth between the sisters, then shrugged. "I kinda know a half Kashgar, and the guy's not half as bad as his freakishly tall brethren. Guess I can't be too picky."

"Go ahead." Tiberius gestured toward the control panels and raised his eyebrows at John. "Do what you came here to do."

"Sure." John headed toward one of the huge iron wheels beside the panel and reached into his pocket.

"Woah, woah, woah. Now hold on there, buddy." Bernie leapt toward him while waving his hands in front of his face. "You don't get to come down here and start playing with stuff you hardly understand. Believe me, I've seen a Peabrain or two try to do that before, and those were under very special circumstances."

"I'd call these pretty special circumstances," Nickie said.

Bernie whirled around and leaned toward her. "Oh, yeah? You think three witches and a Peabrain I've never met before know more about how to run this ship than us mechanics? I heard all about your little family legacy, kid, and it's not nearly as impressive as some others I've seen."

"Oh, come on." Laura rolled her eyes and looked at Tiberius. "Do we really have to explain this all over again so John can start fixing things?"

The gnome studied her with a deepening frown. "No. Bernie, let the guy do whatever he's trying to do."

"Are you kidding me? I've been down here for weeks trying to get this thing up and running again, and you want me to hand it all over to this guy?"

"Yep. And if he can't do what he promised me three different times he could do, these new friends of ours can hightail right on back to the surface and keep flailing around until we figure out how to fix things ourselves. Which is what we do, you know?" he added while casting the sisters a sidelong glance.

Bernie grunted and stepped away from John while pulling down the front of his sweater again. "Fine. But I'm serious. If that Peabrain makes things worse, I am *not* getting blamed for this one. Hey. Jeffrey! Come on, man, that's my dinner."

One of the other gnomes had sat down at the folding card table in the center of the chamber and froze when

Bernie called him out. A Cheeto crunched between his teeth. "I'm hungry."

"Me, too." Emily stared at the table scattered with bags of Cheetos, cheesy popcorn, Skittles, and a half-eaten box of donuts. "Can I—"

"Oh, sure! Why the hell not. It's not like I've been shut up in this room trying to fix this piece of junk that shouldn't need fixing. That's my brain food, you know."

"Thanks." Emily darted toward the table and cupped her hands while the gnome sitting there sprinkled a hefty pile of Cheetos into them.

"That's your dinner?" Laura eyed the snacks.

"Really gets me goin'. Or gimme some nachos with that extra-drippy jalapeño cheese sauce. Mm!" Bernie shuffled toward Laura and Nickie. "Don't let her eat all my food."

"I can still hear you," Emily called through crunching bites of Cheetos. "Don't worry, I won't. I only need something that isn't dirt."

Ronan wheezed with laughter and bent over to slap his thighs. The other Huldus chuckled with him while shooting each other knowing glances. Emily munched away on her Cheetos with a grin.

"I don't know about that one." Bernie pointed at the youngest witch. "She looks feral."

Nickie snorted. "Only when she's hangry."

"Yeah, I get that. Hey, Peabrain! Why's this taking you so long?"

"I'm only looking right now." John gazed at the control panels, taking it all in. "Looking for the right connection."

"The right connection. Psh. Listen to this guy. You call yourself a mechanic up there, buddy?"

"He's a server," Emily said.

"What? That's completely useless."

"Thanks," John said absently, too focused on the controls to fully take in the rest of the conversation.

"He hit his head on something?"

"Not that we know of."

Tiberius stepped toward John with his hands clasped behind his back to get a better view of the Peabrain at work. He scowled the whole time.

## CHAPTER EIGHTEEN

"What's the deal with this one, then?" Bernie looked up at Laura and cut her off before she could get a word out. "Never mind. I don't care. Tell me why the heck you've been running around with one of those tall-bastard cousins of ours, huh? That's instant grounds for suspicion if you ask me."

"He's not—"

"Yeah, yeah. Not full. Only part. Yeesh. Why do they all think that's such an important distinction? But seriously. The only other time I've seen a magical giving any amount of Kashgar a second chance is because they were dating." Bernie shuddered. "Tell me you got a better reason."

Nickie pressed her lips together but couldn't keep back a snorting laugh.

Laura stared at the opposite wall, then glanced down at the taller-than-average Huldu in the ugly sweater. "That's the reason."

"No..." Bernie shook a fist at her, then dropped it by his side. "You're killin' me. I tell ya what. Those tall bastards are trying to take over the surface. I've seen it coming for centuries. And they're gettin' there, all right. What about you, pouty-face?"

Nickie folded her arms and cocked her head. "What about me?"

"What are you doing with your life? You know, when you're not busy making the rest of ours harder."

"Wait a minute," Emily called.

"I know, I know. Fine." Bernie spread his arms. "Sorry about my mouth. Some people tell me I don't have a filter."

"Some?" One of the other Huldus scoffed. "Try everyone."

"Same difference. So?"

Nickie shot him a crooked smile. "I'm a musician."

"Uh-huh. And?"

"And that's it."

"Oh, *wait!*" Bernie slapped his head again and took two steps away from her. "*You're* the witch who started a stage fire at the Mean-Eyed Cat?"

"Wow. Everyone's heard about that."

"I love that place. Had some good times there, man. Good times. And weird times, but those are pretty much always the same thing." He turned around to eye John, who now pulled a thick, jagged piece of broken wood five inches long out of his pocket. "Someone needs to tell that Peabrain he doesn't need a wand. His first attempt was crap, anyway."

"He's not trying to use a wand." Laura frowned at the splintered wood as John tapped it over and over against his open palm and kept searching the control panel.

"Whatever. Speaking of which, where are yours, anyway?"

"We don't need them anymore," Emily said through a mouthful of powdered-sugar donut. "I think."

"The witches bringing a baby Peabrain to us have completely lost their minds. Great. Tiberius, did someone scramble your brains, too?"

"Not now, Bernie." Tiberius raised a finger toward his fellow Huldu but kept watching John intently.

"Not now. Huh. And you ladies can cast spells without your wands?"

"When magic was working, yeah." Nickie wiggled her fingers. "We had these rings—"

"Yeah, yeah. Okay. I don't need all the details. You live around here or what?"

Nickie glanced at Laura and chuckled. "You always ask this many questions?"

"Yeah, I'm curious by nature. Or nosy. Maybe both." He glanced from one sister to the other. "Well, come on. Spit it out. We're gettin' to know each other."

Laura slowly shook her head in amazement. "We live on Pressler Street."

"You live on—ha!" Bernie waved them off. "Of course, you do. That's where all the troublemakers end up these days, isn't it? The same troublemakers that somehow end up responsible for saving the rest of us from all kinds of secret crap most of the passengers on this ship never even hear about. *Pressler Street*. Yeesh. What house?"

"Wow." Nickie cocked her head. "You don't stop."

"Come on, come on. Just answer. What's the big deal?

It's not like I'm gonna show up and start going through your things."

"The big Victorian on the hill," Laura slowly admitted. "Right down the street from—"

"That bright blue bungalow, huh?" Bernie narrowed his eyes at them. "I always knew there was something weird going on in that house. And somehow, I never got around to seeing any of you out there. Psh." He tugged on the bottom of his sweater and turned back toward the control panels as he muttered, "Maggie needs to keep a closer eye on her neighbors."

"Who?"

"None of your business, guitar-burner. I wasn't talking to you."

Nickie hissed out a laugh and ran a hand through her hair. "You're a real peach."

"Yeah. We're all peaches in this city, aren't we?" Bernie chuckled and shook his head. "Ha. Peaches…"

"Okay." John nodded and scratched his chin with one hand while drawing the splintered wood away from the controls with the other. "I think we're good here."

"Don't you dare tell me you worked some souped-up Peabrain mojo on this station just by *staring* at it." Tiberius raised a finger and shook it at John, gritting his teeth. "I wasn't born yesterday."

"You sure would make one ugly baby," Jeffrey called from the table.

Emily snorted and sprayed a puff of powdered sugar from her mouth before holding her hand out to the gnome. Jeffrey gave her a high five, and she burst out laughing even harder before pointing at the Cheetos bag. With a barking guffaw, the Huldu poured more Cheetos into her hand while shaking his head.

Tiberius stared at them. "This day needs to be over right now."

"And it will be." John dragged a finger down the controls and nodded. Then he pulled his arm back and aimed the splintered piece of wood.

"Hey, hey!" Bernie lurched toward him. "You can't—"

John stabbed the broken wood into a seam between the metal panels. The controls sparked with a blue light that buzzed across the array of buttons and dials.

"John!" Laura shouted.

He let go of the massive splinter and stepped back, staring at what he'd done.

"You *idiot*." Bernie clapped both hands to his head and spun in a tight circle. "In what universe is that *ever* a good idea? You just..."

The gnome forgot the rest of his sentence when the piece of wood sticking out of the panel glowed with a blue light. The sparks zipping across the controls faded away, the blue light brightened, then a pebble shot out from the space between the panels and pinged against the metal floor. Two more followed it, then a fourth.

The last one bounced toward Bernie's boot and came to a rolling stop in front of him. "No way. Did you—" The panel spit out one final pebble. It thunked against Bernie's chest before pinging onto the ground. The gnome slapped his chest while sputtering and kicked the stones across the chamber. "Totally uncalled for. Better not have ruined my sweater..."

"It's only a rock," Nickie offered.

"You know what, witch? I've seen rocks do stuff you wouldn't believe. What *was* that, Peabrain?"

"The wrench in your gears down here." John nodded at Tiberius. "You should be able to turn on that emergency generator now."

"Ha! Is that what this black-haired beast called it?" Bernie tromped toward them and patted Tiberius's shoulder. "At least you're trying. I'm the one who got this annoying assignment down here in the first place, so I'll be the one to test this out, thank you very much."

"Uh-huh." Tiberius folded his arms and glanced from the glowing blue splinter to Bernie and finally to John. "You could've simply told us there were a few rocks jammed in the controls."

John scratched the back of his head. "I had to see it to figure out what it was."

Bernie rubbed his hands together as he searched the controls. "Come on, baby. Let's get this thing up and running. Bernie's got way better things to do." He punched a few buttons, turned a dial, then stopped and looked at Tiberius. "Well?"

"Well, what?"

"May I *proceed*?"

Tiberius glanced at one of the giant iron wheels beside him and stepped back. "Don't break anything."

"All right, already! *He's* more likely to break something down here than I am. Yeesh. All the extra time I've put into keeping this place running smoothly and this is the thanks I get. 'Don't break anything.' You know I love you, Tiberius, but you're a real buzzkill."

The black-haired gnome grunted.

Bernie seized the wheel with both hands and paused. "If this doesn't work, you're paying me back for everything your snack-stealing sister ate. Plus interest."

"Deal." Emily dusted off her hands.

"Uh-huh." Bernie gave the wheel a sharp tug, then bent at the knees and yanked it again. "Looks like your fancy stick trick isn't enough to get the job—woah!"

The wheel groaned and jerked downward beneath his full weight. Bernie stumbled backward, his arms flailing. John caught him under the arms and helped the gnome find his footing again.

"All right, all right. That's enough. Thanks." Bernie brushed John's hands away and smoothed down the front of his sweater. "Whew. Look at that, Peabrain. You did something useful."

"No problem."

"Huh." Bernie turned around and gave John another suspicious once-over. "You sure are a cocky one, aren't you?"

"I'm not trying to be."

"Yeah, but your eyes say something entirely diff—hey. Cut that out." The gnome spun around toward Tiberius. "Did you see that? What's wrong with his eyes?"

"It's creepy."

"Took the words right out of my mouth, buddy." Bernie eyed John sideways. "I don't like it."

"Hey, maybe this is the time to say, 'Thanks for fixing our problem, John.'" Emily crammed the last of the Cheetos into her mouth and chewed quickly. "That's exactly what he did."

"We won't know that until the—oh." Bernie studied the

flashing lights on the controls and grinned. "Yeah, that's exactly what he did. Good work, Peabrain. Now get outta here."

Emily joined her sisters in front of the now-working controls and the turning wheel. Tiberius stared at John. "That's it?"

"That's it. The falls at McKinney Falls should go back to—"

"Normal levels. Yup." Bernie nodded and patted his belly. "Already there. Water is falling *down* again. We'll have to check out the flooding and make sure all the fish quit flying around and get back in the river where they belong. But we're good, now. See? No more reasons to keep blaming me for stuff."

John gestured toward the glowing blue stick. "I'd leave that there, though. At least until it stops glowing."

"And when's that supposed to be?"

"As soon as we fix magic, probably."

Tiberius let out a heavy sigh and rolled his eyes. "Come on, then. You four aren't hanging out down here any longer than you have to."

"Nice to meet you, Bernie." Emily clapped a hand down on the Huldu's shoulder and grinned. "Thanks for the snacks."

He eyed her hand, then his gaze flickered across the room. "Yeah, well, you can thank me later. I know where you live, now."

"I'll cook you something."

"Aw, come on. Witches don't cook."

"That one does." Nickie nodded at her little sister and turned with Laura toward the open control room door.

"Hmm." Bernie narrowed his eyes at Emily, then quickly glanced at his shoulder when she removed her hand to join her sisters. "Aw, come on. Hey!" He brushed at the combination of Cheeto dust and powdered sugar streaked across the fuzzy material of his sweater. "Look what you did."

Jeffrey ripped open a bag of cheesy popcorn and laughed. "What's the big deal? That's not a new look for you."

"Yeah, but *I'm* the only one who gets to wipe their hands off on me."

Tiberius burst into roaring laughter while thumping a fist against his thigh and pointing at Bernie with the other hand.

"Psh. Everyone's going insane."

Tiberius held his belly as he kept laughing and gestured weakly toward the door before leading the Hadstrom sisters and John out of the room. John raised a hand to the gathered Huldus and smiled. "Have a good one, guys."

"Yeah, you too, Peabrain. Try not to blow anything up."

"Don't make us come after you again."

"If you get into trouble, don't call us!"

The gnomes laughed, and the other five who'd led the witches down to the control room gathered around the card table to dig into the snacks.

"Oh, no. Guys." Bernie stalked toward them. "You know what? Gimme this." He snatched the popcorn bag from Jeffrey's hand and pointed at the open door. "I'm not throwing a party down here. Go find your own food. Hey, where are all the Cheetos?"

Jeffrey pointed at the door. "Witch."

"Damnit. That's what I get for being nice. Get out of my chair."

His Huldu friends chuckled as they made their way across the chamber. "You comin' to the main market tonight, Bernie?"

"Maybe. But I'm not buying any of you ungrateful thieves anything."

The gnomes waved him off as they filtered out of the room, and the metal door slid shut behind them.

Bernie stared at his mostly eaten snacks and scratched his head. He grabbed the last powdered-sugar donut and took a huge bite. "Huh. Peabrains."

# CHAPTER NINETEEN

"Are you sure there isn't a faster way to get back up there?" Emily let out a heavy sigh and climbed up the stairs behind her sisters.

"Elevators and transport bubbles to the surface don't work right now," Tiberius grumbled as he stomped up the metal steps. "Not even the escalators. And I'm not making my guys work overtime to power up and shoot all four of you back up where you belong. So yeah, I'm sure. And you can quit whining about it, 'cause we're almost there, anyway."

"Finally."

Laura glanced at her watch. "We've been walking up these stairs for half an hour."

"Yep. And then you'll be free. Lucky you."

They reached a door at the end of the staircase, and Tiberius knocked on it before pressing his ear to the metal. "This should be the right one."

"What?" Emily wiped the sweat from her forehead. "It better be."

The Huldu shoved the door open and peered out. "We found you outside the burger joint, right?"

"Yes." Laura peered through the open door.

"Well, then we're good. Just watch out for the trash. They missed putting it out for pickup this morning, so it's gonna be a mess here 'til next week." Tiberius stood aside and gestured toward the open door. "Go on. Have a nice night. Don't screw anything else up while you fix magic and bring this whole disturbingly drawn-out hiccup to a close."

"Such encouraging words, Tiberius." Laura slipped past him with a chuckle. "Thanks."

"Yeah."

Nickie smiled at him before she stepped through. "See you around."

"I seriously hope not. Unless you're playing another show. Then maybe I'll show up."

Emily shot him a sidelong glance.

"I get it, okay? Look before I memory-sweep." Tiberius rolled his eyes. "You still need to let that go."

"I know." She almost laughed when he did a double-take and blinked at her in surprise. "You let us come down here to fix whatever that was so we could help you out a little. I can let it go."

"Good." Tiberius leaned forward and muttered, "Between you and me, it doesn't look like he's missing all that much, anyway."

"No, he's not." With a goofy salute, Emily left the gnome on the staircase and followed her sisters through the door.

"Thanks for lettin' me do my thing," John said.

"Yeah, well... Aw, hell, Peabrain. You have me convinced." The Huldu gestured up and down John's body and snorted. "Whatever you got goin' on with this weird Gorafrex thing, whether or not that story's true, at least you did what you said you'd do. And I guess the rest doesn't matter. So thanks."

John grinned and clasped Tiberius's outstretched hand. "We're all trying to do our part, right?"

"Oh, sure. And some of us are more successful than others, all right. Don't prove me wrong about you."

"Not planning to." With a final nod, John left the Huldu on the stairs and stepped through after the Hadstrom sisters. The heavy metal door shut behind him with a clang, and he almost tripped on the two industrial-sized trash bags at his feet. "What's going on here?"

"They missed trash day. Tiberius wasn't kidding." Nickie stepped over the last heap and turned back to look at the door they'd stepped through. "That looks like the back entrance to the gas station."

Laura shook her head. "Apparently, not *all* the Huldu magic stopped working."

"If we opened that right now, those stairs wouldn't be there, would they?"

"Probably not, Em." Laura headed for the street and tried to orient herself. "Okay. Nickie, I think your car's up here a few blocks."

"Let's go."

The witches and John walked up the street toward the restaurant where Nickie had parked. Pedestrians filled the sidewalks, and the street was busy enough for a

Wednesday night in Austin's thriving summer nightlife. When they all got into the car and Nickie started the engine, Emily sighed and strapped herself in. "All things considered, I'd say it was a good day of relatively few giant problems."

"Feels like the longest day ever." Nickie buckled her seatbelt and paused. "There's no way those snacks made you full, Em."

"Nope. But they were delicious."

"I'm gonna call Chuck and have him grab us something." Nickie pulled out her phone. "I'm done trying to order food."

"Thank you." Laura settled her head against the headrest. "This has been one of the longest days ever."

John leaned forward. "Can you guys drop me off at my place? I can meet you somewhere in the morning if it's easier than coming to pick me up again."

"We don't mind coming to get you."

Emily set her hand on his shoulder. "You want dinner first?"

"No, that's okay. I have a ridiculous amount of Ramen noodles at home. And some beans."

"That's not dinner."

"Neither are Cheetos, Em."

She laughed and sat back in her seat. "Fair enough."

After Nickie made her call to Chuck, she followed John's directions to his apartment building, and the sisters told him goodnight.

"We'll be up fairly early," Emily said. "Call me when

you're ready, and we'll come get you."

"Sounds good." He pulled her in for a long kiss, and Nickie and Laura smirked at each other in the front.

When John pulled away, Emily blinked quickly and swallowed. "Um... Okay, then. See you tomorrow."

"'Night." John hopped out of the car, softly shut the door, and headed toward the entrance of his apartment building, his hands shoved into his pockets.

"You okay, Em?"

The youngest Hadstrom sister slumped back against the seat with a groan. "I am so ready for this whole thing to be over."

"We're almost there. You could probably catch up to him if you wanted." Nickie pointed at John moving quickly down the walkway. "We'll come get you in the morning."

"I'm not gonna spring that on him. And he didn't invite me in, so..."

"That doesn't mean he won't."

"Can we go home, please?" Laura asked. "I'm starving, and all I wanna do right now is sit and not think about everything else we have to do in the morning."

Nickie gave her big sister a quick glance before pulling away from the curb. "Everything okay with *you*?"

"It will be."


Both Chuck's and Nathan's cars were parked outside their house on Pressler Street when Nickie pulled up along the sidewalk. Laura stared at Nathan's car. "I did *not* think he'd be here."

"I didn't know that would be a bad thing." Emily unbuckled her seatbelt. "Is it?"

"I don't know." Laura shook her head. "I mean, I like Nathan. I like having him around. But now I'm not gonna be able to relax all the way."

"Uh-oh." Nickie turned off the car. "I don't think you have anything to worry about with that one."

"You can totally relax around Nathan. I bet he'd even massage your feet if you asked him to."

"Gross, Em."

"What? How is that *gross*? That's like one of the best things ever about relaxing around somebody."

"Nobody needs to rub my feet. And Nathan's already helped enough. I don't want him to feel obligated. This is our mess to clean up, and he's not—"

"Okay, stop right there." Nickie turned toward her sister and raised her eyebrows. "We wouldn't be where we are right now without Nathan. Or Chuck. Or John, now. That's what he's been saying all day, too. That we're all in this together. If any of the guys were done with our craziness, they wouldn't be here right now."

"If he's willing to put up with us through all this," Emily added, "he's worth it."

Laura stared at her lap and drew a deep breath. "This is a ridiculous conversation. Let's go eat and call it a day." She quickly got out of the car and headed up the cement steps.

"That sounds like grumpy Laura, right?"

"Yeah, Em. Hangry applies to all of us. She's fine."

They got out of the car and followed Laura up the stairs and along the walkway at the top of the hill toward their front door. Before Laura could grab the handle, the front door swung open, and Chuck greeted them with a huge grin. "Welcome home."

Emily laughed and eyed him sideways. "You feelin' okay, Chuck?"

"I feel great! You guys were gone for the rest of the day, and I didn't even worry about it once. 'Cause you know what? No more Gorafrex to fight. No more kidnappings or giant potion battles or explosions. I already feel like this whole thing is over." He stepped aside to let the witches into their house while puffing up his chest with a deep breath. Then he grabbed Nickie around the waist and shoved the door closed. "I missed you."

"I—" Nickie laughed and flung her arms around his neck when he pulled her in for a kiss and wouldn't let her go. She finally had to push him away to come up for air. "That's one hell of a way to greet someone at the door."

"You're welcome."

"What's going on?"

Chuck squeezed her again, pecked her cheek, and turned toward the kitchen. "Nothing. I'm happy. Maybe I'm crazy, babe, and after everything that's happened, I'd say all of us are entitled to lose our minds a little. But it…it feels like things are working out."

"Well, we're not done yet. We still have a bunch of places to go tomorrow. Including going to talk to Dave. You're still coming with us for that, right?"

"Of course, I am. That dude needs some backup. I mean, it seemed like you guys handled it okay when he showed up in your basement, but I'm pretty sure John isn't enough of a friendly face to cancel out the Gorafrex effect. Where is he, by the way?"

"John?" Emily shrugged. "He wanted to go home. Can't blame him, though. He hasn't been alone since almost dying and agreeing to host that thing in his body forever. So, okay. He wanted to be alone." Her eyes widened when they walked through the living room and she saw the kitchen table. "Woah. You guys really went all out."

# CHAPTER TWENTY

Nathan stuck the last serving spoon in the takeout box and smiled up at them. "It's about time you guys sat down for an actual meal, right? You know, without being interrupted or rushing or needing someone else to step in and finish cooking it for you."

Emily pointed at him but stared at the Chinese-food feast laid out on the table. "I know you're talking about taking over my egg-cooking, and I'm not even a little offended."

"Babe, I only asked for some takeout." Nickie hugged Chuck tighter around the waist. "You didn't have to do all this."

"No, but we wanted to. Also, I'm starving too, so this is for all of us."

Laura pulled an extra chair to the table from the dining room. "This is great. Thanks."

Emily rubbed her hands together and scooted toward the table in her chair. "I'm so ready for this."

Nickie dipped her head and playfully batted her

eyelashes when Chuck pulled a chair out for her with a goofy bow. Then he plopped down beside her and pointed at the dishes still in their boxes. "Got a little of all the favorites. Think five full dinner orders is enough?"

Nickie squeezed his thigh, then picked up a pair of chopsticks set out by the plate in front of her and cracked them apart. "I think we'll manage."

"I don't know. I feel like I could eat all this myself."

"Well, I'm not giving you the chance to try." Chuck scooted forward in his chair. "Hand me that Kung Pao chicken, will ya?"

"Yeah." Emily scooped a helping onto her plate first and grinned as she handed it over. "Just making sure I get some."

"Uh-huh."

Nathan set down glasses of water, then walked around the table toward Laura with a small frown of concern. "Not hungry?"

"I'm starving, actually." She looked up at him and shrugged. "I just…"

"What?"

*That smile makes me feel ridiculous now.* Laura let out a wry, exhausted laugh. "I wasn't expecting all this. It's been a weird day."

"You okay?"

"I don't know. Maybe everything's starting to catch up with me now that we're so close to the end. And coming home to this and you guys not freaking out about where we were almost makes things feel normal again."

"That's a good thing."

She looked up at him and bit the inside of her cheek. "It

is. But it feels a little wrong to be celebrating something when we're still not done. Magic is still going nuts for everybody. We have at least five more stops to make tomorrow. And there's that stupid magic show—"

Chuck choked on his water, forced it down, and cleared his throat. "Say what, now?"

"Oh, yeah," Emily said around a mouthful of mu shu pork. "We kinda roped ourselves into putting it on at the main library."

Nickie pointed a chopstick at her. "*You* roped us into that one."

"At least I *had* an answer. A bunch of parents and their kids saw some flying books at the library the other day. I had to come up with an explanation on the fly."

"And you picked magic show." Chuck slowly lowered his chopsticks toward his plate again. "That's such a weird go-to excuse."

"Hey, I said we were *practicing* for a magic show. Isabelle's the one who turned it into a real thing."

"The librarian," Nickie clarified. "Fairy who watches the restricted magical section."

"Uh-huh." Chuck cocked his head and kept eating.

Nathan ran his hands down Laura's shoulders while chuckling. "That's what's making you feel guilty?"

She rolled her eyes. "Not *only* the magic show."

"All right. Listen up, Dr. Hadstrom."

Emily kept herself from laughing by shoveling more food into her mouth as she briefly glanced up at her sister and the professor in the dining room.

"It's a lot harder to make it to the end if you don't give yourself a little break first." Nathan grabbed her hands and leaned toward her, smiling with his chin almost touching his chest as he looked down at her. "You're not letting anyone down by taking some time to relax and enjoy yourself a little."

"See?" Nickie raised her chopsticks in the air. "Relax, Laura. *Relax*. Nathan can help."

Laura glared at the back of her sister's head until Nathan wiggled her hands.

"Hey, I'm serious."

"I know you are. And I know you're right, but I still can't wrap my head around it." She let out a self-conscious laugh and stared at the far wall of the dining room behind him. "Or why you're still hanging around when we keep hitting one wall after another. I think *I'm* even getting fed up with myself."

Nathan brushed the loose pieces of still slightly damp and now much wavier hair away from her face and tucked it behind her ear. It spilled loose again almost instantly, and he smirked. "I know I've already told you, but I get how easy it is to forget sometimes."

She rolled her eyes and felt a crooked smile twitching on her lips. "What's that?"

"That I really like you. And unless you tell me straight up to get lost, I'm not going anywhere."

"Whew." Emily shook her head and stared at her plate. "There it is."

Nathan pulled Laura in for a tight hug and bent to whisper in her ear, "That includes after dinner."

She playfully slapped his back and laughed, then rested her forehead against his chest. "I'm so hungry."

"So come sit," Nickie called. "And hurry, too. Em's mowin' through this stuff like nobody's business."

"Don't touch that shrimp 'til I get some."

"Too late." Emily pointed at the takeout box and shrugged. "But there's plenty left."

Laura took the open chair between Emily and Chuck, who raised a fist when Nathan walked past. The professor gave him a quick fist bump before pulling out the last chair and sitting to dig in.

Emily finally looked up from her plate, slowed her chewing, and gazed at the food before looking up at everyone else sitting around the table. "Okay, guys. Time for a new deal."

Nickie snorted in her water glass. "Did we have any old deals I need to remember?"

"Probably too many to count. Chuck, Nathan, you guys outdid yourself trying to make takeout look like a home-cooked meal."

"Just a lotta blood, sweat, and tears, Em." Chuck shot her a thumbs-up.

Nathan scooped a helping of chicken onto his plate. "And a split bill."

"And the next time we all sit down and do this, it better be when John's here, too."

Everyone else around the table paused and slowly looked up at her. Laura and Nickie exchanged a wary glance. Chuck cleared his throat and poked his food with his chopsticks.

"What now?" Emily folded her arms and sat back in her seat. "Oh, come on. Simply because he's the Gorafrex's next host doesn't mean he can't be a part of this, too. Seriously, I thought you guys already realized that."

"It's a deal, Em." Nickie nodded. "If John wants to sit down with us and be a part of this, of course, he can. That's up to him."

"Yeah, we have no problem with it." Laura shook her head. "Like, at all."

"I like John." Nathan shoveled a bite into his mouth.

Chuck pointed his chopsticks at the professor. "What he said."

"Okay…" Emily's gaze flickered from one face to the other. "Why did you guys get all weird and silent and creepy when I brought it up?"

Laura tapped her finger against the table. "You tend to get a little emotional whenever John comes up in conversation, Em. I think we were kinda waiting for another—"

"Emily Hadstrom explosion?" The youngest sister threw her head back and laughed. "Was I really that bad?"

"Yep."

"Uh-huh."

"Definitely."

"I really had you guys trained to expect that?" Emily lunged forward and grabbed one of the takeout boxes from the center of the table before spooning more onto her plate. "You can chill out about it. I'm fine."

"Okay…" Laura watched her sister with an unsure smile. "Good to see you working some of that out, Em."

"Yeah, you know what? It feels good. Who knows? When we fix magic and go back to our regular lives, maybe I'll stop having feelings that light stuff on fire and try to stab people." She shrugged and stuck a huge bite in her mouth.

Chuck laughed and widened his eyes as he reached for another takeout box. "That would be a definite plus."

Nickie elbowed him in the side, and he flinched away from her, smirking.

"Just wait, man." Emily pointed her chopsticks at him. "Once all this is over, things are gonna be better than they were before they fell apart."

"I like that outlook, Em." Nathan met Laura's gaze and smiled softly. "I can't think of anything that would be better, though."

"Speak for yourself." Emily caught her sister and the professor staring at each other over the dinner table. "I mean to say, maybe Laura won't blush all the time and give you both away."

"What?" Laura stared at her sister, her face growing even redder.

"I think it's cute," Nathan said.

"You're not helping." They all laughed, and the oldest Hadstrom witch shook her head. "I can't believe I'm saying this, but that magic show can't get here soon enough."

Nickie grimaced and shook her head. "I refuse to look that far ahead into the future. And I'll probably do the whole thing with my eyes closed."

Emily snorted. "The kids are really gonna love *you*."

## CHAPTER TWENTY-ONE

T he next morning, Emily rolled over in her bed and blinked at her buzzing phone on the nightstand. She slapped at it and squinted while trying to focus on the text from John.

*'You awake?'*

She had to try three times to unlock the screen before she could reply.

*'Just got up now. Everything okay?'*

She watched the three dots blinking at the bottom of her screen and smiled.

*'All good. Just thinking about you.'*

*'How'd you sleep?'*

His reply took longer than the last one. "He still has to sleep, right?"

*'Like a baby. Can you guys meet me at Walnut Creek in an hour?'*

*'You don't want us to pick you up?'*

*'I've been up for a long time. Went for a walk.'*

Emily chuckled sleepily, rubbed her eyes, and rolled onto her back.

*'Yeah, we'll see you there.'*

At the foot of her bed, Speed grunted and kicked in his sleep.

"All right, buddy. You can stay here as long as you want, but I'm getting up. Got another long day, and there is no way it can be as weird as yesterday." Emily threw the covers off herself and staggered out of bed. When she stepped into the hall, she found Nickie's bedroom door already open. Then she heard Chuck's low voice coming from downstairs, followed by Nickie's snort of laughter before she hushed herself.

Emily peered into her sister's bedroom and the rumpled sheets on the twin-sized bed. *How do they both sleep on that?*

The instant the smell of coffee hit her, she didn't care about the answer anymore. She raced down the stairs, trying to be quiet, and found Nickie and Chuck standing by the coffeemaker still burbling and hissing out freshly brewed coffee. "Morning."

"Hey, Em." Nickie pulled another coffee mug down from the cabinet and set it on the counter. "How'd you sleep?"

"Really well for how late we passed out. Didn't think you guys would be up."

"It kinda happened." Chuck shrugged. "Guess we all wanted a head start today."

"Well, I woke up 'cause John texted me."

"Yeah? How's he doin'?"

"Fine. Wants us to meet him at Walnut Creek in an hour."

Nickie glanced at Chuck. "Yeah, that should work. Wanna come with?"

"To the park?" He cocked his head. "I mean, sure. We're gonna go see Dave at some point too, right?"

"Definitely. Yesterday was less of a set plan and more like one thing on the list rolling into the next without warning. Which was kind of weird, but it worked out. So if you're with us all day, at least you'll be around whenever we get to Dave."

"Sure. It's not like I'm doing anything else right now." He ruffled his short blond hair and sighed. "Man, I'm seriously ready to get back to work, too."

"You put everything on hold?"

"Not everything." He slid his arm around Nickie's waist and grinned. "You're my favorite client. My focus is more on you, anyway."

She laughed and walked her fingers up the side of his neck. "As flattering as that is, I don't want you to stop working because I'm not playing any gigs right now."

"No, wait a minute. You're not playing any gigs because *I* stopped working. It's not your job to book yourself. That's what you have me for."

"Among other things…"

Emily cleared her throat. "Hey, look. Coffee's done. Pour me a cup, huh?" She quickly went to the fridge and pulled out the flavored creamer before taking it straight to the table. *Note to self. Those two get weird first thing in the morning.*

Nickie and Chuck joined her at the table with the full, steaming mugs of coffee, and they all sat, passing around the creamer and the spoon. "You think Laura's getting up soon?"

"No idea. She looked pretty exhausted last night. Then again, she's probably dreaming about fixing magic, and that'll wake her up that much sooner."

The door to Laura's bedroom creaked open and shut softly upstairs.

Nickie grinned. "Perfect timing."

Laura shuffled down the stairs, rubbing the sleep from her eyes before pulling her robe tighter around her. When she stepped into the kitchen, her eyes were barely open. "I'm so glad somebody already made coffee."

"Good morning to you, too." Emily watched her sister cross the kitchen to pour herself that first cup. "You ready to hit the road again today?"

"Give me a sec." Laura filled her mug, took a few quick sips, and sighed. "Okay, what did you ask?"

Emily scooted the spoon and creamer across the table as Laura joined them. "Ready for round two of Gorafrex-amends roulette?"

"That sounds so weird."

"And accurate," Nickie added, holding her mug with both hands under her nose. "That's exactly what it feels like."

Chuck swallowed his coffee and blinked heavily. "Well, doesn't that make the whole thing sound so much more appealing? You sure you don't wanna pick me up right before heading to Dave's?"

Laura shook her head. "No. The way things worked out to be so weirdly convenient yesterday, we could literally run into Dave on the street. And it would be a lot easier if you were already with us."

Emily snorted. "Otherwise, we'd have to string him up, throw him in the trunk, and bring him *to* you so you're there to help him process whatever John has to say to him."

Chuck and her sisters stared at her.

"What? Not funny? I just woke up, guys. Come on."

"John wants us to meet him at Walnut Creek in an hour," Nickie said. "Or a little less, now."

"We're not picking him up?"

"Nope." Emily lifted her mug toward Nickie. "Here's to saving all that extra gas."

"Ha." Nickie drank more coffee. "You'll be funnier when we've all had a chance to wake up."

Forty-five minutes later, the Hadstrom sisters and Chuck got out of Laura's car in the access parking lot at Walnut Creek. John stood at the trailhead with his hands in his pockets and smiled at them.

"Day two as a Peabrain, and he still looks okay with the whole thing."

"Yep." Emily unbuckled her seatbelt and couldn't get out of the car fast enough. *Don't run, don't run.* She made it halfway to him before skipping forward and throwing her arms around him.

"Woah." John laughed and hugged her back. "Hey."

"Hi." She leaned back and grinned at him. "Too much?"

"Nope. You could do that every time you see me if you wanted."

"Don't push it." She felt like her cheeks would fall off with how much she smiled, and his laughter made it worse. *I shouldn't have pushed him away for so long.* "We'll see what happens."

He studied her eyes and pulled her closer. "I can be patient."

"Yeah, I bet you—"

John cut her off with a kiss, and the rest of her breath filtered out of her in a sigh.

Nickie whistled as she, Chuck, and Laura headed toward the trailhead. "That's some hello."

Emily pulled away from John, brushed her hair out of her face, and smiled at him before turning toward her sister. "Yeah, well, you got your special hello last night. Now I get mine."

"What happened last night?"

"Chuck and Nathan set up a takeout feast." Laura stuck her thumb out toward Chuck. "Between the time we dropped you off and the time we got home."

"Sorry I missed it."

"We'll do it again," Chuck said. "You'll have to put some work in for that one if you wanna reap the benefits, though."

Nickie nudged his arm. "Which are what, exactly?"

"Really good food, babe. And lots and *lots* of gratitude." He winked at her, and Nickie ran a hand through her hair while chuckling. "Totally worth it."

John ran his hand slowly up and down Emily's back. "No problem, then. I can set up a feast like nobody's business."

"Yeah, but you gotta get the *experience* in, man."

"Dude, you realize what I do for a living, right?"

Chuck blinked. "Oh, yeah. Then maybe we should let you do the whole thing." He stuck his hand out for a quick handshake. "How you doin'?"

"Pretty well, all things considered. Had some weird-ass dreams, though."

Emily shot him a curious frown. "Like what?"

John shot her a quick sidelong glance. "That's something we can talk about later."

"Oh..."

"I guess you wanted us to meet you here to call on the Tree Folk, right?" Laura nodded toward the trailhead and the thick woods leading into the park.

"Yep. Figured we'd start here. Mostly because it's gonna get really hot today."

"Good thinking." Emily linked her arm through his and turned them toward the trailhead. "A nice walk in the park at eight in the morning. Throw a little chat with monkey-like tree elves into the mix, then move on to the next person on the list. Doesn't get any better than that."

John chuckled and watched her staring up into the trees as they headed down the path. "Are you always this optimistic first thing in the morning?"

"That's a definite no," Nickie called from behind them. "She's in rare form today, John. Enjoy the moment."

Emily shrugged and squeezed his arm. "She's not wrong. I feel good today. Hey, Chuck. Maybe your weird cheeriness is rubbing off on me."

"Not a bad thing," Chuck replied. "But you have enough of that all on your own."

"Thanks. I think."

Laura leaned toward Nickie and muttered, "She seems a lot better today."

"Yep. And it looks nothing like crazy-happy Emily when she hasn't had enough sleep."

"Maybe she's happy-happy," Chuck offered. "Nice change of pace after the last few weeks."

"Well, she's had her moments in there, too. But yeah."

Emily leaned back and looked at them over her shoulder. "And she can hear everything you guys are saying about her."

"Whoops." Nickie pointed at her. "But they're all good things, Em."

"Yeah, *today*."

After they'd walked a mile down the footpath, Laura frowned up at the overhanging branches bursting with green leaves and sending flickering streams of light onto the forest floor in the light breeze. *The Tree Folk knew we were here the second we headed into the park. What are they waiting for?*

"Hey, John?"

"Yeah?"

"Is there something specific we're looking for? Waiting for?"

"Not really." He slowed down and grabbed Emily's hand. "I've been enjoying the walk."

Laura frowned. "Okay, but we're here to talk to the Tree Folk."

"Yeah. You wanna do that now?"

"Yes. That's why we're here. I thought you had some kinda plan for this."

"Loosely. They know we're here." John slowly looked up into the trees. "We can talk to them whenever we want."

"Like, we could've called them as soon as we got here?"

He nodded. "Yeah."

She pinched the bridge of her nose. "We're kind of on a time crunch."

"Not exactly." John gently pulled Emily with him as he doubled back to join Nickie, Laura, and Chuck on the path. "Everything's gonna work out the way it needs to."

"Not if we don't *do* anything about it. We can't sit around and wait for magic to fix itself."

"That's not what I meant."

"Hey." Emily waved a hand between them, mostly to get her sister's attention. "Can we kill this conversation right now? We're here and we can call the Tree Folk, so let's do that."

"Yes, please." Laura widened her eyes at John, who gave her an apologetic smile. "Nickie, do you wanna start singing or something?"

"Yeah, I can." Nickie glanced from John to her big sister. "You wanna clear the air first?"

"Not really."

"Laura, I'm sorry." John nodded. "I know what we have to do. I get it. I'm still adjusting. Time goes by fast in the woods."

She stared at him and let out a long sigh. "It's fine. Sorry I lost it. I really want to be done with this whole thing."

"No problem. And Nickie, you don't have to sing for these guys."

"I don't?"

John shook his head and glanced up in the trees with a barely concealed smile. "No, they're already here."

## CHAPTER TWENTY-TWO

"Are you serious?" Laura looked up into the trees. "I really wanna ask how you know that, but I already know the answer."

"Hello?" Emily called. "Wouldn't they normally be out here laughing at us by now?"

"I think they're surprised." John slowly released her hand and spun in a slow circle. "Maybe a little scared."

Chuck laughed softly and scratched the back of his head. "*They're* scared? It's not like we're the ones popping in on them from between tree branches. I only got a quick look at one yesterday, so I don't really know—ah!"

He leapt back when an upside-down face with two bright blue eyes swung down from the branches overhead and dangled in front of him.

"There you are." Nickie grinned at the elf and gently patted Chuck's shoulder. "Get a good look, babe. They're not scary at all."

"I never said they were."

"You've come a long way, Nickie Hadstrom," the

upside-down elf murmured. "Still, we are disappointed that you did not bring music for us this time."

"Oh, I always have it. Just hadn't gotten around to that point before you dropped in on us."

"Hmm." The elf tilted his head, then instantly swung back up into the trees and scrambled away.

"That can't be it." Emily turned and scanned the trees. "No way."

The branches rustled all around them, followed by a heavy wave of unintelligible whispers. Leaves broke free and fluttered to the ground. Chuck swallowed. "Lots of 'em, huh?"

"They're called the Tree *Folk*," Emily muttered.

Dozens of pairs of eyes materialized in an instant above the branches and between the leaves, all of them wide and slowly blinking as the Tree Folk made themselves known to their visitors.

The elf woman who served as one of their leaders leaned far forward on a branch, holding herself steady with a grip on the thinner branch above her head. "Your spell was successful."

"It was," Laura replied. "And now we're—"

"Making amends." The elf woman dropped from the tree and barely made a sound when her bare feet touched the ground. "We felt it when that curse lifted, Laura Hadstrom. We'd spent so long in this ship, existing beneath the gravity of what was done far before this vessel set sail, that we had forgotten the last pieces of the truth. We remember now."

"We remember." The whisper came from dozens of voices filtering through the trees.

The elf woman looked John up and down, standing perfectly straight in her frayed green jumpsuit that looked like it was sewn from leaves. "Yes. You broke the curse, but we are not yet sure if the one you freed from two different prisons is truly what it claims to be."

"John's not lying." Emily stepped toward the elf woman, who turned and faced her with a sharp glare. "The Gorafrex saved his life. And he agreed to be its host. They helped each other, and they've been helping us put everything back together again. That's exactly what this is."

The elf's bright green eyes narrowed. Then she slowly walked in a wide circle around John while looking him up and down, peering closely at him once before returning to her original spot on the footpath. "We want to hear it from *you*."

"Really? You don't believe me?"

"It's okay, Em." John extended his hand toward her, motioning her to stop, and gave her a reassuring nod. "It's totally okay. I can tell the same story."

"No, not you." The elf stepped in front of him and stopped mere inches away. "We want to hear it from the other in your body."

"The Gorafrex?" John smiled. "It'll tell you the same thing."

"That is the proof we wish to see." She dipped her head as an afterthought, never looking away from his eyes. "Peabrain."

"Okay." John glanced at Chuck and the Hadstrom sisters and shrugged. "Don't freak out, okay? I'll be fine."

"When you tell someone not to freak out, man, that's generally the first thing they do." Chuck slowly folded his arms, his shoulders hunching in anticipation as he stared at his fellow Peabrain.

"I get that. It's temporary." He nodded at them and drew a deep breath before closing his eyes.

The rustling and whispering in the trees settled into complete silence as the Tree Folk waited for what they wanted to see.

Emily stepped toward Laura and grabbed her sister's arm. "What is he doing?"

"I don't know, Em. He seems pretty sure about it, though."

When John opened his eyes again, they weren't his eyes at all but the brilliant, glowing silver of the Gorafrex's eyes staring out of John's face. Emily grimaced and willed herself not to look away.

"There *you* are." The elf woman clasped her hands behind her back and raised one furry eyebrow. "Tell us what you are doing with this Peabrain."

"Seeking peace." The Gorafrex's unearthly voice spilled from John's mouth like it had with all the other hosts the Hadstrom sisters had seen the creature control. "I am free. Free to choose between blood and life. Free to aid the ones who pulled me from my chains."

"Free to undo the warning you put into place." The elf woman lifted her chin. "You broke magic. And now you want to fix it."

"Yes."

"So you can utilize this Peabrain's magic as your own."

"Yes."

"Wait." Emily lurched forward, but Nickie grabbed her shoulders and pulled her back.

"Hold on, Em. Let them finish."

Emily bit her lip and tried to calm her heavy breathing. *No way is that thing trying to screw us all over. I felt it. It has to be good.*

The elf woman's gaze never left the Gorafrex's silver eyes, and now that the interruption was over, she continued. "What will you do with your host's magic when your gifts have been given and reccived?"

"That is up to John." The Gorafrex spread John's arms and tilted his head. "We have had enough time for him to know this is my wish. We will use what we each possess together, but it is his choice. I was freed, and it is only right that he too is free in this."

"How long will you stay?"

"As long as it takes."

"And then?"

The Gorafrex slowly lowered John's arms. "Then I will search. If John wishes to help me, he may. For him, that is a very long time from now."

"What is he talking about?" Chuck asked Nickie.

She mirrored his gawking expression and shook her head. "No clue."

"Very well." The elf woman peered up at her people, who watched them from the trees. "You understand we cannot freely give our blessing without something given to us in return."

"I do."

"What do you wish to offer us?"

"I..." The glowing silver eyes blinked. "John wishes to return for that."

She nodded, and the Gorafrex closed John's eyes. The

woods were silent but for the birds and the buzzing drone of insects.

John blinked rapidly, his eyes perfectly normal again, and cleared his throat. "Still getting used to that."

A small smile lifted the corner of the elf woman's mouth as she gazed intently at him.

"We have—*I* have two things for you. Technically, a little more than that, but I'm counting basic groups, here." He reached into his pocket and dug around in it.

Tittering laughter came from the branches, shaking the limbs and spilling down another cascade of green leaves. "The number does not matter, Peabrain."

"I know." John pulled out one closed fist and reached into his other pocket next. Then he handed that item to the elf woman first.

She accepted a miniature version of the jagged wood fragment he'd jammed into the Huldus' control station and stared at the chunk in her open palm. "Explain."

"That built a boy's treehouse he created with his dad, who's gone. He's a Peabrain who—"

"Gave this city its first taste of true imbalance. Yes."

"You already know. Okay..." John chuckled and nodded at the piece of wood. "I used the rest of that piece to help the mechanics with a technical issue the Gorafrex caused in its madness."

Laura smoothed her hair back from her face and smiled in disbelief. "He's tying everything together."

"What?"

"The people on the list, Em. Taking something from one to give to the other. He's working a giant spell."

"No..." Emily scoffed and turned back to watch John's

exchange with the leader of the Tree Folk. *But it makes sense.*

The elf woman blinked slowly and held out her other palm. "And your other offer?"

"Um…" John held his other fist over her palm and dropped a small handful of pebbles into it. "Also from the Huldu chamber. A piece of the ship's response, and not a Peabrain's."

Someone in the trees hooted. Then another, and the cry echoing from one of the Tree Folk to the next filled the woods. Nickie laced her fingers through Chuck's and looked up at the shaking branches as the Tree Folk bounced up and down on the boughs, hooting at one another and staring at John. *They sound way too much like monkeys.*

The elf woman gave John a coy smile, then stepped back and spread her arms. The Tree Folk screeched and whooped, rocking the branches so much now that the trees swayed wildly back and forth. She slowly closed her hands around the offered gifts and lowered her arms. "We accept. From both of you."

"Yes," Chuck muttered while pumping his fist by his side.

Nickie squeezed his hand. "Did you get a little nervous, there?"

"This whole thing makes me nervous, babe. I'm simply over here in the cheerleading section."

The Tree Folk's monkey-like cheer rose to a deafening pitch, and the odd voice rang out with encouragement.

"We accept!"

"The blessing!"

"Ask. *Ask!*"

Their leader grinned up at her people from the forest floor and shook her head. "We are pleased by your gifts and what you two are doing as you near the end. You may ask for one thing, Peabrain. Name it."

John didn't hesitate. "A piece of your clothing."

# CHAPTER TWENTY-THREE

The Tree Folk burst into wild laughter while shrieking and bouncing. Some of them slipped from their perches in their mirth, catching themselves easily with a hand or a foot striking out at the right moment. The ones closest to the meeting pointed, jabbing their fingers down at the elf woman and once again taking up the chant of, "Accept. Accept."

The elf woman smiled politely as she held John's gaze and reached up to rip a piece of leaflike fabric from the neckline of her frayed jumper. She handed it to him with a slow nod.

"Thank you." He stuck both hands back into his pockets and cleared his throat again. "This'll make things a lot easier for us."

"We know. We look forward to seeing you again after you and these witches have accomplished your goal. Things will be very different."

"Naw, they won't change that much."

That sent the Tree Folk into another explosion of laughter and cheering.

"What of your brethren?" The woman nodded up the footpath.

"Chuck?" John turned around to eye Nickie's boyfriend. "What about him?"

"Does he wish to see?"

Chuck swallowed and squeezed Nickie's hand so tightly, she grimaced. "I can already see just fine, thanks."

"With new eyes," the elf woman added. "As a Peabrain fully awakened."

"Uh, no." Chuck's gaze shifted back and forth across the path. "Nope. I'm all good, but thanks."

Nickie tapped his arm and muttered, "Are you sure? You're always talking about being the one Peabrain without any magic yet. They're handing it over on a silver platter."

He looked down at her while frowning in confusion. "Do you want me to?"

"I want you to do what *you* want, babe. Doesn't change a single thing for me."

"Okay, good." Chuck looked back up at the elf woman and nervously licked his lips. "I appreciate it. For real. Now's not the right time."

"Very well. When the right time arrives, our offer will stand. Now we must go. He's waiting to speak with all of you." The elf woman disappeared from the footpath, and a second later, the branches above the Hadstrom sisters creaked and rustled.

"Wait, who?" Laura gazed up at the quickly retreating

faces of the Tree Folk as they disappeared. "Hey, you can't say something like that and leave!"

"Laura." Nickie nudged her sister's shoulder. "Hey."

"What?"

"Look."

Laura turned down the path toward John and saw someone else standing six feet farther down on the path. "Oh. That's—"

"Yep."

The wizard they'd saved from becoming the source of the Gorafrex's blood magic stood stock-still, his eyes wide as he tried to process what he'd seen. "I seriously never thought I'd see you three again. Or that. Whatever that was."

"The Tree Folk," Emily explained. "And something like a peace agreement."

The wizard pointed at John with a trembling finger. "What's wrong with his eyes?"

"Oh, boy." Nickie ran a hand through her hair and stepped down the path, pulling Chuck along behind her. Her boyfriend let her lead him along as he stared up into the trees. "Looks like this was exactly the right place and time. You have a few minutes for a little chat?"

"I don't know. Depends on how you answer *my* question."

"Fair enough." Laura waved the wizard forward. "You're heading back to the parking lot, right?"

"Maybe."

"Come on." She passed John with an exasperated smile and gently pushed the wizard down the footpath with a hand on his back. "We're heading that way, too. So we have plenty of time to explain what's happening."

"I…" He glanced over his shoulder at John again and blinked. "I don't know if I want anything to do with this."

Nickie and Chuck turned to walk beside Laura and the wizard. "I know the last time we saw each other felt like a big deal. And it was. But it's nothing compared to this. In a good way, though. Trust me."

"Uh-huh."

"What was your name again?" Laura asked.

"Willard."

"Willard. That's right. I'm Laura. Nickie and Chuck. Emily and John back there." She looked back at her youngest sister and widened her eyes, nodding for Emily to hurry up. "Some of this might be a little hard to believe at first, but hang in there with us, okay? I promise you won't be disappointed."

Emily stepped slowly toward John, ducking her head and peering up at him. "You okay?"

"Huh? Oh. Yeah, Em. I'm fine." He settled his arm around her shoulders, and she hooked hers around his waist before they took off after her sisters. "Got a little distracted there for a bit."

"That might be an understatement. I meant are you okay after…you know. Letting that thing take over."

"Uh-oh. I told you not to freak out, didn't I?"

"Yeah, you did. Would've been nice to know exactly what I wasn't supposed to freak out about, though. That was super weird."

"Yep." He pulled her closer when he saw her concerned

frown. "I'm okay. Really. That whole switcheroo thing was totally my choice."

"Right. But it doesn't bother you that that thing might take over and never give you back?"

"That's not gonna happen. The being-in-my-head thing works both ways. Yeah, the Gorafrex tells me things in the moment if it needs to. Most of the time it's simply trickling into my brain in the background. Like one steady stream all the time. But if I want to, I can go through all its thoughts, too. What it wants. What it knows. What it's thinking. There's not really a separation there."

"Except for it can still use you like a puppet."

John laughed. "Only when I want it to. It won't be a regular thing, Em. Besides the fact that it creeps out pretty much everyone who sees it, the Gorafrex doesn't like doing that. I had to push a little to get it to talk to the elf."

"So it's not, like, always trying to fight for the front seat?"

"No way. Nope. I don't really know how to explain it, but I guess it's like...like a building. Part of the same thing but all the pieces are still separate, and none of them are doing anything but existing there all put together. Otherwise, the whole setup would come crashing down."

"Huh." Emily tightened her grip on his opposite hip and gazed at the sunlight filtering through the rustling leaves. "I wouldn't have chosen a building as your comparison, but I think I get it. The Tree Folk sure enjoyed it."

"I guess. Wasn't really expecting to put on a show, but hey."

"And you got a piece of her jumper in return." She

narrowed her eyes. "What's that supposed to be for, anyway?"

"I won't know 'til we get there. So we'll both have to see."

"Okay… You sure you're not simply trying to keep it a secret from me?"

"Hey, come on. I don't keep secrets from you."

Emily swallowed and stared straight ahead, the tips of her ears burning. *No. Not like I kept one giant secret from him.*

"What? What's wrong?"

"John, I *couldn't* tell you."

"I don't get it."

She pulled away from him. "About me being a witch. My whole family. That *I'm* the reason all the crazy stuff happened at Meadowlark. That I had to lie to you every single time about where I was going and what my sisters and I had to do. Because that's the only rule, okay? You don't tell anyone until they find out on their own. And then you did, and—"

"Woah, woah. Hold on a second." John stopped and grabbed her hand, making her stop too. "Hey, that's not what was I was talking about at all."

"Okay, but that's immediately where my brain went." Emily blinked at the trees beside them. "I wanted to tell you everything. And I almost broke that rule a little that night at the park. Then Rutilda had to go stomping around Austin and blow up everything in her path. I was *glad* that she was doing it, too. I mean, yeah, you looked terrified. And it probably would've taken some time and a lot of talking it out to get you to half of how comfortable you are with it now. But at least I wouldn't have had to lie to you for a week." She drew a deep breath and closed her eyes. *Great. Now I'm rambling.* When she opened her eyes, she found John studying her with a small frown. "I know we've only been hanging out for a few weeks, but it feels like a lot longer. And I ran away from you. I don't run away from anything."

John nodded slowly and brushed her hair away from her face before cupping her cheek. "I get it. It's okay."

"Not really."

"Look, Em. I'm not saying this for any reason other than I don't want you to do anything you don't wanna do. So I really hope you can hear it that way." He dipped his head toward her, and she forced herself to look at him. "If you need some time after all this is over, after we fix magic—"

"No, I don't need some *time...*"

"I'm serious, though. Hey." He brought his other hand up to her face too and looked at her with wide eyes. "I'm not going anywhere. But if being around me right now, especially with this whole Gorafrex thing, is making things hard for you, I understand."

Emily bit her lip. "Do *you* want time? You know, away from me."

He chuckled. "Not really."

"But kind of."

"No, Em. Straight-up, flat-out, resounding no. Does that clear it up?"

She touched his hand against her cheek and pursed her lips. "I'd have to be pretty dense not to get that message."

With a surprised laugh, he leaned down and kissed her.

The tingling warmth of his magic spread through his hands and into her face.

Emily kissed him back until she had to pull his hands away. "Okay, woah. Slow down, there."

"Um…" With a crooked smile, he glanced over her head and studied the trees before shrugging. "That's pretty much as slow as it can get right now. Unless you changed your mind about kissing me."

"No, I mean this." She shook his wrists and laughed. "You were spreading the love with the Peabrain energy again. And you had no idea, did you?"

John glanced at his hands. "Nope. I was a little preoccupied."

"Okay." She laced her fingers through his and turned to keep walking with him down the path. "We'll have to work on that, then. It's pretty distracting. And it reminds me of walking through the broken wards at the library. Not two things I really wanna mix together."

"Uh-huh." He squeezed her hand. "So we'll work on it, yeah?"

Emily smirked at the path ahead of them, feeling his curious gaze on her. *You already know your answer, Em. Put him out of his misery.* She huffed out a breath and playfully rolled her eyes. "Yeah, that was me telling you I don't need any time away from you. Only more time *with* you. Does that clear it up?"

"Oof." John laughed and ruffled his hair. "Sending it right back at me."

"Wasn't that how our first conversation started?"

"Yep. Keep it up."

## CHAPTER TWENTY-FOUR

By the time they reached the parking lot, the Hadstrom sisters had filled Willard in on everything he needed to know about the Gorafrex that kidnapped him and the Gorafrex now peacefully coexisting inside John.

"Yeah, okay." The wizard scratched his head and gazed from one smiling face to the next. "I mean, I appreciate the explanation. Puts a lotta things into perspective. So thanks."

"You still look a little unsure about something." Laura tilted her head. "Anything we can clear up for you?"

"No need." Willard cleared his throat. "I'm gonna pour myself a few fingers of whiskey and repeat the process until everything makes sense again. I honestly thought the Tree Folk were a story. You know, urban legend and all that."

Nickie forced back a laugh. "Not that urban, though. They've been on this ship since it set off."

"Part of the legend, yeah. Only it's real." Willard shook

his head. "And I'm gonna have dreams about monkey elves, now."

Emily snorted. "They're not dangerous or anything."

"Doesn't matter. That was some weird shit. So, uh… good luck, Peabrain. And witches. Do we need to do some kinda ceremony or…"

"Nope." John laughed and held out his hand. "You made this really easy. Thanks."

"Uh-huh." They shook, then Willard pointed at his car across the lot. "I'm gonna go. Any idea when magic's gonna start doing its thing again?"

The Hadstrom sisters looked at each other.

"Saturday, probably," Emily said.

"Yeah, Saturday's a good bet."

Willard narrowed his eyes and slowly turned away. "Okay. I'll be watching for it. Have a good day doing the rest of whatever you…" He waved them off and quickly headed toward his car while shaking his head and muttering to himself.

Laura folded her arms. "He took that as well as Marlin."

"To be fair, I'm pretty sure being kidnapped by a Gorafrex is a heck of a lot easier to deal with than being possessed by a Gorafrex." Emily waved at the wizard as he pulled his car around in the lot and headed for the street.

"True," Nickie said. "You think he bought any of it?"

The oldest Hadstrom sister stared after the car. "I don't know."

"Yeah, he bought it." John nodded and opened the back door of Laura's car. "It's the Tree Folk that convinced him we weren't making everything up."

"He did say he was gonna dream about them…"

Emily went around the back of the car and slid into the middle to leave room for Chuck. "Did you know Willard was gonna be there?"

John slowly shook his head. "Seems like it worked out perfectly. You know, when we stopped. When Laura wanted to talk to the Tree Folk."

"Oh, you're giving *me* credit for that?" Laura pulled the driver-side door closed and buckled up. "I wouldn't take it that far."

"Not giving you credit, per se."

She turned in her seat to look at him. "But if we'd stopped any earlier and met the Tree Folk any closer to the parking lot, Willard would've missed the whole thing. And then he wouldn't have been as convinced as he is right now."

John scratched his jaw and tried to hide a smile. "Something like that. But I didn't know that was gonna happen."

"Sounds like a subconscious kinda knowing, man." Chuck closed his door too and strapped on his seatbelt while Laura started the car. "You knew, but you didn't *know* you knew."

Nickie snorted in the passenger seat. "Jeeze, you're making my head hurt."

"Babe, that's a thing."

"I'm sure it is. Don't know if I can handle it right now."

They pulled out of the parking lot and headed away from Walnut Creek.

"I don't really feel like driving aimlessly around right now." Laura glanced in the rearview mirror. "And I know things kinda pop up when they're least expected, but does anyone have a—"

"Let's go see Dave." John slid his hands down his thighs and smiled at her. "Feels like a good time."

Nickie leaned toward her big sister. "Maybe you should take that as him not knowing he knows."

"As long as we keep moving, it's good enough for me."

Chuck offered directions to his best friend's house, and fifteen minutes later, Laura pulled up to the curb and turned off the car.

"How are we gonna do this?"

Chuck opened his door. "I'll go knock first, yeah? Kinda ease him into it. Then I'll give you guys the signal, and you come on in."

Nickie turned in her seat. "The signal?"

Emily grinned. "Sounds really top-secret, Chuck."

"Oh, come on. I'll wave, all right? You don't have to ruin it." The Hadstrom sisters laughed, and he smirked as he shut the back door and headed toward the house.

"Yeah, good idea." Nickie patted the dashboard. "We'll stay in here with the AC."

"You talkin' to me or the car?" Laura asked.

"Yes."

They watched Chuck knock on the front door and wait for Dave to answer. He turned around and shot them two thumbs-up, then raised a hand for them to wait when the front door opened.

"He's getting his signals mixed up," John muttered.

"I think he's the only one who thought we'd mistake a thumbs-up for a wave." Emily leaned against John's shoulder to get a better view out the window. "At least they're talking."

Chuck turned from the front door and nodded toward

Laura's car. They exchanged a few more words, then Dave stepped back into his house and slammed the door in Chuck's face.

"Oh." Nickie covered her mouth and laughed anyway. "Looks like the 'easing him into it' part wasn't as easy as he thought."

"Chuck's a straightforward guy," Emily said. "That's why I like him. He doesn't try to butter things up."

"Yeah, like you, Em." Nickie opened her door and got out as Chuck walked dejectedly back toward them. "Didn't go like you planned, huh?"

He rubbed the back of his head and shot Dave's house a confused scowl. "I was sure I had that one in the bag."

"Well, what did you tell him?"

"The truth."

Laura closed her door and stared at him over the roof of the car. "All of it?"

"Well, yeah. Was there something else I should've told him instead?"

"Maybe the smallest, least terrifying parts to get his interest first." Emily walked around the car as John got out. "Which is the hardest part to get right, because it's totally boring."

"He doesn't wanna talk to me."

"Sure he does, man." John clapped Chuck on the back and nodded toward Dave's house. "He just doesn't know it yet. Come on."

"You sure that's a good idea?" Chuck hurried after him. "I mean, the dude's been through a lot. And he tried to kill me. Well, not *him*. Just the Gorafrex *in* him. And actually, he was trying to kill Nickie, probably, but I got in the way, and apparently that doesn't mean anything to—You're walking right up to his door, huh? Okay."

"He'll be fine."

"Chuck has a point," Nickie said. "If Dave's not gonna talk to his best friend about this, I'm not sure he'll wanna talk to us."

"Maybe not. But he'll listen." John knocked on the door. "And that's the first step."

"Whew." Emily scratched her arm with an unsure smile. "You're pullin' out all kinds of philosophical nuggets today."

He turned to wink at her. "They're simply comin' to me."

The door slowly opened by a foot, and Dave peered around it onto his front stoop. "Oh, come on, man. I told you no, and you brought the whole damn party right up to my—"

"Hey, they brought themselves." Chuck spread his arms. "I told them you didn't wanna talk."

"And they decided they'd come on up here anyway, huh? Sorry, Nickie. And friends. I'm not having this conversation about—" Dave finally noticed John and looked him up and down. "Who are you?"

"John."

"Have we met?"

"Not sure."

Dave's left eye twitched. "You look familiar."

"I get that a lot. But we definitely have a few things in common."

"Oh, yeah? They drag you out here to have a talk you didn't want, either?"

John chuckled. "Not exactly. But out of everyone here right now, I know the most about what you've been through. What you're going through."

"Yeah, right. When you've had your body hijacked by some crazy, bloodthirsty psycho and almost bleed out from a bunch of stab wounds only to find out that the whole thing activated your freakin' *magic*, then you can come back and we'll talk. Not interested." Dave closed the door again and turned the lock.

## CHAPTER TWENTY-FIVE

"Babe, I thought you said you told him everything."

Chuck glanced quickly at Nickie and shook his head. "I did."

"Including the arrangement John and the Gorafrex have going on?" Emily asked.

"Duh. I told him your boyfriend's walking around with the Gorafrex now by choice, since the curse is off and it suddenly turned good. Or not evil, at the very least. And that it wants to apologize to him for all the... Why are you guys looking at me like that?"

Laura folded her arms. "You didn't give him John's name, then."

"Oh. Nope."

Emily clapped him on the back. "Way to unintentionally leave a little mystery in there, Chuck."

"Okay..."

John knocked on the door again, and Dave's growl of frustration came from inside before the locked turned again.

The door jerked open, and Dave's eyes practically bulged from his face. "*What?*"

"I'm back," John said softly.

"You didn't leave."

"True. But let me start by saying all those things you laid out have already been checked off my list."

Dave looked John up and down again, then glanced at Chuck. "Is this guy stoned or something?"

"Naw, man." Chuck clicked his tongue. "John's the guy I was talking about."

Emily linked her arm through John's and grinned at the baffled Peabrain standing in the doorway. "Tada."

"Jesus." Dave forgot about holding the door open by only a foot and reeled backward away from them. "You gotta be kidding me." His back thumped against a standing armoire in the entryway, and he patted the side of the furniture before skirting around it to peer out at them from the other side. "No way. Don't even think about coming in here, man. And *you!*" Dave pointed at Chuck, then waved his finger toward each of the Hadstrom sisters. "All of you. You brought that thing right to my front door? You're supposed to be my friends. Well, at least you, Chuck. I thought I was pretty cool with the rest of you, but this is crossing a major line—woah, woah, woah. No!"

John stepped through the front door, his hands raised in front of him. "Look, Dave. I only wanna talk."

"Too bad! Get the hell outta my house!"

"Hey, Dave." Emily slipped through the door and set a hand on John's arm. "Remember when you showed up at our house?"

"Uh... Which time?"

"All of them, I guess. Your magic was going crazy all over the place."

"Emily, now's not really the time to talk about all the things I've been doing wrong since—"

"No, no. That's not where I'm going with this. I'm talking about the fact that you couldn't control it, right? That it took a lot of focus on distractions *from* your magic to keep it from spilling out and doing a bunch of damage, right?"

Dave peered up at the ceiling of his entryway, where tiny black spots dotted the white plaster. "Yeah. You guys were pretty helpful with that."

"Okay, so what if I told you that we're *this* close to fixing magic? And I mean like a day or two from now." Emily cast John a sidelong glance and got him frowning at her. *Little white lie. He doesn't need to know we're waiting for Saturday.* "That close."

"That's what you said yesterday when you guys headed out to the Greenbelt." Dave clutched the corner of the armoire. "And it obviously didn't work. Look what happened to *this* guy! Look at his eyes!"

"Yeah, that's the point. Well, sort of."

Nickie stepped around them to stand beside her sister. "What she's trying to say is that when we get magic all sorted out in a few days, you'll have everything you need to control *your* magic. To make it do what you want it to do."

Dave blinked quickly and gazed at his hands. "It works like that?"

"Yeah. When it works. Which used to be all the time until a few weeks ago. That's partly on us, and partly on the Gorafrex, but we're all trying to fix it now. Together."

"But we can't do that without you," Laura added as she stopped on John's other side and squeezed his arm. "That's why we're here. John's helping us, too. *And* the Gorafrex—"

"That doesn't make sense!"

"Dude." Chuck grabbed the sides of his head. "I *told* you what's going on."

"Yeah, and you sound insane."

"Dave, please." Nickie spread her arms. "Hear us out, okay? Try to hear what we need to tell you. None of us are exaggerating when we say we literally can't do this without your help. I mean, you've already helped us out in huge ways already, so maybe this is a lot to ask on top of that. But we're asking."

After glancing between the sisters, Dave took a tentative step out from behind the armoire and squinted. "I did? I helped you that much?"

"Are you kidding?" Emily laughed. "You saved us *so* much time by going through all those bones and artifacts—"

"The what?" John looked at her in surprise.

"Again, part of the long story we need to talk about. But seriously, Dave. We got to where we are that much faster because you were there to help us."

"And we would've spent a lot more time trying to find something to trade with the Tree Folk if you hadn't blown into our basement and found that family picture for us."

"That's right." Laura pointed at her. "I didn't know we had that in our house."

"We'd be in a whole different place without you." Emily nodded. "And none of us will be able to use magic the way we're supposed to if you don't help us out one last time with this. Not to mention the fact that things will only keep getting worse for everybody. And we're not sure that this broken-magic thing won't spread outside Austin if we take too long."

John nodded. "Exactly. How 'bout this? Can we make a deal?"

Dave chewed on the inside of his cheek and squinted. "What kinda deal?"

"If anything weird happens coming from me or the Gorafrex, even something you simply don't like, you have a free pass to punch me in the face."

Chuck whirled toward him. "What?"

"Seriously?"

"John…"

Dave didn't break away from the other Peabrain's gaze as he cocked his head and considered the proposal. "Will the Gorafrex thing feel it, too?"

John chuckled. "Definitely." His eyelids fluttered for half a second. "And it promises it won't try to hit back."

"Huh."

"Dude, you can't seriously be considering that." Chuck rubbed his chin. "John's a nice guy."

"What, are you trying to say nice guys can't take a hit?" Dave stepped fully out from behind the armoire and sniffed. "'Cause they can. I can. And I'll take your deal, John." He stuck out his hand, and John didn't hesitate before shaking it. "Despite how much better it would make me feel to hurt that thing, I hope it doesn't come to that."

"Yeah, me too."

"All right. Come on. I'm pretty sure there's enough

space for everybody." Dave nodded and led them through his house into the huge living room.

Emily's eyes widened. "Yeah, I'd say three couches is enough."

"This is insane." Laura shook her head and leaned toward Nickie. "Right when I thought we were getting through to him with telling him how much we need his help, John has to go all bro-pact on the guy and offer free punches." Nickie snorted. "I mean, what's that about?"

"Okay, lemme put it like this." Chuck stuck his hands out in front of him. "The three of you have your sister thing, yeah? This is a guy thing."

Laura rolled her eyes. "That's seriously the best you can come up with?"

"It's true. We're that simple. If another dude gives you permission to whale on him with no repercussions, that's when you know *he* thinks he has something, at the very least. Checks and balances, you know?"

"Babe, I don't think that's the term you're looking for."

He wrapped his arm around her shoulders and kissed the top of her head. "It's definitely what I'm looking for."

"The whole point of this is to avoid other people getting hurt."

"And that's exactly what this will accomplish." Chuck nodded, his confidence fully returned. "We simply need to get Dave to listen first. Which looks like we're covering pretty well right now."

"This is insane."

"No, Laura." Chuck wiggled his eyebrows at her. "This is a fun, harmless little chat. You'll see."

## CHAPTER TWENTY-SIX

An hour later, Dave rubbed a hand through his hair and snorted. "I can't believe I'm gonna say this, but I think I get it."

"Finally." Emily slumped back into the couch between Laura and John and stared at the ceiling. "I was about to give up hope."

"I mean, does it make sense when you look at it head-on? Hell, no." Dave turned his head and eyed them sideways. "But when you come at it from any angle, even a little off dead-center, it makes a freaky-weird kinda sense."

"If that's the way you've been thinking about using your magic, no wonder you were having such a hard time keeping it under control." Laura leaned forward over her lap and propped her forearms on her thighs. "But you got it now."

"Yeah, I got it now." Dave stroked his chin. "And I was really looking forward to socking that bastard in the face."

"Watch it." Emily pointed at him. "This bastard is the only one who can make any of this work."

"Thanks, Em." John wrinkled his nose. "I think."

"It really is inside you right now?" Dave slung his arm over the couch's armrest and frowned. "I mean, like, alive and kickin' and everything?"

"Oh, yeah."

"Did it… You know." Dave gestured to himself. "Did it say anything about me?"

John chuckled and rubbed the back of his head. "Yeah, actually."

"All right, well, now you gotta spill it, man." Dave pulled his feet up onto the couch and leaned farther into the armrest. "Seriously. This has gotta be good."

"Yeah. The Gorafrex… The Gorafrex wouldn't have left you if it had a choice. Which, fortunately, it didn't, thanks to our Hadstrom witches."

Nickie shook her head when Emily gave a mocking bow over her lap. Laura folded her arms.

John's eyelids fluttered. "It says you were the strongest. More power in your magic than any of the others, which gave it a better grip, I guess?"

"Woah." Chuck leaned back in the couch beside Nickie and crossed one leg over the other. "You were the favorite, dude."

"Man, that's like a fox saying, 'Sorry I ate all your chickens, Mr. Farmer. But for real, that reddish one was literally the most delicious bird I've ever stolen from a chicken coop.' Not exactly the kinda compliment that gets a lot of appreciation."

John shrugged. "You asked. I'm only the messenger in this case."

"Yeah, I picked up on that." Dave blinked quickly and

stared at the large glass coffee table in the center of the three couches. "So what now? We have to make some other kinda deal or put it down in writing that we talked it out and everything's right as rain for magic to slip back into place again?"

"Nope. You acknowledging what's up is enough."

"But?"

"What?" John shook his head. "But nothing, man. That's it."

The living room fell silent while Dave stared at the other Peabrain. "Okay, what's up with you and my fireplace, huh? You've been staring at it since you sat down."

"This is gonna sound weird, but can I take some of that ash outta there?"

Dave choked on a laugh and gestured toward the fireplace. "Dude, have at it. Not like I need it for anything. Wait, you're not gonna, like, use it against me or anything, right?"

John had got up off the couch but paused. "I didn't know that was possible."

"Just checking. These guys went and dug up a bunch of their family members, and that was creepy enough. I guess I'm trying to cover my bases, but I don't know what those are anymore."

"No worries. Not gonna use anything against you. Especially not now."

Dave sat back on the couch and nodded. "Yeah, we're cool."

As soon as John finished stuffing a handful of fireplace ash into his pants pocket, the Hadstrom sisters rose from Dave's couches and nodded.

"I guess that takes care of that." Laura stuck her hands in her back pockets. "Thanks for not trying to blast us out of your house or anything."

"Honestly, that didn't even cross my mind. Weird, right?"

"Not really," Nickie said. "When something doesn't work the way it's supposed to or ends up making things worse, it's easy to forget it was ever an option."

Emily dipped her chin at Dave and raised an eyebrow. "And thanks for not punching John in the face."

"Ha. I wanted to. But I get why he made the offer. And we're all good."

"All right, man." Chuck leaned forward to shake his best friend's hand. "I *would* thank you for something, but turns out you slammed a door in my face. So…"

"Yeah, sorry. Slipped into autopilot."

"Well, I guess it's better than shooting Peabrain magic at me, so we're a step up from worst-case scenario."

Dave snorted. "Get outta here."

Chuck waved him off and followed the Hadstrom sisters and John out of his best friend's house. When he pulled the front door closed behind him, he drew a deep breath and let it out with a contented sigh. "That went well, right?"

"Minus the minor freak-out and the offers of unnecessary violence, sure." Nickie wrapped her arm around his waist. "Could've been a lot worse."

"Yeah, like real violence."

Emily caught up to John as he reached the car. "How many random things do you have stashed away in your pockets right now?"

"What? I dunno." He reached for his pocket, and she pulled his hand away while laughing.

"I'm kidding. I mean, it's a little weird that you didn't ask for a jar or something for a bunch of ash, but I know you're doing your thing. Whatever that happens to be in the moment."

"Yeah, and I figure it out in the moment, too." John opened the back door and waited for her to crawl into the middle of the back seat before he slid in beside her.

Emily grabbed his hand and smiled as Chuck and her sisters got into the car and Laura started the engine. "Okay. Next stop?"

Nickie buckled her seatbelt and huffed out a sigh. "You know, I was kinda hoping we'd run into whoever else we needed to talk to next."

"Guess it wasn't in the cards."

John squeezed Emily's hand. "You guys need to call a family meeting."

"A *what?*" Laura turned around to stare at him. "You getting some kind of warning messages now about our family being in trouble?"

"No. Only a regular message about needing to talk to them." John shrugged. "Look, your whole family was involved in this part, too. Only on the Hadstrom side, obviously. But this whole thing...they have to know what your legacy was. Not a legacy at all."

"Just a seriously intense curse." Emily frowned. "I thought we'd already made things right with Hadstroms in general when we broke the curse."

"You did. This is more specific. Have you guys told your

family what's been going on here since this ship left Arenya V?"

Nickie grimaced. "No. I guess we were kinda hoping that could wait until after we'd fixed this giant mess."

Chuck leaned forward and shook his head at John. "Dude, it's so weird to hear you talking about this stuff like you've been in on it the whole time."

"Tell me about it. Seriously, though. Your parents need to know about all this. Your aunt and uncle. The Hadstrom ones."

"Mark and Julie. Yeah." Laura readjusted the rearview mirror and sighed. "That's gonna have to wait 'til later tonight. Dad's the only one who doesn't have a regular nine-to-five."

"That's fine. Can you set something up now? Then we'll know that's taken care of."

Nickie ran a hand through her hair. "And I guess this sense of urgency is coming straight from the Gorafrex."

John stared out the window as Laura pulled the car away from the curb. "That's the only answer I have right now, yeah."

"All right." Emily pulled her phone from her back pocket and pulled up a group text with her parents and both of Gregory Hadstrom's siblings. *None of them will be too happy about being lumped into the same message together. But we can't let anything get lost in translation.*

"And while we wait for them to be ready," John added, "we might as well get the soothsayer out of the way."

Nickie grimaced. "See, I knew we still have to go see him, but I hoped that one would work itself out a little more conveniently."

"But we gotta do it." Laura flipped on her blinker and nodded resolutely before turning off Dave's street. "So let's go see him."

Chuck turned to Emily. "This is the guy who gave Laura that weird prophecy?"

"Yep. Same guy who invented the potion the Gorafrex made and almost killed us with, too. And our mom's *mentor*."

"Weird. He's a wizard, then, or…"

"Not a wizard, babe." Nickie shot him a quick look. "A soothsayer. Whole different breed. And this one's a pain in the ass.

"Fantastic."

Emily chose her words carefully in the text to her parents and the last generation of Hadstroms chosen to guard the cursed Gorafrex prison.

*'We need to meet with all of you tonight after you're done with work re: broken magic and what we're trying to do. And we need your help. Yes, Mom, you too.'*

She sent it and stared at her phone, waiting for the explosion of denial and refusal and excuses all four of these people were sure to give her lumped together in a message like this. Julie was the first to reply.

*'I have room for all of us. I'll be home at 5:30. Just come over.'*

Emily smiled. *Okay, that wasn't so bad.*

Then Mark sent a thumbs-up emoji followed by a second text.

*'I'll be there shortly after that. Am I bringing wine or beer?'*

The next message came from her dad.

*'Sounds like we'll need both. You hear that, Nancy? You can't get away from us.'*

"Oh, jeeze." Emily slapped her forehead and closed her eyes.

"What's wrong?" Laura asked, glancing anxiously in the rearview mirror.

"I texted them all to meet up tonight. And Dad's being Dad."

Nickie snorted. "That's nothing new."

"Right, but we're all supposed to be on the same page here. He's gonna turn Mom off to the whole thing before we even have a chance to—"

Her phone buzzed with a new text, this one from their mom.

*'Well, I certainly tried.'*

Emily laughed sharply at the emoji of a shrugging person at the end of her mom's text, which was followed immediately by Greg Hadstrom sending a devil-face emoji in reply. "Wow. Guess they're better at getting along than I thought."

"They've always been good at getting along," Laura said. "Only not in the same house."

Nickie chuckled. "So everything's good?"

"Yeah. Meeting at Aunt Julie's at five-thirty."

"Great. We can get a lot done between now and then." Laura breathed deeply and smiled. "I like having a plan."

"Now I hope Dad doesn't do something stupid to screw it up." Emily stuck her phone back in her pocket and leaned back against the seat. "He tends to do that."

"He'll be fine, Em."

"Is this something you guys want me to come to?" Chuck asked.

"You wanna be there?"

He stared at Nickie's profile and scratched his head. "I mean, meeting up with your parents for the first time since I found out about this whole magic thing and witches and Peabrains… You know I like your parents. And this kinda feels like meeting them for the first time all over again."

Emily laughed and nudged his arm. "So you get a chance to impress them all over again, too."

Chuck cocked his head and smiled when he pictured a repeat of that day three and a half years ago. "Yeah, okay. I can live with that."

"And John gets to finally meet the parents, too." Nickie shot him a thumbs-up from the passenger seat. "They'll love you."

John let out an unsure chuckle. "Well, thanks. You think they'll feel the same way about meeting the Gorafrex?"

The car fell silent as the Hadstrom sisters processed that thought. Then Laura shrugged. "We'll play that one by ear."

# CHAPTER TWENTY-SEVEN

Laura pulled up to the curb outside Astro the soothsayer's house and jerked her keys out of the ignition. "Let's get this over with."

"Couldn't agree more." Emily waited for John to open the door and get out before she slid across the back seat after him.

Chuck got out and shut his door, hesitating on the other side of the car. "You sure I should go in there?"

"Up to you, babe." Nickie walked backward across the sidewalk and spread her arms. "The guy's rude and pushy and doesn't give a crap about what anyone thinks of him."

"So, kinda like Harry."

She laughed. "Yeah. Forty years older, bald, and with a cane."

"Huh." Chuck shrugged. "I guess I can handle that."

"Who's Harry?" Emily asked as they walked up the path toward Astro's front door.

"Another manager. He showed up at all my gigs last

year trying to get me to ditch Chuck and start working with him instead."

"Oh, so he's an idiot."

Nickie laughed. "No. But he doesn't take no for an answer."

"But he stopped eventually."

"Uh-huh." Nickie glanced at her little sister with a coy smile. "I might've convinced him it was in his best interest to back the hell off."

Emily's eyes widened. "You didn't."

"I don't know what you're talking about, Em." Nickie shrugged. "All I know is he stopped showing up pretty quickly after that."

The group stopped on the front stoop, and Emily scrunched her eyes shut to keep from laughing. *And I thought I was the only one trying to use magic to my advantage.*

With an already irritated frown, Laura stalked toward the door and knocked sharply. The door swung open five seconds later, and Astro's bald head and beady eyes peered out at them from the dark, smoggy confines of his house.

"What do you want?"

"We need to "

"Yeah, yeah, whatever." The soothsayer waved off Laura's explanation and eyed John up and down. His wrinkled face broke into a leering smile, and he wheezed out a laugh. "Well, looky what the cat dragged in! Or maybe I should say the Gorafrex did it, eh? Isn't that what all this is about? Don't answer that. I already know."

The man spun away from the door and hobbled down the entryway, and his cane thumped against the floor with every step.

Chuck peered into the soothsayer's house. "Wow, you weren't kidding."

"I know."

"Come on." Laura pushed the door open all the way and stepped inside. "That's about as much of an invitation as we're gonna get."

The house wasn't nearly as smoke-filled as the last time the Hadstrom sisters visited Astro, but the box fan mounted on the wall in his study hummed away just the same. The soothsayer let out a hacking cough, laughed at himself, and said, "Would you believe we have last-minute visitors this morning? Pah!"

The witches led John and Chuck into the study, and Laura peered around the corner. *I wouldn't put it past him to suddenly start talking to himself.*

When she saw the redhead witch sitting on the edge of one armchair, her hands nervously pressed against the tops of her thighs and her back rigidly straight, Laura paused inside the study doorway. "What?"

Vanessa jerked her head toward the doorway, and her already wide eyes grew even wider. "What?"

Emily pushed past her big sister and grinned. "Oh. Hi, Vanessa."

The other witch blinked furiously. "What are you guys doing here?"

Nickie smiled at the woman as she, John, and Chuck entered Astro's study. "Same thing as you, probably."

"*That* is a bald-faced lie." Astro pointed at the Hadstrom sisters and tittered. "And I thought Nancy Milton's spawn were working so hard to get rid of all the damn lies. Huh. Shows you how much a soothsayer knows, doesn't it?" He slapped a hand against his thigh and hobbled toward his recliner, still wheezing with laughter.

When Vanessa saw John and the brilliant flash of the Gorafrex's light behind his eyes, her already pale complexion blanched. "I should go."

She started to stand from the chair, and Astro thumped his cane against the floor. "No, you should not! Sit down, Vanessa. What these thick-headed young people came to say to me is the same thing they'll say to you. Might as well get it over with now, or you'll have some serious déjà vu in…oh, say another two hours. Sit."

Vanessa stared at the old man, her surprise morphing into resigned disdain as she slowly lowered herself into the armchair again. "What's going on?"

Astro grunted and plopped down into his chair. "I don't think it's the nightmares addling your brain, woman. Maybe you were born this stupid, huh?"

"Hey, that's not necessary," Laura said.

"Oh? Look at you, Dr. Know-It-All. You're gonna step into *my* house and start telling me what's *necessary*? Ha! You're as thick as this one. Go on, then. Give your little song and dance performance. Sure, it'll cost me a customer, but I was about to tell her my potions won't help with those boring subconscious messages anyway. You." Astro jabbed a crooked finger at John. "You have the cure for what ails this rabbit in a snare, don'tcha?" He winked at John and fell into a fit of cackling and coughing at the same time.

Chuck leaned toward Nickie and muttered, "So he's insane, then."

"Ha!" Astro thumped his cane against the area rug beneath his chair. "I'm insane, and you, Peabrain, are an idiot. Should've taken the Tree Folk's offer when you had the chance. Or maybe you're a coward."

"Okay, wait a minute—"

"Babe." Nickie grabbed Chuck's arm and slowly shook her head. "We still need his help."

The soothsayer blew a wet raspberry at them. "Yeah, everybody needs Astro's help. And everybody lets the damn soothsayer say whatever he wants because of it. Isn't that right? Ha! I'm *waiting*."

John approached the armchair where Vanessa sat and extended his hand. "We met at the party you threw for Nathan."

Vanessa slowly looked him over from head to toe. "I remember. You're a lot different since then."

"Yeah. A few things have changed." When she didn't take his hand, he lowered it by his side. "It's good news that you're here right now. We have a few things to explain."

"Like why your eyes are doing the same awful thing as the eyes of the last Peabrain I met?" The witch's lips trembled. "She kidnapped me from my house. During a *party*. And I...I can't get those eyes out of my head. It's not helping that you—"

"Blah, blah, blah." Astro groaned and shifted in his chair. "Let's cut through all the bullshit pleasantries. You have no idea how insufferable it is to listen to stuff I've already heard like it's already happened." He slapped his thigh with another croaking laugh. "So I'll do everything for you instead, huh? That's how this ends up. *You* were kidnapped by the last Gorafrex-infested Peabrain and almost used to power the thing's blood magic. Boo-hoo. Get over it."

The soothsayer's crooked finger jabbed at the Hadstrom sisters again, who all stared at him in varying degrees of disbelief. "*These* bozos, who only got half their mother's brains, if that, saved you and managed to buy the rest of us some time before they figured out their whole family's been doing it wrong for centuries. So they did the work, broke the curse, thought it would be perfectly fine to forget one seriously important minor detail and bam! This flashy-eyed freakshow came barreling into utter destruction at the worst possible moment. Add impending death to certain chaos for all of magic as we know it, and you have the perfect recipe for a host who needs the Gorafrex and vice versa."

Vanessa closed her eyes. "What?"

"You heard me. Host needs to live. Gorafrex needs a host. Even a complete moron could figure that one out. And now that manipulative bastard without a body wants to hitch a ride into *my* house to—" Astro burst out laughing. "To *apologize* for…ha-ha…for stealing my potion from the ether and binding to whatever scraps I've been leaving in the sludge of knowledge for hundreds of years. Bah!" He fell into a fit of cackling again as he slumped back into his chair and thumped his cane against the rug repeatedly.

Vanessa looked up at John and shook her head. "Why would you want to apologize to *him*?"

John huffed out a laugh and scratched his head. "That's a good question. It has to happen. We'll be able to put things right after this."

"Oh, *sure*." Astro propped himself up on his cane, his laughter dying. "Sure, you need *all* our help. Vanessa, accept the man's apology so we can all move on with our pointless lives."

"Apologize to *me*?"

John nodded. "That's part of all this. I know I wasn't involved, but I know what happened. The Gorafrex has to clear the air with everybody. To apologize. You're part of that, too. This is how we put everything behind us, and then magic will be up and running again before you know it."

"You're serious."

"Completely."

"Damnit, witch!" Astro spread his thin arm out toward the Peabrain standing beside the armchair. "Tell the man what he wants to hear."

"What, you mean you want me to say that everything's okay and I'll forget about the whole thing? That I can move on from this? I haven't slept for *days*."

"I know. And you have every right to be upset about it still."

"Oh, just stab me in the gut now." Astro rolled his eyes. "I have to sit here and listen to *this* touchy-feely crap?"

Everyone ignored the soothsayer as John crouched in front of Vanessa's armchair. "You don't need to forget about it. That's probably impossible anyway, and too many things have been forgotten already. We only need to know that you understand. What the Gorafrex did, it did under a millennia-old curse. It might be hard to believe, but it had about as much control over what happened as you did."

"I almost died."

"Yes. A lot of people did. We're trying to make sure that doesn't happen again. Things are still getting worse with magic being so dangerous and unpredictable. We're doing this for everyone."

Vanessa let out a heavy, shaky sigh. "What do I do?"

"Take my hand and say you understand."

The witch studied the Peabrain's face, reassured when she didn't see the Gorafrex return behind John's eyes. "Sure. I understand." The minute she grasped John's outstretched hand, the redhead witch gasped.

John smiled and dipped his head. "Thank you."

"Oh."

Astro hooted with laughter and swung his cane up before bringing it down to point at Vanessa. "That's *way* more powerful than any potion I could make you, woman. Hoo, yeah. You'll sleep like a rock tonight!"

John slowly stood, Vanessa's fingers slipping out of his hand as she faced forward in the armchair and sagged back against it while blinking in surprise.

"All right, Peabrain. Time for our little exchange, eh?" Astro wiggled his fingers and leaned forward. "Yeah, yeah. I understand, and all's forgiven, yadda, yadda. Come on. Hand over what you brought me and get the hell outta my house."

With a confused smile, John stepped toward the soothsayer and reached into his pocket. He pulled out as much as he could grab of the fireplace ash from Dave's house and dropped it into Astro's open palm.

"Oh-ho! That sure is somethin', isn't it?" Astro raised the handful of ash with a conspiratorial wink and jammed it into his mouth. Black and gray dust puffed away from his face, spilling down the front of his sweater and pluming into the air around him as he chewed.

"Ugh. For real?" Chuck's nostrils flared.

"I did *not* see that coming," Emily muttered.

Laura grimaced and ran her fingers over her lips. "Who knows why the guy does anything?"

Nickie simply puffed out a sigh and shook her head.

"Yeah." Astro smacked his lips, then gave his ash-covered palm a long lick and grinned. "There it is. We're done here. Go save the people who give a shit." Then he sat back in his armchair with a sigh, a satisfied smile curling his lips as he closed his eyes. Ten seconds later, he was snoring.

Vanessa stood quickly from the armchair and scurried past the Hadstrom sisters toward Astro's front door. "I can't believe I came here for his help. Good luck with everything."

"Yeah, you too," Nickie replied.

"I hope you guys succeed with this. I don't feel right without being able to pick up my wand when I need it."

"We're on the same page." Laura nodded. "Not much longer now."

"Good." Vanessa jerked open the door and hurried across Astro's front lawn without bothering to close the door again.

Chuck cleared his throat. "Yeah, she has the right idea."

"Uh-huh." Nickie turned to follow him out of the house.

Laura stared at the snoring soothsayer and shook her

head. "I feel so bad for Mom right now. She's still coming over here to make potions for this nutjob."

"And she agreed to it without hesitating even a little." Emily grabbed her sister's wrist and tugged Laura toward the entryway. "She dealt with him for years when they were both a lot younger. She can deal with him now, no problem."

They left Astro's house, and John shut the door behind him with a soft click before dusting off his ash-covered hand. "That went nothing like I expected."

"Never does with that guy." Emily waited for him to catch up with her as they headed back to the car. Wherever Vanessa had parked, she was already gone. "You okay?"

"Oh, yeah." His crooked smile was more from confusion than amusement. "But now I think I understand what goes through all your heads when I say something that's impossible to know without a Gorafrex rolling around inside you."

Emily snorted. "That's a soothsayer for you, I guess. That guy's been dipping into all the timelines for who knows how long. It's all the same to him."

"Yeah, and it's creepy."

"You got that right."

They filed back into Laura's car, and no one said a thing as she drove them away from Astro's house. Once she turned off the soothsayer's street, Chuck leaned forward to look at John. "I have one question."

"Sure."

"Did you know he was gonna eat Dave's ashes?"

Nickie burst out laughing.

"I mean..." Chuck laughed too. "Not *Dave's* ashes. Obviously. You know what I mean."

"I'm as surprised as you are, man. That was one of the weirdest interactions I've had. Gorafrex included."

Chuck's cheeks puffed out with his next exhale. "No kidding."

## CHAPTER TWENTY-EIGHT

Two hours later, Laura pulled into the back parking lot behind Austin's downtown history museum. She parked her car and let the engine and the AC run. "Anyone else feel like we're going through a real-life *Groundhog Day*?"

"You're talking about the movie, right?" Chuck ruffled his hair and sent a shower of sawdust all over the back seat.

Laura didn't care about the mess. "Yeah, Chuck. The movie."

"I mean, probably not as much as you guys right now, but yeah. If things weren't weird enough already, they're officially there."

Emily brushed the stray sawdust off her pants and blinked. "Annie wasn't happy to see us a second time."

John drummed his fingers on the armrest of the door. "No, she wasn't. Did you guys have any idea the last two wizards on our list were her neighbors?"

"Nope."

"We never saw them."

"I was a little busy playing myself into a coma." Nickie shrugged. "Didn't notice much of anything that night."

"At least they got her to calm down long enough for us to talk." Laura's eyes widened. "I thought we were gonna have to pull out the way-too-unstable magic to get her to stop blowing up the trees in her yard."

"Good thing she likes music. Huh, Nickie?"

"Sure. Just a little weird that she already knew who I was."

John patted the back of her seat. "Anyone who listens to your music knows who you are, Nickie. And I was also a fan before all this happened."

"Well, thank you very much." Nickie sighed. "Last stop here before we wait for that Hadstrom-family meeting, right?"

Laura pulled the list from her back pocket and skimmed over the pages, reviewing everyone they'd already spoken to. "I can't believe I haven't crossed a single thing off this list."

"We've been a little busy."

Emily leaned forward between the front seats. "I bet it'll still feel good to burn that list when we finish. I'll even help you conjure a bonfire in the back yard once magic's working again."

"And not before then, Em. The last thing we need is for one of your explosion spells to take off the top half of our house or something."

"Naw. The neighbor's house, maybe…"

Laura playfully rolled her eyes and stuffed the list back into her pocket. "This is our last stop. Let's get it done."

"And then we can stop for lunch, right?" Chuck patted his stomach. "I'm feelin' it right now."

"You know what, babe?" Nickie unbuckled her seatbelt and turned back to grin at him. "We'll get some subs, and I won't try to take a single bite from yours. How's that?"

His eyes widened in mock surprise. "Are you feeling okay?"

"Come on. We have a deceased Engineer's lair to...I don't know what we're doing here, but whatever."

They got out of the car and glanced around the parking lot. "It's amazing that we never see anyone back here," Emily said.

"I'm gonna go with the theory that we have impeccable timing, Em." Laura headed toward the manhole cover behind the museum. "John, you *do* have a plan for this one, right?"

"Yep. Gonna need a power boost from you guys, though. If you don't mind."

"For what?" Nickie squeezed Chuck's hand when he laced his fingers through hers.

"You'll see."

Laura and Emily slid the heavy metal plate aside while grunting under the weight, then the group surrounded the dark hole in the ground and stared down into it. Laura shrugged. "I'll go first."

"What's down there again?" Chuck scratched his chin as Laura climbed down the rebar ladder.

"A whole bunch of tunnels and the giant cavern where a giant woman's been living since she climbed aboard the ship in the very beginning."

"Giant woman, huh?" He snorted.

"Yep. Like, ten feet tall at least." Emily pulled out her phone and turned on the flashlight app to light the way down for her big sister. "Probably bigger. She liked eating giant cockroaches, bad jokes, and stomping on things when she made the rare trip out of her lair and all the way up here."

"No kidding."

She looked up at Chuck and raised an eyebrow. "No kidding."

One by one, the group climbed down the rebar ladder and joined Laura at the bottom. Five flashlights from five cell phones swept back and forth across the tunnels on the route the Hadstrom sisters had memorized by now.

When they reached the end of the twisting, downward-slanted corridors and stepped out onto the platform of Rutilda's massive cavern, Chuck's jaw dropped. "This actually exists."

"Better get used to it, babe." Nickie patted his back. "There's a lot more of this ship underground than there is aboveground. And you are one of the lucky few who get to see it."

"I guess."

Laura gestured toward the metal-mesh catwalk stretching from their small platform to the much larger one on the opposite side of the cavern. "We wanna go down there, right?"

John eyed the metal column rising from the other platform up to the darkness of a ceiling they couldn't see.

"Yeah, that should work."

They moved across the catwalk single-file, the rope nets on either side swaying as their footsteps echoed through the expanse around them. Chuck grimaced the whole time and stared at the back of John's head. "Don't look down. That's all you gotta do. Don't look—"

"You okay?" Nickie asked behind him.

"Nope. But I'm still going."

"That's *the* definition of bravery, buddy." Emily turned and peered past John to grin at Chuck. "Way to be."

"Doesn't make me any less afraid of heights, but thanks."

Once they stepped onto the platform where Rutilda the Velikan Engineer had hidden away for centuries, Chuck immediately sat six feet from the edge and pulled his knees up to his chest while drawing slow, deep breaths. "Do what you gotta do, guys. I'll sit here and exude calm, yeah?"

"That's an excellent way to help out." Nickie rubbed his back and gazed around the last Velikan's lair. "Those Huldus cleared this place out."

"I don't get why they had to take all her stuff in the first place." Laura brushed her hair away from her face and walked a wide circle around the metal column in the center of the platform. "It's not like anybody else was in a hurry to buy the place and move in."

"Recycling her gear, maybe?" Emily folded her arms with a sympathetic frown. "Doesn't feel like her place anymore without all the junk piled everywhere."

"Doesn't mean it's not her place anymore." John approached the metal column and knelt in front of it. "She was here since the ship set off. This place has a stronger link to her than most places are connected to anything else. I mean, if you think about it, the Engineers are the parents of the whole world."

Chuck shook his head, which he'd dropped between his arms wrapped around his knees. "Blueprints of Earth. Still getting used to that one."

"Sounds like this is the right place to make those amends to Rutilda, then." Laura approached John and watched him swiping away the thick layer of dust from the platform in front of the metal column.

"And the two witches who died for the energy cores." John blew out a long breath. "They're part of this, too."

"What do we do?" Emily knelt beside him and set her hand on his shoulder.

"Link up. I need a power boost for a few seconds, and that should be it."

"Okay." Nickie knelt beside Emily and put a hand on her little sister's back. Laura knelt on the other side of John and did the same with his other shoulder.

"Right." He straightened enough to reach into his pockets. One hand brought out the rest of the ash from Dave's fireplace, which he dropped on the dusted circle of the platform. His other hand produced the Eternal Heart from Brightwing Emporium, and he quickly uncorked it. The glowing blue liquid pulsed when It opened to the air.

"Now the secret's out." Emily's eyes lit up with the glowing blue light. "We get to see what that thing's for, right?"

"If I knew what it did, Em, I'd tell you."

"We know." Laura patted his shoulder. "Ready when you are."

"Okay." John scooped the ash into as tall of a pile as he could, then slowly poured the Eternal Heart on top of it. The blue light shimmered as it seeped into the blackened dust, still pulsing. He pressed both palms against the concrete platform and closed his eyes. None of the Hadstrom sisters could make out the words of the spell he whispered, but they focused on lending him their energy and their magical power boost for whatever it was.

The same shimmering silver light that occasionally flashed in John's eyes now blinked beneath his palms as it spilled across the platform and spread toward the ash and the potion.

"Woah. Are we growing something?" Emily leaned down toward the shifting pile of ash as a glowing blue shoot emerged. It sprouted quickly, jerking back and forth as it split in two and kept growing.

John opened his eyes and blinked at the glowing young tree quickly maturing in front of them. "Yep. Might as well call it Rutilda's tree, right? Back up."

They got to their feet and stepped slowly away from the blue tree widening and rising higher and higher into the chamber beside the metal column.

"It's beautiful," Laura whispered.

"Sure is." John smiled. "Looks like the ship and the last Velikan's personal space have accepted." He gave the tree two thumbs up and chuckled. "That was easier than I—"

The platform trembled beneath them, followed by a grumbling roar from down below.

"What the—" Chuck scrambled to his feet and spread his arms to steady himself while quickly glancing around. "Guys?"

"We felt it." Laura carefully stepped away from the tree. "This isn't a sign that we messed up, right?"

John shook his head. "I don't think so."

Stone cracked and split below them, then rumbled down into the bottom of the cavern. The glowing blue tree kept growing, branches spreading out higher and farther as the trunk itself twisted around the metal column. The platform bucked and sent the magicals reeling away. A hanging chunk split and crumbled away from the edge.

"Time to go." Nickie raced toward Chuck, grabbed his wrist, and pulled him with her toward the catwalk.

"This is a seriously bad idea!" he shouted.

"It's the only option we have, Chuck." Laura stumbled forward and tripped on a fallen chunk of rock when the platform shook violently. She saw the edge of the platform and the gaping darkness below her and tried to stop in time.

John grabbed her around the waist and hauled her away from the edge. "We're not going that way."

She laughed and shook the close call out of her head. "You got that right."

"Come on!" Emily waved them forward onto the catwalk, then looked up when a crumbling boulder dropped from the ceiling. "Hey!"

"Go, go, go." John practically shoved Laura forward onto the mesh walkway, and they ran. The boulder smashed into the catwalk a foot away from the platform's edge. The walkway shrieked with twisted, bent metal and sent a rippling wave beneath the group's feet.

"Ah!" Chuck stumbled forward onto his knees and caught himself with his hands. His eyes widened when he looked down through the holes in the mesh. "Not good. So not good."

"Close your eyes if you have to." Nickie grabbed his arm and pulled him up. "I gotcha."

Chuck froze, still staring at the chasm beneath his feet.

"Babe, come on!"

Another chunk of rock and earth dropped from the ceiling. Huge pieces caught in the netting on either side of the catwalk, which swung wildly under the sudden weight. The group staggered against the side of the walkway and the nets.

"We need to keep moving!" John shouted.

"Yeah, yeah. I..." Chuck saw another falling boulder heading straight for them and shoved Nickie out of the way. The giant rock smashed into the catwalk and bounced, making the whole thing shudder violently with another squeal of ripping metal. He grabbed Nickie's hand and pulled her forward, racing toward the opposite platform now.

"That's about to—"

"Yep. Em, go!" Emily scrambled across the tearing pieces of the catwalk and booked it for the platform at the end.

Laura followed quickly, John behind her. As he skirted around the boulder sitting in their path and pulling the catwalk apart, something else snapped. The walkway buckled as Laura leapt onto the platform, then the whole thing snapped in the middle and sent the boulder hurtling down into the chasm.

"John!" Emily darted toward the edge of the platform and stared at him as he dangled from the broken end of the catwalk swinging wildly up and down beneath his weight. "Okay, okay. Hold on."

The tree had grown so tall, most of its branches had risen into the darkness of the chamber above them, and it wasn't finished. Stone cracked and rumbled in the cavern. Emily shut her eyes. *Come on. Please. Just let one thing work.*

Her sisters grabbed her hands and nodded. "We can at least try."

"We only have one shot." Emily's voice squeaked as she stared at John clinging to the swaying catwalk, his fingers hooked painfully through the holes in the metal grate.

"Worth it. Come on." Nickie and Laura both reached out toward John while focusing on their magic.

The catwalk groaned and pulled free of its setting in the platform's edge.

"No, no, no…" Emily tried to lunge forward, but her sisters pulled her back as the edge of the platform crumbled away. "John!"

He didn't make a sound.

They stared down into the darkness, stunned and momentarily forgetting about the chamber falling apart all around them. Chuck stumbled sideways against the wall of the tunnel and couldn't breathe.

"We…" Emily fell to her knees, swaying. "He."

"Woah. Em." Laura swallowed and tried to pull her little sister back. "Watch out. I don't know what that—"

The cavern flashed with blue light, growing brighter by the second. Loud rustling and creaking rose from below, and the tree growing on the opposite platform shuddered. Then a mass of glowing blue tendrils whipped through the air right in front of Emily's face. She stared blankly at it. *I don't give a shit about tree roots right now.*

"Holy…" Nickie's eyes widened as a silhouette rose

inside the mass of thrashing, tangled blue roots. The light flashed rapidly and dimmed as the tree roots set John gently onto the platform in front of them.

He blinked with wide eyes and tried to smile as he clutched one bleeding hand. "We need to—"

Emily leapt to her feet and threw her arms around him, nearly knocking him back over the edge. Laura and Nickie pulled them both forward as even larger chunks of the chamber ceiling dropped in front of them.

"Hey." John pulled Emily gently away and nodded toward the tunnel. "We need to go. Right now."

"Emily." Laura grabbed her little sister's hand and jerked her toward the opening. Nickie and John raced after them as the tree roots slithered away from the platform. The twisting blue tree let out a violently blinding burst of light and grew another ten feet with a roar of groaning wood and cracking stone.

The Hadstrom sisters, John, and Chuck darted into the tunnel seconds before the entrance caved in behind them while spewing dust and chunks of rock and cold air after them.

Emily jerked her hand out of Laura's and spun toward John. "You're okay."

"Yeah, Em. I—"

She grabbed his face and pulled him in for a fierce kiss. His back thumped against the wall of the tunnel, and he wrapped his arms around her without trying to pull away again.

Chuck gazed at the tunnel ceiling and put a hand against the wall to feel that it was solid and steady. "Not sure this is the best time for that..."

Laura cocked her head. "At least it's quiet in here."

Nickie looked around. "And nothing's falling apart."

"We can give 'em a minute, right?"

Emily finally pulled away from John and choked out a laugh through her tears as she brushed dirt and root hairs off his face. "Twice in two days. Are you kidding me?"

John let out a heavy breath and tightened his arms around her waist. "I'm not trying to be an asshole. I promise."

"It's impossible not to believe you. Let's get the hell out of here." She grabbed his hand and hastily wiped away her tears with the other. Then she nodded at her sisters as she and John moved quickly past them down the tunnel. "We did what we came here to do. And I'm never coming back."

"Agreed."

"Fully on the same page."

Chuck raced after the Hadstrom sisters while puffing out breath after breath. "That'll get you moving."

# CHAPTER TWENTY-NINE

At 5:28 p.m., Laura's car pulled up in front of their Aunt Julie's house in northern Austin. "We're ready for this, right?"

"Yep." Nickie looked at Laura and raised her eyebrows. "We have to be."

"Chuck, you don't have to come with us if you'd rather stay out of it."

"Are you kidding me? I'm neck-deep in all this now. There's no way I'm sitting out the last part of it."

"Then let's go have this family meeting."

Emily only let go of John's hand so they could get out of the car with the others, then her fingers slipped right back between his. He pulled her closer and kissed the top of her head as they headed toward Julie's front door. "Almost there, Em."

"That's the only 'almost' I'm okay with."

When they reached the wraparound front porch, two more cars pulled down the street and parked on the other side of the driveway. Nickie glanced over her shoulder and rolled her eyes. "Here comes the dynamic ex-duo."

"Wow. I can't remember the last time Dad was this on-time."

"I told them we needed their help," Emily muttered. "Guess that got his attention."

Greg Hadstrom leaned against the door of his car to shut it and grinned as he raised a case of beer in one hand and a bulging wine bag in the other. "You can relax now, kids. I took care of it."

"Oh, jeeze." Laura covered her eyes with her hand and shook her head.

Nancy Milton stepped onto the sidewalk and raised an eyebrow at Greg. "You trying to invite everyone in the neighborhood with that?"

He laughed. "Come on. Mark and I will go through at least half of this."

"I'm sure you will." With a patient smile, Nancy headed toward her daughters, Chuck, and John standing on the front porch. "Everything okay?"

"It will be after this." Nickie hugged her mom, who slowly pulled away from her to blink at Chuck.

"Hi, Chuck."

"Hey." He accepted her hug and looked at Nickie with wide eyes. "How's it goin'?"

"You know, same old thing day in and day out." Nancy quickly glanced at her daughters and chuckled. "I didn't expect to see you here for this."

"Uh…" He scratched the back of his head while smiling sheepishly. "Well, I've learned a lot since the last time you saw me."

"Mm-hmm? Like what?" She raised her eyebrows.

"Like magic, this ship, that you're a witch, the whole Hadstrom legacy and the Gorafrex, and that I'm a Peabrain although my magic's still sleeping my life away." He shrugged. "You know, the usual."

"Okay…" Nancy patted his shoulder and blinked. "You sound like you've had some time to process that. I'd love to hear how you found out."

"We'll lay it all out once we're all together." Laura hugged her mom next and whispered in her ear, "We didn't tell him if that's what you're thinking."

Nancy squeezed her oldest daughter's shoulders, then stepped forward to knock on the door. "Let's get out of the heat, huh?"

"Won't matter once we crack these open." Greg stepped onto the porch. "I'll give you all hugs once I lighten the load."

The front door opened, and Julie greeted them with a curious smile. "Gotta say it's a little weird to see all of you standing on my porch at the same time. Come on in."

They walked into Julie's massive entryway. "I like what you've done with the place." Nancy gazed at the light-painted walls and the natural light spilling through the large windows lining the front of the house. "It's bright."

"Just trying to decorate to my moods." Julie pulled Nancy in for a quick hug. "Good to see you, Nance."

"Yeah, you too."

"Where do you want me to put these?"

"Jeeze, Greg. I'm not throwing a party."

"Well, not yet."

Julie rolled her eyes and pointed to the dining room. "We can all go in there now and wait for Mark."

They all filed into the dining room. Greg thunked the alcohol down on the table and pulled out a chair. Nancy sat across from him, and everyone else filled in around them.

"All right. Who wants to start?" Greg pulled a beer from the case and cracked it open.

"Everyone needs a drinking buddy." Chuck shrugged and nodded at the case. "I'll join ya."

"Yeah?" Greg pulled out another beer, started to hand it over, then paused. "What are you doing here, bud?"

Nancy set her elbow on the table and tossed up a hand. "He knows, Greg."

"Knows what?"

"Everything."

He blinked at his ex, then snorted. "Well, it's 'bout damn time. I'll drink to that."

Chuck took the offered beer and cracked it open, smiling as he raised the can to his lips.

"Wait, this isn't some kind of official 'welcome to the family' meeting, right?"

"Dad, did you read my text?"

"Sure, kiddo." He smiled at Emily. "Said you needed our help."

"Yeah, with broken magic. Not with Chuck."

"Hey, you never know. But nobody answered my question."

"No." Nickie grabbed Chuck's hand under the table and stared at her dad. "This isn't about Chuck and me."

"Okay. So what's it about?"

Sitting next to Emily, John cleared his throat. "Should we wait until Mark gets here, too?"

"Well if it's that important, we can—" Greg did a double-take at the Peabrain he hadn't met and set down his beer. "Where did *you* come from?"

"Oh, boy." Laura rubbed a hand across her forehead.

"He's been with us the whole time." Emily bit her lip. "You okay, Dad?"

"I'm fine. Absolutely fine. Greg." He leaned over the table to shake John's hand.

"John. Nice to meet you."

"You too." When their hands clasped, Greg's eyes widened. "Have we met before?"

"No, sir."

"Oh, cut it out with that sir stuff, huh?" Greg sat again and picked up his beer. "Just Greg, man. That's it."

"I'm so sorry, John." Nancy leaned forward to look at him. "I never even said hi."

"No problem."

They shook hands in front of Emily, who raised her eyebrows when her mom gave her a questioning glance.

"Are you in the same boat as Chuck?"

Chuck snorted. "I mean, if you're talking about dating one of your daughters and being a Peabrain who knows about all your family stuff, then yeah. But John's at a whole different level."

Nickie huffed out a laugh. "Way to put it all out there, babe."

"Nah, that's not all of it." Chuck stared at the table and drank his beer.

"How'd you two meet?" Greg wagged his finger at Emily and John. "I'm curious."

"At work."

"No kidding. Okay. Things still going well at the restaurant?"

"Things are… Well, they're—"

The front door opened, and Mark stepped into his sister's house with a heavy sigh. "Let me start by saying how much I hate traffic." He closed the door behind him and stepped into the dining room. "People need to learn how to drive. And it's not even the end of the week—oh. Everybody's here."

Julie raised her eyebrows and gestured to the last empty chair at the table. "Waiting on you."

"All right, Greg. Looks like I took your place."

"Only today."

Mark sat at the head of the table and sighed again. "Hey, girls."

The Hadstrom sisters greeted their uncle. Then Mark glanced at John and Chuck. "New faces, huh? Mark. Nice to meet you."

"Chuck."

"John."

"Great." Laura clapped her hands together and propped them on the table. "This is gonna be a weird conversation. Just so everyone knows ahead of time."

Greg stared at her hands. "Where's your ring?"

"What? Oh. Yeah, that's part of it."

"Laura…"

"I gotta start at the beginning, Dad."

Greg glanced at his other daughters. "What about you?"

"No ring, Dad," Nickie muttered.

Emily stared at the table and shrugged.

"What the hell is going on here?" Greg folded his arms and sat back in his seat. "I made it clear what those rings mean for our family. The kind of responsibility you three were taking on when we passed them on to you. What were you thinking?"

Nickie ran a hand through her hair. "Dad, that's what we're trying to tell you."

"Tell me what? That you hawked your rings after you let that thing out of prison?"

"Greg." Nancy shot him a warning glance.

"No. That I could deal with. But this? This is sheer stupidity. What did you do? Melt 'em down? *Lose* them, for crying out loud—"

"Dad, the whole thing's a lie!" Emily shouted.

"Well, show me the rings, then."

"No, I mean the legacy. Our family's role with the Gorafrex. All of it."

Laura leaned forward. "You guys had it all wrong. All of our family had it wrong. We were powering a curse with those rings."

"I don't know what kinda Kool-Aid you girls have been drinking—"

"Let them talk, will you?" Nancy glared at him across the table. "They wouldn't have asked all of us to meet here if this wasn't important."

Greg ran a hand over his mouth, then dropped it to the table. "At least tell me where the Gorafrex is."

The Hadstrom sisters and Chuck all slowly turned to

look at John, who dipped his head with a self-conscious smile.

Chuck tapped his beer can. "That's the new level I was talking about."

The dining room fell utterly silent. Then Julie stood from the table and paused. "I'm gonna get a bottle opener and some wine glasses."

"Great idea," Nancy added and sat back in her chair.

Greg stared at his daughters, his nostrils flaring. He turned sideways and kept eyeing them as he tipped his beer back and gulped the rest of it down in twenty seconds. Then he silently grabbed another out of the case and cracked it open.

Nickie let out a slow breath and cocked her head. "Here we go."

They spent three hours in their Aunt Julie's house, revealing the truth of their misunderstood Hadstrom legacy and the curse cast by the one Hadstrom wizard back on Arenya V who went dark. It took several rounds of hashing out the same details in slightly different variations until Greg finally had to face the fact that all of it was true.

When that happened, he excused himself from the table and stormed through his sister's house. The back door slammed shut behind him, and his muted shout traveled back into the living room.

"Despite that," Julie stuck her thumb over her shoulder, "you did the right thing by telling us."

"We had to." Laura drained her only glass of wine. "That's the only way we fix magic."

"And you're sure this is the last thing you have to do before that happens?" Nancy asked.

"Well, we have one more minor thing on Saturday morning." Nickie wrinkled her nose. "But I'd say after that, we're good to go."

"That'll be the end of it." John nodded.

"Okay. Then that's what has to happen."

They waited around the table in silence, then Emily stood. "I don't think Dad's coming back in for a while. We should go."

Julie and Mark gave her matching sympathetic smiles. "He'll be fine, Em."

"Yeah, I know. I just don't wanna be around until he is."

Mark reached out and brushed her arm when she passed him. "See you soon, kiddo."

"Have a good one, Uncle Mark."

Laura set a hand on her mom's shoulder and nodded. "We'll see you soon, too."

"Oh, I'm counting on it. Love you, girls."

"Love you too, Mom. Thanks for having us here, Aunt Julie."

"It's as good a place as any for something like this." Julie nodded. "Good luck with everything."

Chuck and Nickie said their goodbyes and followed Laura and Emily toward the front door.

John stood and cleared his throat. "Nancy?"

"Yes?" She blinked and slowly looked up at him.

He approached her chair and reached into his pocket. "The choice you made to start working with your mentor again was yours, of course."

"How do you know about—oh." She laughed softly. "Right."

"And that was another side effect of what happened with the Gorafrex. You're still part of this whole thing even without being a Hadstrom."

"Thank you, John."

Julie and Mark exchanged curious glances.

"This is for you. We stopped in to see Astro today, and working with him would be…" He chuckled wryly. "Difficult. Maybe this'll help." John pulled the piece of the Tree Folk leader's jumper from his pocket and handed it to her. The ripped fabric that wasn't quite fabric shimmered under the dining room light.

Nancy's breath caught in her throat. "Is that…"

"Straight from the Tree Folk, yeah."

She laughed, clapped a hand over her mouth, then held open her other hand so he could drop the item into her palm. "John, you…you know what kind of potion work I could do with this, right?"

"I do now. Glad it's something you can use."

"Something I can use." Nancy stood quickly and wrapped him in a tight hug. "I can do anything with this. Thank you."

"You're welcome."

She pulled away and nodded toward the door. "Now get out of here. I know they're waiting for you."

"Okay. Nice to meet all of you."

"You too, John." Julie and Mark nodded at him.

He made it halfway to the door before Nancy called, "So, you and Emily, huh?"

John gave her a self-conscious smile as he turned and nodded. "I'm all in. The rest is up to her."

"Ha." Mark slapped a hand down on the table and pointed. "Smart man."

"Yes, he is. I'm sure I'll see you again soon."

"Probably." John bit his lip, ducked out of the dining room, and swiftly stepped outside to join Chuck and the Hadstrom sisters.

"I was about to go back in there and rescue you." Emily stepped toward him and took his hand. "Everything okay?"

"Yeah. We're good."

"Oh, crap." Laura spun around on the driveway, her eyes wide. "I can't believe we missed this. We haven't talked to Jessica. The second host."

"No..." Nickie clenched her eyes shut. "I thought for sure this was it."

"Don't worry about that one," John said.

"We can't leave something out." Laura pointed at him. "That's how you became host number six."

He nodded toward the car and kept walking. "No, I mean I have that one covered. You don't have to worry about it."

"How's that?" Nickie asked.

"A feeling I have."

Chuck snorted. "Man, your *feelings* have been spot on so far. Might as well keep trusting them."

"Fine by me." Nickie frowned as she pulled her phone from her pocket and blinked.

"What's wrong?"

"Dave's calling me."

Chuck cocked his head. "Huh. Well, see what he wants."

She answered the call. "Hey, Dave."

"Hey. Look, I know we all talked this morning, but I've spent the day thinking, and I feel good about it."

"Okay…" Nickie looked at her boyfriend and shrugged.

"Magic's coming back in the next few days, right? Everything's gonna go back to relatively normal. I want you to come into the office on Monday so we can finally sign the paperwork, then we'll get you in the studio."

"Wait, say that again."

He laughed. "Come on, Nickie. We've put it off long enough, and I owe you this much at least, if not more. Chuck knows how much I've wanted to sign you for a while now. Let's make it happen."

"Yeah. Yes! Monday. We'll be there."

"Perfect. Good luck with the rest of it."

"Thanks, Dave."

He hung up first, and Nickie stared at her phone.

"Wanna share?" Chuck studied her face with a hesitant smile.

"We're going into Dave's office to sign that record deal on Monday."

"What?"

"That's what he said."

"Yes!" Chuck picked her up and spun her around in a quick circle. "We're back on track, baby!"

"Okay, okay. Put me down." She grabbed his face and kissed him, then let out a huge sigh and grinned. "Finally looking up."

"Hey, that's awesome," Emily said.

Laura nodded. "That was bound to happen eventually. Perfect timing."

"I know. I can't..." Nickie pumped a fist. "Awesome."

Laura's cell phone rang with an obnoxious built-in ringtone, and she whipped it out of her pocket. "Woah, okay. Hold on a sec." She accepted the call and tossed her head. "Hi, Winston."

"Dr. Hadstrom." Her elf colleague at the university chuckled. "Listen, a friend of mine in Waco's been leading a dig somewhere around there, I think. Brand-new find. He asked if I knew anyone who was available and particularly suited to some delicate work, if you get my drift. You're the first person who came to mind. He's looking for someone to start next week. You interested?"

"Am I interested?" Laura stuck a hand on her hip and turned away from her sisters. "Have you ever known me to not be interested?"

"That's a yes, then."

"Absolutely."

"Great. I'll email the details. Feel free to call me back if you have any questions."

"Thank you!"

"Enjoy your summer, Laura."

She shoved her phone back into her pocket and barked out a laugh. "I have a dig to get to next week."

"Nice."

Emily wrinkled her nose. "Not a cemetery, is it?"

"I seriously doubt that, Em." Laura brushed her hair away from her face and grinned. "I'd resigned myself to slogging through lesson plans for the rest of the summer. This is perfect."

"Should be fun." John stuck his hands in his pockets.

Emily turned toward him and narrowed her eyes. "Did you have anything to do with this?"

He gazed down at her until she felt her phone buzzing in her back pocket. She took it out and groaned. "Despite how weird it is that we're all being called right now about our jobs, I don't wanna answer this."

"Who is it?" Laura asked.

"Chef Ansler."

"Em, you really should."

Gritting her teeth, Emily stalked away from them down Julie's driveway and answered. "Hello?"

"Hadstrom. I don't remember firing you."

"Um… No. You didn't."

"Good. Marino told me you called in and quit."

"No, no. I didn't quit. I only needed a shift covered. But I know that's way too much to ask, so I figured…"

Her boss scoffed. "You figured you were expendable, huh? We need to fix that. You still have your place in my kitchen, Emily. Can we meet up for coffee on Saturday? Go over the next steps and what I have planned for you? I think that might convince you to stay."

"You…you want me to stay?"

"You're a lot better at processing information when you're on the line, aren't you?" Chef Ansler chuckled. "Yes. I want your skills. So how about it?"

"Oh, um… I have another commitment on Saturday. It's not job-related. Family stuff."

"Sure, whatever. Give me a time that's good for you. We need to make this work."

"Yeah. Yeah, how about Sunday morning?"

"Sounds good. Meet me behind the restaurant. We'll

find a place."

"Okay."

He hung up without another word, and Emily swallowed as she pocketed her phone again. Then she pointed at John and didn't even try to hold back a laugh. "Now I *know* you had something to do with this."

John raised his eyebrows. "Did it work?"

"I'd say that's a resounding yes. Ansler just worked around *my* schedule so we could have coffee and discuss *his plans for me*. What just happened?"

Laura and Nickie turned toward John to wait for his answer.

"You guys are on the list, too. Your lives were overturned as much as anyone else's."

"How did you..."

John stepped toward her and wrapped his arm around her shoulders as they headed to the car. "I told you I got up early this morning."

"Jeeze. You get more done in a day than anyone I know. Even more than Laura."

"I'm not even offended by that, Em." Laura laughed. "It's true."

"Yep." Chuck nodded and followed them. "He's in."

"And now we only have to wait for Saturday."

Nickie groaned. "Right when I'd forgotten about the whole thing."

"It's forty-five minutes, Nickie." Laura grinned as she opened the driver-side door of her car. "That's nothing compared to magic finally working again. Hopefully forever."

"Sure. I'll keep thinking about it like that."

## CHAPTER THIRTY

At 10:15 a.m. on Saturday, the Hadstrom sisters pulled into the back parking lot of Austin's main library. "You guys ready for this? Last errand."

"Feels more like a punishment." Nickie pulled her guitar case out of the back seat and shut the door. "I'll feel so much better when this is over."

Emily wiggled the deck of cards in her hand. "The kids are gonna love it, though. No real magic, but I've had thirty-six hours to brush up on a few card tricks."

"If they're even old enough to care about card tricks," Laura added. "We're gonna bomb this so hardcore, and I don't even care."

"Hey, look."

Nathan's car pulled up, then both he and Chuck got out. "We decided to carpool," Chuck declared as he spread his arms. "And my car battery died. Figured I'd rather jump it later than show up late to this!"

"No..." Nickie scrunched up her face. "Don't say it like that. You can't be excited about this."

"Nope. I'm thrilled." He kissed her, then pulled out her cord bag and a new portable amp from the back of Nathan's car. "Stopped by your place and brought you this. And picked this up earlier."

"Hey, that's sweet, but I'm going acoustic today. You knew that."

"Well, yeah. Got a call from John. He told me to swing by and make sure I brought these."

"Oh, boy." Laura slipped her arm around Nathan's waist and tried not to laugh. "He has a never-ending stream of surprises, doesn't he?"

"I'd say yes." Chuck shrugged. "And I honestly hope that doesn't stop when magic works again. It's great entertainment."

"I'm so glad you're entertained by all this." Nickie gave him a playful frown. "You might be the only one."

"Nah. The kids are gonna love this. As long as you smile, they'll laugh at anything."

"It's not a comedy show for kids, babe. It's a magic show."

"Same thing when they're that age."

"Hey, there he is." Emily grinned at John's white truck pulling into the parking lot. "Okay."

"Why's she breathing like that?" Chuck asked.

Nickie watched her little sister watching John's truck. "I think not seeing him at all yesterday made her a little nervous."

Chuck pulled her in for a hug, the cord bag bouncing against her back, and muttered, "Dude almost died twice. I'd be nervous, too."

John hopped out of his truck with a wide grin. "Hey!

Hold on a second." He opened the back door and pulled out a navy blue Stratocaster, the body shimmering in the sunlight. "Nickie, come grab this."

"Wow." She approached him and took the guitar. "Looks like my old one. John, you didn't have to do this."

"I know. I was walking around yesterday. Went past the music store and saw this thing in the window. It's not brand new, by the way."

"Oh, yeah?" She slipped the strap over her head and wrapped her hand around the fretboard.

"Yep. Another donated guitar. This one came from Jackie Venson. Thought you might be the same vibe."

She looked up at him with wide eyes. "Hell yeah. Thank you."

"Yeah. Glad you like it." John leaned into the back seat again, fiddled with something, then pulled out a tiny furry thing and held it against his chest.

Laura tilted her head. "What's that?"

"A kitten."

"A kitten?" Emily slowly approached him while staring at the tiny bundle of gray fur. "What are you doing with a kitten?"

"Finding it a good home." He shrugged and showed her the tiny creature pawing at his chest. "A lady was giving them away yesterday. This little guy was the last one."

Emily gave the kitten a quick pet and snorted. "Are you keeping it?"

"Who knows? You guys ready for some magic?"

Nickie rolled her eyes. "The kind that comes back for real, sure. Not the fake kind for a bunch of kids."

"So let's go set you up and get it over with as soon as

possible, huh?" Chuck hugged her closer and headed toward the library's back door.

Laura and Nathan followed them, and Emily frowned at the kitten as she and John fell in at the back of the line. "I can't see you with a kitten."

"Really? I'm holding one."

"Very funny. You know the Gorafrex killed Jessica's cat the first time it handled blood magic, right?"

"Yeah, I know, Em. That's not gonna happen this time. I promise."

"Okay." She gave the kitten another little scratch behind the ears as they stepped into the library.

Isabelle smiled at them from behind her desk and pointed toward the front. "Right in the main room. People are filing in."

"Thanks, Isabelle."

They reached the front room of the lobby, where the chairs and tables were pushed aside and a long table set up to act as their stage. Emily laughed. "This is ridiculous."

"It'll be great." John pulled her in with one hand for a long kiss that made her forget all about the magic show.

"Um... What was that for?" She scrunched up her face, then opened her eyes.

"For good luck. Or for breaking a leg, I guess. Please, not literally."

"Uh-huh. Thank you very much." She squeezed his arm and turned to join her sisters in setting up for the show. *We have no idea what we're doing. Doesn't matter, if a little fake magic brings back the real deal for good.*

. . .

Fifteen minutes into the show, Nathan stepped toward John with his arms folded. "I honestly thought they wouldn't pull this off half as well as they are."

John snorted. "Surprising, yeah. But they make anything work, don't they?"

"I get that general feeling, too." Nathan scratched his head when Emily pulled two puffy red balls out of her sleeve instead of one and the second one bounced across the floor. She lurched after it, and the kids screamed with laughter.

"Magic 101, kids." She snatched up the ball and grinned. "Don't drop stuff."

Behind her, Nickie struck a goofy-sounding chord and hit the whammy bar, shaking her head with a smile of disbelief.

John glanced around the gathered crowd and found exactly who he was looking for. He bumped Nathan with his elbow. "I'll be right back."

"Yeah, sure."

John worked his way around the half-circle of laughing kids and their slightly amused parents and stopped next to Jessica. The woman watched the show with a slight frown, as if she couldn't figure out why three real witches were pretending to be very bad magicians.

"Hey. You showed up."

Jessica glanced at John and straightened. Then she let out a wry chuckle. "Guess I wanted to see what all the fuss was about. This is not what I expected."

"I know. Doesn't look like it now, but there's a lot to learn from those three."

"When they're not performing, right?"

"Right."

They laughed softly, and the woman's gaze fell on the kitten in John's arms. "Oh. How old is your kitten?"

"Nine weeks."

"He's so cute. Can I pet him?"

"Sure." John held the kitten out toward her and waited for the rest to play itself out.

"I just…" Jessica smiled at the kitten and wrinkled her nose. "I lost my cat a few weeks ago."

"I'm sorry. That's always hard."

"Yeah. This one especially. Seeing this little guy makes me wonder about when I might look for another fur baby."

"You'll know when the time's right. This one's the last of a litter that…well, wasn't technically planned for. Now I'm waiting to find him a good home."

Jessica stopped petting the tiny animal and looked up at John. "Really?"

"Yep."

"I'll take him."

"Yeah? I haven't gotten his shots or anything yet—"

"I'll take care of that. No problem."

John grinned at her. She was so focused on the kitten that she didn't see the Gorafrex's light flashing behind his eyes. "Sounds good to me. Looks like you found the right time."

"I think so, yeah." She reached for the kitten and pulled it into her arms with a sigh of relief. "This is exactly what I needed. Thank you."

"You're welcome."

A wave of warm, tingling energy burst through the

library, unnoticed by the humans who hadn't yet woken up to magic. But the magicals felt it.

Before she knew what was happening, the objects Emily was trying to juggle started spinning through the air all on their own, flashing with multi-colored lights.

"Em?" Laura whispered.

"Ha." The youngest Hadstrom sister stuck one hand behind her back and pretended to keep juggling with the other hand.

The kids cheered and jumped up and down, their eyes wide in awe. Some parents were impressed enough to clap.

"This is why you stay in school," Emily said with a grin and pointed at the children. "So you can study chemistry and make magic that looks like this. Flashing lights and everything. Just don't try it at home, kids."

Nickie picked up the pace of her guitar song, changing it to something a little more upbeat as the full return of her magic coursed through her. She laughed as she shook her head at Emily's antics and looked at Laura. Laura sidled toward her and whispered, "Did you feel that?"

"Oh, yeah." Nickie strummed a louder chord and drew her arm all the way around and back. "We did it."

Laura laughed. "Don't go full rock show quite yet, okay?"

"I'm tryin'."

When the oldest Hadstrom sister looked at Nathan and Chuck, she saw them staring at her and her sisters with wide, questioning eyes. She shot them a covert thumbs-up by her thigh and winked.

On the other side of the library, John laughed and returned Emily's goofy salute.

*We did it.* Laura didn't care about getting ready for their next 'trick'. *That was it. During a freaking magic show.*

At the Barton Creek Greenbelt, a huge flock of grackles swooped down through the trees where the berm and the willow tree had sunken back into the water. Cawing and flapping, they wheeled over the cool waters and darted back up into the sky, banking north again to head toward downtown Austin.

Every magical they passed on their flight looked up to see the messengers of the magical world back in the sky. Those who listened heard the greeting. Magic was back.

The grackles swooped down over the back parking lot behind Austin's history museum and cawed in surprise when a loud bang came from inside the dumpster. The birds fluttered around, then took off again to keep spreading the word.

"Ooh. That's a good one. I think my work's done here." Bernie the mechanic climbed up out of the dumpster while sucking Dorito dust and donut glaze off his fingers. He wobbled at the edge of the dumpster, caught his balance, then leapt to the asphalt. "Whew. Climb out of one dumpster, you can climb out of 'em all. Now where did I put that—"

A heavy metallic clang from behind startled him, and he whirled around to search the parking lot.

"Who's there? I'm warning you, I know some serious stuff. And magic's back. So come on out and... What is that?"

From the uncovered manhole behind the museum came

a pulsing blue light. A thick, glowing tree branch bursting with blue-glowing leaves snaked its way up out of the hole. Leaf-covered vines snaked up with it and quickly spread across the asphalt, growing and snapping as they spilled out of the tunnels below. In under twenty seconds, the open hole in the ground looked like nothing more than a new bush planted right there in the parking lot.

"Not the best placement, but I guess it gets points for thinking outside the box." Bernie sucked the last of the donut glaze from his fingers and shook his head. "I swear, this town gets weirder every day. Nowhere else I'd rather be."

THE END

Have you read the Goth Drow series from Martha and Michael? Book one is ONCE UPON A MIDNIGHT DROW and it's available at Amazon and through Kindle Unlimited.

Get your copy here.

Get sneak peeks, exclusive giveaways, behind the scenes content, and more.
PLUS you'll be notified of special **one day only fan pricing** on new releases.

Sign up today to get free stories.

or visit: https://marthacarr.com/read-free-stories/

# AUTHOR NOTES - MARTHA CARR

## JUNE 8, 2020

I'm thinking of doing a mural down my hallway in the dream house. The idea has been percolating in my brain since the start of the pandemic. Maybe even earlier.

It's starting to take shape – at least the idea of greyscape buildings representing most of the cities I've lived in and laid over top gradually emerging butterflies that go from shades of grey to full color.

Ever since I ran away to New York at 48 I've felt like with each year I've set myself free a little bit more. Turns out freedom can be more a state of mind than anything else. I left for New York because I had to find out if I could actually figure out life on my own. It's a chaotic, fast paced, jumble of people and buildings and it was like my lungs were filling with some kind of rarefied air.

I was constantly running into people dressed as angels performing a play on the street, or subbing on my cousin's cable talk show as a panelist, or listening to Broadway stars on their day off singing in a local church and constantly listening to someone's big dreams. New York is full of big dreams said out loud. It was so deeply, divinely wonderful and scary and fast paced.

Eventually, I took off for Chicago to add a little more practical into the freedom mix. Chicago was perfect for that. Midwesterners are practical in their bones. And I was still surrounded by actors and writers and dreamers. I went to a play in a living room with the actors sitting with us and it was fantastic.

That was the city where I really started to figure out who I was. Sure I was fifty years old, but it turned out that didn't matter. There was still time. I just needed to start asking the question and being brave enough to answer it and then act on it.

Now, I'm in Austin learning how to put down roots. I've never been particularly good at that. The first time I bought a large piece of furniture was in Chicago and at first it filled me with panic. I couldn't just get up and go anymore. Here I have a big house and I'm putting in a garden and there's even a pressure washer and an actual dining room. No more running away or to anything. I guess I'm making my stand here at 60. This is the biggest change since that initial run to New York.

I tend to grow into big changes and become comfortable with them. It's not instantaneous. Kind of like a butterfly. Caterpillars don't just go into a cocoon and emerge as an entirely different form with wings. They have to be willing to completely let go of their old self and dissolve into mush that reforms itself into something unknown. Pretty brave stuff. And they're rewarded with color and wings that can take them across an entire country.

My new wings are going to help me put down ever deeper roots and find out what that means. That's where the mural comes in. It's my stamp on the house that says, I'm not selling any time soon. It can be the Offspring's problem after I'm gone for good, turning into a butterfly somewhere much further away. More adventures to follow.

# THE KACY CHRONICLES
# MIDWEST MAGIC CHRONICLES
# SOUL STONE MAGE
# THE FAIRHAVEN CHRONICLES

# OTHER BOOKS BY JUDITH BERENS

# OTHER BOOKS BY MARTHA CARR

# OTHER BOOKS BY MICHAEL ANDERLE

# JOIN THE TERRANAVIS UNIVERSE FAN GROUP ON FACEBOOK!

# CONNECT WITH THE AUTHORS

## Martha Carr Social

Website:
http://www.marthacarr.com

Facebook:
https://www.facebook.com/groups/MarthaCarrFans/

https://www.facebook.com/terranavisuniverse/

## Michael Anderle Social

Michael Anderle Social
Website:
http://www.lmbpn.com

Email List:
http://lmbpn.com/email/

Facebook
https://www.facebook.com/TheKurtherianGambitBooks/